THE PSYCH DETECTIVE
and the case of the trapped souls

JACK LEWIS

FABLE BOOKS

Published by
Fable Books
PO Box 291
Gravesend
Kent
DA12 2WG

A catalogue record for this book is available from
the British Library.

ISBN 0 9548748 0 3

Printed and bound in Great Britain by
Antony Rowe Limited
Bumper's Farm Industrial Estate
Chippenham, Wiltshire SN14 6LH

Cover Design, Val Horn
Cover Artwork, Fluid Strategic Designers Ltd.
www.fluid-ideas.co.uk

ACKNOWLEDGEMENTS

I would like to express my gratitude to my sons, Symon and Jeremy, Don Horn, Jenny and Howard Lewis, Patricia Deadman, Gillian and Hamish Turner and Judy Blackett.

Without their help and support, my first journey in writing a book would have been a much rougher road.

Thank you for lightening the load.

ONE

Nancy Harnetty tried to contain her excitement as she pulled her new blue taffeta dress over her head, struggled with the buttons at the back and tied the sash into a bow. She scrambled onto the two-foot-six inch bed and surveyed her image in the small mirror over the equally small table. She loved it and couldn't wait to show it to her best friend, Laura. She was a small child for her age, with thick, dark hair tied neatly at the back and a delicate oval face, which at this moment was slightly pink with anticipation. She looked like any other pretty child about to celebrate her birthday, but she was not what she seemed.

Nancy Harnetty was psychic and had been for as long as she could remember. As a tiny child she had played with other children, who just seemed to appear when she wanted to play, and disappear when she was tired, so she had never felt lonely. She was fortunate that her grandmother shared the same gift, so had not made her try to "push it away" as is normal with well-intentioned parents who, if *they* could not see what their children saw or heard, then it was "a silly game"; the sooner they grew out of it, the better. Children, on the other hand, soon realised that talking to others no one else could see, was regarded as very odd, and with time instinctively closed down this channel.

Nancy had never been subjected to this pressure. Her grandmother neither encouraged nor discouraged the habit, so as Nancy grew and flourished, her link to the other side had increased with each passing year.

She jumped off the bed and sat on the rug that covered the linoleum. She was just doing up the buckles on her black patent shoes, when she heard her grandmother calling.

'Nancy, how many times have I asked you not to jump off that bed? It sounds like a herd of elephants down here.'

1

'Sorry, Grandma, I forgot.'

Her grandparents' were standing in the tiny hall of the two-up, two-down terraced house in Fulham they had rented for the past forty years. Nancy leaped down the stairs two at a time. Her grandmother opened her mouth to reprimand her, when she felt her husband's hand on her arm. She looked up at him and smiled.

'You're right,' she said. 'She's too excited. Let's go.'

It was Friday, July 27th, 1952, Nancy's tenth birthday. Her best friend Laura's tenth birthday had been three months earlier and somehow it had put a barrier between them. She had never experienced this before, but being ten was different. It was a double-digit birthday, and double- digit birthdays pushed you much closer to being a teenager. When Laura reached the age of ten she had, in Nancy's eyes, been elevated to the position of being more grown up. But not any more; the barrier had been lifted.

Her grandparents must have thought it was a special birthday too, because they were taking her out to a restaurant, which was rare indeed. If they ate out, it was at a fish and chip, or pie and mash shop, but she had never felt deprived; most of their neighbours didn't frequent restaurants either.

The restaurant was only a few streets away. It was a lovely evening and Nancy held her grandparents' hands as they walked. The restaurant had only been open for a few months and was run by an Italian couple; it was called The Pasta House. Nancy had never had savoury pasta before, but Grandpa had. He had lodged for two years in a four bedroom house run by an elderly Italian widow and had acquired quite a taste for it. Pasta was what she cooked and if you didn't care for it, then you just moved out. Grandma only used pasta in puddings but they were both quite keen to try it.

She felt her grandfather's eyes on her and smiled up at him.

He smiled back. Every year she reminded him more and more of their only child, Alice.

Dear Alice - he briefly recalled that terrible night, nearly nine years ago. They were baby- sitting Nancy while Alice and her husband, Joseph, attended a wedding reception. Tragically, they never arrived; they were involved in a car accident. Joseph had died instantly, but Alice had hung on for nearly a week, against all odds. She had tried so hard to live for her baby, but when she knew she was losing the fight, she had asked them to take Nancy.

'Just love her as you have loved me,' she had asked, and they had. They had taken this fourteen-month-old bundle and had never regretted it. She had helped soften their terrible grief.

As they walked, Nancy suddenly saw an abandoned hop-scotch game some children had chalked on the pavement. She ran ahead, but as she hopped and skipped over the squares, she suddenly stopped and wondered if she was now too old to play hop-scotch. Perhaps it was childish? Oh well, she was only *just* ten, so she skipped on.

Her grandfather was just short of six feet with a weather-beaten face acquired during many years as a professional gardener. He was sixty-seven years old, but still had a good bearing. Her grandmother, a couple of years younger, was a little on the short side and quite plump, but she was one of those rare women who never lost any sleep over being somewhat overweight. They were a loving and close couple, even though they were total opposites in many ways. When he had decided to ask her to marry him, some of his well-meaning family had said he should think twice about it. Yes, they liked her, but he had to admit (they reasoned), she was "a little odd".

He had taken their advice and thought about it for a good six months, but the waiting only confirmed what he already knew; she was the one for him.

Nancy reached the restaurant first and waited for her Grandparents to arrive.

Grandpa opened the door and stopped dead. The restaurant was empty except for a man and woman seated on stools at a small bamboo bar, positioned near the entrance.

Nancy sensed her grandparents' hesitation. She looked up at them. They were definitely looking a little uncomfortable.

The man seated at the bar stood up and walked towards them. 'Just because our restaurant is empty, it don't mean the food is no good,' he said with a strong Italian accent.

'Oh, no,' replied Nancy. 'The food is very good. Where shall we sit Grandpa?'

Her grandfather relaxed. If Nancy said it was good, then the food would be good. She knew these things, just like her grandmother - only more so. Anyway, they were a little early; it would probably fill up as the evening wore on.

The Italian man (whose name was Antonio) didn't need any prompting. He was already stepping back with his arms outstretched.

'Please,' he said. 'This is my best table; you will be very comfortable here – Rosa,' he called over his shoulder, 'bring the menu. What would you like to drink ah? I got good red or white house wine. But you want beer? I got beer.'

He rushed around with a genuine permanent smile on his face, pulling out chairs, laying out paper serviettes, and generally fussing. He lit the candle on their table with a flourish. Nancy felt so important; she didn't need to be psychic to sense how welcome they were.

'This is my wife, Rosa, who, I promise you, is a wonderful cook, and her fettuccini….' He closed his fingers and kissed the tips. 'Magnificent! What you like, ha?'

'Well, the fettuccini sounds good,' her grandfather replied, 'but let's look at the menu first.' Antonio passed them around.

Nancy opened the handwritten list and peered at the selection. She really hadn't got a clue what to order. She looked at her grandfather for guidance and noted grandmother doing exactly the same.

Her grandfather's twinkling eyes appeared over the top of his menu. 'Need my help, ladies?' he asked.

Antonio seemed to appear from nowhere. 'Please, ladies, let me tell you what we got.' He reeled off the list at what seemed breakneck speed, with an equally quick description. Things like spaghetti Bolognaise, spaghetti Milanese, cannelloni and lasagne. The menu seemed never ending. 'What you like, ha?'

'I think I'll have the fettuccini,' said Grandpa.

The "ladies", still not at all sure what they would like, decided on the fettuccini too.

The restaurant was quite basic in design. It was furnished with small square wooden tables and chairs, with some tables pushed together to seat larger parties. Each table had a small narrow vase which held two carnations, and a cheap enamel candle holder, housing a candle. Only the candle on their table was lit. Nancy watched the flame dance for a while then turned her attention to the walls of the restaurant.

There were large colourful posters showing scenes of the Vatican City, Florence, Venice, the mountains and the sea. In between the poster were ropes of onions and garlic, which looked real, and bunches of grapes that didn't.

The food duly arrived, and Antonio was right: Rosa's fettuccini was magnificent.

There were only five people in the Pasta House Restaurant that night, but it was a magical evening. It was an evening (although none of them realised it at the time) they would never forget.

'I can't understand it,' Grandma was saying. 'The food is so good and inexpensive. I really can't understand why the restaurant isn't doing well.'

There was a note of anger in Antonio's voice as he replied. 'What does it matter that our food is good and cheap. Good and cheap to the English is fish and chips or pie and mash. They only put pasta in their puddings.' Grandma felt a little

5

uncomfortable. Without realising it, Antonio had reminded her of one of her own failings.

As Nancy sipped her lemonade and listened to the conversation, she became aware of an old man sitting at the next table. He was listening intently to the conversation, when he suddenly realised Nancy was watching him. His eyes widened in surprise.

Oh dear, thought Nancy, a ghost. She looked at her grandmother. Her grandmother quite often sensed another presence, even though she did not always see them, but Nancy realised she was totally unaware of this man.

'You can see me, little girl, can't you?'

Without waiting for a response, he became very agitated. *'You have to help me, little girl, I need to talk to my son, Antonio.'*

Nancy had learned from a very small child that you didn't have to communicate with ghosts by speaking. You could just hear their thoughts, and they yours. When she was about three years old, she used to talk all the time to the little spirit children that came to play, but as she grew older, she communicated as they did

'Grandma says I shouldn't talk to ghosts when we're out. She says people don't understand and some don't like it.' She paused for a moment as a thought occurred to her. *'You wouldn't have wanted a message like this when you were alive.'*

'I am a good Catholic.' he said defensively. *'But now,'* he moved his head forward slightly and pursed his lips, *'I understand more.'* She sensed he was becoming impatient with her. *'You must speak to my Antonio for me.'*

Nancy's grandmother bent down and whispered in her ear. 'What is it, Nancy. What can you see?'

'There's an old man sitting at the next table, but I've told him I can't speak to Antonio for him. Honest, Grandma, I did.'

'Don't upset yourself, dear. Tell him to just go away and we wish him well.'

6

Her grandmother stared at the next table. She began to sense him too, but she couldn't see him as Nancy could. Grandma decided to add her support to Nancy by sending her thoughts too.

'I'm sorry old man, you'll just have to go, we can't help you. She's too young and you shouldn't burden her with your problems like this.'

The old man was pleading now. *'Please, let me speak to my family through this child, they will lose everything they have if she does not help me.'*

'No.' Grandma was emphatic now. *'It's her birthday. We came here as a special treat for her and anyway, people don't like getting messages like this, it upsets them when they're not expecting it. We don't know Rosa and Antonio well enough to do what you ask, they might even ask us to leave.'*

'Is that why people like you are given such a gift, so that you can ignore the pain of a caring father like me, whose only concern is to help his son and family?'

As Grandma began to sense his sorrow, coupled with anger, she started to feel uncomfortable. Her mind was in turmoil and she could feel Nancy's eyes on her, which she now knew were disapproving.

While her grandfather chatted to Antonio, Nancy bent forward and whispered to her grandmother. 'Don't worry about me Grandma. I don't want to leave here, but I know I will feel worse if we leave Antonio's father so unhappy.'

She looked nervously at Rosa and Antonio. How would they react? They were Italian, so it was odds on that they were Catholic. Catholics didn't like dabbling in things like this, or usually seek messages from people who had passed on. Oh goodness, what am I to do she thought?

'Help me,' came back the man's thoughts loud and clear. *'If Rosa and Antonio refuse my help, I will have done all I can. But if you do not let this child help me and ignore my plea, how will you live with yourself when eventually my family lose the restaurant they have saved so hard for all these years?'*

7

Grandma could not help but be concerned. *'Are you sure they will lose everything?'*

The old man sighed heavily before he slowly replied. *'Yes,'* and she knew it to be true.

'Oh dear, then I must try, I have no choice.'

Nancy watched her grandmother with interest now. She knew she felt very uncomfortable about situations like this and wondered how she would handle it. Her grandmother looked at Antonio and Rosa and decided the only thing to do was to take the bull by the horns; if she offended them, they would pay their bill and leave.

'Antonio and Rosa,' she began, 'I am going to tell you something that under normal circumstances I would never do.' She paused. She had their total attention now. Ignoring her husband's slightly startled look, she continued. 'I'm one of those people who either see or sense people who have passed over to the other side.'

Nancy noticed how carefully her grandmother phrased her words: she never said "dead" or "ghost".

'I do hope this won't be too much of a shock for you, Antonio, but your father is here. He says he's very worried about you and your family and he wants to give you some help with the restaurant. Would you like me to continue?' she asked hesitantly.

Antonio looked stunned and for a moment could not move. 'I'm not sure,' he said, not taking his eyes off Grandma for an instant. It was almost as though he was mesmerised, unable to think quickly or clearly.

'Yes', replied Rosa in a firm voice.

Antonio looked questioningly at Rosa.

'I trusted your father in life, Antonio, and if he is here, I know he would never want to hurt us. I also know he would help us if he could, and right now, we need help.'

'You are right as always, we have nothing to fear from my father.' Nevertheless, he was apprehensive as he said: 'I would be very grateful if you could tell us why he is here.'

'I'll do my best.' Grandma was as uncomfortable as he was. 'He says he passed over about three years ago,' she paused. 'He had lung cancer.' They nodded. 'He says his wife is living with you and helps look after the children now you have your own business.'

'Yes,' said Antonio. He was starting to feel quite emotional but trying not to show it.

'He's talking about the restaurant now. He says the restaurant will be a success but...'

Here she hesitated. 'He's saying something very odd; I can't quite catch it - something about giving it away.'

'No, Grandma,' said Nancy, 'that's not what he said.'

'You had better continue, love. I can't quite get it and it's obviously important.'

'What he's saying is the food is good and the people here will like it very much, but they are poor and not used to throwing money away on trying new things. You have to talk to the local newspaper and tell them the food will be free for one night only. Your father says the newspaper will love the story and they'll recommend the restaurant's food too after they have tried it. He says the restaurant will then be a great success, and you and Rosa will be happy, so he won't need to worry about you all the time, as he does now.'

Rosa looked at Antonio and, with a note of irritation in her voice, said, 'How many times did I tell you we should spend money advertising our little Pasta Restaurant?'

'We did', he replied, gesturing with his hands in the air.

Rosa pursed her lips. 'But such a little advert, Antonio, I needed my glasses to find it.'

He shrugged by way of an answer. 'But what Papa is saying is different. He's saying we open our restaurant free for a night. Can we afford to do this? What if nothing happens?'

Rosa sighed. 'We only have enough money left to carry on for a few weeks and the bank has already told us they will not help us to continue any longer.' She took his hand in hers and kissed it gently. 'Antonio, we are finished anyway, it doesn't

9

matter whether it's now or in a few weeks time.' She looked at him with an almost pleading expression. 'Do you trust your father?'

He looked anxiously at Grandma. He didn't want to offend her. 'Of course, but he is dead, Rosa. I want to believe that he is here to help us now, but it's so hard, especially as when he was alive he was so against trying to speak to the dead. Let them rest in peace is what he always said.'

'I know, but you forget one thing: you did not try to speak to him, he came to you, so my heart and feelings say we should trust him. We have always made our decisions together, but this decision must be yours. He is your father'

Antonio left the table and walked slowly to the bar. He leaned over and helped himself to a beer. 'I have always trusted your instinct, Rosa and I don't want to ignore it now because you are usually right.' He took a few sips of his beer, then ran his hand through his hair as he tried to decide the best thing to do. He was an astute man but had no experience of making decisions like this. Suddenly he relaxed. It was simple really: they only had one chance left.

'I will contact the Fulham Chronicle first thing in the morning and tell them what *we* have decided to do.' His voice held a note of excitement now. 'Yes, we will do that, Rosa.'

She smiled. 'And when we are a big success, you must buy me that beautiful diamond ring you have always promised me, yes?'

'The biggest and best I can find.' He looked lovingly at Rosa.

Grandpa was a little embarrassed and deciding it was high time they left, asked for the bill. He didn't know it, but he was about to become even more embarrassed.

'You will pay nothing,' said Antonio. 'Rosa and I are very grateful to little Nancy and your wife for their help, so you have been our guests this evening.'

No matter how much he insisted on paying, Antonio and Rosa would not hear of it.

10

Grandma came to his rescue. 'I'll tell you what: why don't we pay this evening, because we know how tight things are financially at the moment, and perhaps you could invite us to your free evening instead?'

'Done', said Rosa.

It happened just as Antonio's father had predicted: Rosa, Antonio, his mother and their three children never looked back. Antonio never spoke about the child who helped change their lives until much later; not, in fact, until Nancy Harnetty had grown up and her "gift" was no longer a secret from the world. He had respected her grandmother's wishes when she had asked him to say nothing of Nancy's clairvoyance.

'She needs to remain a normal child for as long as possible. How long that will be; only God knows.'

Fame came to Nancy without her seeking it. With time, she learned to cope and adjust her life, so that her unusual talent did not lie too heavily on her shoulders, relying on the help and guidance of those who reside in the spirit world, to whom she had always felt very grateful and had learned to trust above all else.

TWO

The telephone rang beside Nancy's bed. She could hear it in the distance, as she hovered between deep sleep and a semi-conscious state. She slowly picked up the phone and then replaced it quickly, as she realised it was the automatic alarm she had set the night before in her hotel room.

She switched it off as she swung her legs out of bed. There was peace again. God, she was tired. This tour had been too long, with hardly any rest periods. She sat with her head between her hands and decided this was the last time she would ever agree to travel for two months, virtually non-stop.

Nancy made her way to the bathroom and, as she showered, she recalled the lectures, seminars, workshops, clairvoyant demonstrations and private readings of the last few months.

She couldn't fault the arrangements; everything had gone like clockwork. John Dale, her tour organiser, had worked as long and as hard as she had, but America and Canada were vast countries and the travelling, combined with a heavy schedule had taken its toll on them.

She always had breakfast in her room, because so many people wanted to talk to her if she ate in the restaurant, and was pleased to see the breakfast tray waiting for her when she had finished in the bathroom. Three-quarters of an hour later, she was just about to leave when the phone rang.

'Hi, Nancy,' said a soft American voice.

'Hello, John. I'm just on my way down.'

She left quickly and made her way to the lift.

Next week would be her 41st birthday and she was glad she would be celebrating it at home with friends. She didn't have much family, now that her grandparents had died. She missed them so much, especially at birthdays and Christmas. People had said they could not understand why she had grieved nearly as much as they did at losing a loved one. After all, she

12

could still communicate with them, couldn't she? That was true, of course, and she always sensed and knew they were near, but it wasn't the same as a physical cuddle or a fireside chat.

She walked through the lobby of the Cedar Hotel in Toronto, continuing through a walkway to one of the conference rooms. As she entered, John gave a little signal from the back of the room which meant that he had already checked everyone was present, so she could start on time, which was a blessing.

'Good morning, ladies and gentlemen. If you could all take your seats, I'd like to press on. We still have a lot to get through.'

There were a few stragglers still looking at the books for sale which were laid out on one of the tables to the side of the room. She waited until they were all seated and it was totally quiet, before she began. She always expected their total attention and usually got it. Apart from the faint noises still audible from the hotel, the room was now quiet.

Nancy had developed from a petite child into a slim, attractive lady that belied her 40 years. Her face was unlined and her hair still had no trace of grey in it, but her pale blue eyes looked tired.

'All right,' she said, 'before we start our meditation this morning, I'll quickly go over a few points from yesterday.'

As Nancy looked around her, there was the usual very mixed bag of people from all walks of life, cultures and ages. One of the main reasons that people came to these workshops was to learn to meditate to counteract the stress in their lives. The student who was finding it hard to cope with his exams; the thinking 'whiz kid' who had found success but not quality of life; the agitated housewife with her family traumas; the family doctor who had read about the benefits of meditation, and begun to notice the change in those of his patients who had either taught or learned the art. It was also evidently becoming fashionable. Whatever the reason, meditation certainly would not hurt them, and most would gain some benefit.

It was approximately two hours into the course: Nancy and the rest of the group had their eyes closed and were just starting twenty minutes of quiet meditation, when she sensed a presence. At first, she tried to keep her eyes shut and ignore her, but in the end she was compelled to open them. The woman was standing quite still, at the back of the middle aisle, with her eyes focused on Nancy. She was fairly tall, with a slim, erect build; Nancy guessed her age to be in the mid- sixties when she had died. Nancy mentally sent her thoughts to the woman that she was not here to give messages to those in the group, so if she wanted to communicate with anyone here she was very sorry, but she could not oblige.

The woman's thoughts came back gently to her. *'I must apologise for disturbing you, it was not my intention and I do not know anyone here.'*

Nancy's curiosity was aroused now, and she focused her full attention on the woman. *'What is your purpose in being here then?'*

'I came to observe you.'

'But why?' Nancy was more curious than ever now.

Her face saddened at this point. *'Because we will be together in times to come, when I will help and protect you. Yes, it should be my responsibility to protect you.'*

The woman disappeared as quickly as Nancy supposed she had arrived. Nancy looked around the meditating group, who were totally unaware of the last few minutes - except one. A young girl of about eighteen years was looking over her shoulder in the direction the woman had been. The girl turned her head again to look at Nancy who, by now, had her eyes closed like everyone else. The girl closed her eyes, but her puzzled look remained. There was usually one who was psychically aware, thought Nancy, without knowing what it was they sensed. Usually one.

The two-day workshop finished and she knew it had been a success. As usual, quite a number of the group were still hanging around, nearly an hour after it had ended. A few would remain in contact with each other, but all had enjoyed the comfortable camaraderie that had developed, and they were loath to end it and go their separate ways, as they must. Nancy eventually said goodbye to them all and left.

* * *

A pleasant Canadian voice announced over the speaker that passengers on flight number 352, Toronto to London, should make their way to gate number 16, as the plane was now ready for departure and apologised for the four hour delay, due to technical reasons.

Nancy Harnetty picked up her travel bag and followed the long line of passengers, as they slowly made their way. A young couple in front held the hands of two children, who had become both irritable and whiney due to the long delay. Nancy prayed silently that she would not be seated too near them; she was tired and planned to sleep as much as possible on the way back to the UK. She handed her ticket to the stewardess, who directed her to a window seat half-way down the plane. She put her hand-luggage in the overhead compartment and settled down into her seat. She turned her head towards the window, closed her eyes and just listened to the general bustle around her.

These tours left her with a deep physical and mental fatigue, but she knew that once she was home, her "safe place", she would re-charge her batteries within a week. Her home was a modest one-bedroom flat that had been converted from a large detached house. The medium-sized, ground-floor flat was self-contained with a side entrance and its own small, private garden. Her favourite armchair faced the large window next to the tall glass door which led into the garden. As the garden was quite shady, she had stocked it mostly with evergreen shrubs, planting smaller ones to the front and taller ones to the back. It had flourished into a slightly wild, yet very symmetrical and balanced garden, which was in harmony with itself.

The same could be said of her home; the odd table and armchair acquired here and there blending with soft-coloured carpets and curtains, made it both comfortable and cosy. A home - not a show piece. She looked forward to her return.

Eventually, the general activity around her began to subside. Everyone was now on board and virtually all seated; just the last minute rush before take-off. She would soon be in the air and on her way home; she slipped slowly down into her seat, as she became more and more relaxed. What bliss.

Suddenly her eyes were wide open and she sat bolt upright. What was wrong? Something was wrong - but what? Was there a problem with the plane? No. She knew immediately it wasn't the plane. She had been jolted out of a fairly relaxed and drowsy state. Calm yourself, she thought, and then you'll know. It was the same feeling she'd had twice before in her life. The first time was a few days before her grandmother had died unexpectedly; the second time was a few hours before she had seen a child run out in front of a car and die. She knew these feelings came to forewarn and prepare her for some impending disaster, but this time the feeling had been so strong, she had not recognised it.

She leaned wearily back in her chair. There was nothing she could do but wait. She would know soon enough.

***

Many hours later, Nancy put the key in her front door. She paid the cab driver and as she opened the door, he kindly helped her in with her luggage. Being away for two months doesn't allow you to travel light. She thanked him and closed the door as he left.

She kicked off her shoes before making her way to the kitchen to make a cup of tea. God, how she had missed a decent cup of English tea. She picked up the kettle just as the

16

phone rang. She looked at her watch. It was 10.30 p.m. Who could be calling at this time of night? Well, whoever it was would have to wait; they could leave a message on the answer machine. She stopped. She had a sudden overpowering impulse to pick up the phone.

'Hello, Nancy Harnetty speaking.'

The Cockney voice that spoke to her was agitated. She sensed a mixture of embarrassment and fear in his voice.

'I'm sorry to bother you, Miss Harnetty, and I ain't never had a reason to call the likes of you before, but I'm desperate and that's a fact. I got your number from a Mr Jessop, after I told him about something that happened recently - upset me it did. So I went to see him, and all I know is, he ain't happy either, so he suggested I call you. He said he didn't know of anyone else who could help me.'

Nancy's sense of unease returned. 'Are you sure he couldn't help you; he's a very competent clairvoyant? Were you dissatisfied with the information he gave you?'

'He didn't give me any information. He listened to what I had to say and said I should call you as soon as you got back from abroad, which he said was today. Been ringing all day, I have.'

Her thoughts suddenly returned to the female presence she had encountered in Toronto. 'I can see you about six tomorrow evening, if that's convenient for you,' she said.

'I'll be there', replied the Cockney voice, which held a much happier note now.

She gave him her address and said, 'By the way, you'd better give me your name'.

'Oh yeah, it's Georgie Wells, and I'll see you sharp at six'.

As Nancy slowly replaced the receiver, she knew her feelings of apprehension and unease on the plane were somehow connected not only with Georgie Wells, but also the Toronto "presence".

Now it begins, she thought. Now it begins.

THREE

Nancy slept in late the next morning and felt much better for it. She rose, had a leisurely bath and decided her next priority was a visit to the supermarket.

She dressed quickly and after an equally quick cup of tea, made her way to the car park at the back of the flats. When she was away from home for any length of time, one of her neighbours would turn the engine of her car from time to time, just to keep it ticking over.

It took her a while in the supermarket, as she needed to replenish most things, but she enjoyed the slow amble up and down the food aisles, knowing that her time was now her own.

As she put the groceries away, her thoughts returned to the telephone conversation with Georgie Wells the night before and her sense of unease returned. Why had Alan Jessop referred Georgie to her? She had been too tired to contemplate it last night, but the question had played on her mind since she opened her eyes this morning.

She had met Alan about fifteen years ago, when they had both been asked to give a demonstration of clairvoyance to mark the fiftieth anniversary of one of the Spiritualist Churches. She knew him to be a competent and honest medium, which was why Nancy was at a loss to know why he had referred Wells to her. In all the years she had known him, he had never sent one of his clients to her directly. Yes, they would sometimes discuss interesting phenomena and the latest news in their profession, and occasionally Alan had asked her opinion on various matters, but he had never actually asked her to see one of his clients and Nancy was curious to know why. There was only one way to find out.

Alan answered the phone almost immediately and was obviously pleased to hear from her.

'How did your tour go?' he asked, and for a few minutes they talked as old friends. Then Alan said: 'I've been expecting this call. It's about Georgie Wells, isn't it?'

'Yes, I was just curious as to why you gave him my number. I'll see him of course. You obviously had good reason, but not one that springs to mind.'

'I felt I was out of my depth. I'm a respected medium, but I'm not in your league and I know it. Unravelling this mystery is going to be very difficult even for the best, and you're the best, but above all, something is very wrong.'

'Mystery, I don't understand. We relay messages or information we receive, most of which are simple details that the sitter can understand and draw comfort from. Where's the mystery in that, Alan?'

He sighed heavily. 'Nance, I didn't give him any information.' He was the only one who ever called her Nance, but she knew it was a form of endearment on his part.

'I did not, and could not give him any help or comfort, even though I knew he was sorely in need of it, he came to me looking for answers and I had none to give. Nance, just see him. Let him tell you his story and then make up your own mind, that's all I ask. If you decide you can't help him then he will have to accept it.'

She was silent for a moment. 'He's coming to see me at about six o'clock. Why don't you come along as well Alan and sit in on our discussion.'

'I was hoping you'd say that. I'll see you tonight at six.'

* * *

Nancy looked at her watch, as she had done for the last hour or so. It was five-forty pm. Not long now, but why was she feeling so agitated? She could not remember feeling so apprehensive about a meeting before.

As the time drew nearer to meeting Georgie Wells, she had, for a fleeting moment, resented Alan for passing the problem to her, but it was only a brief thought. Nancy knew that

19

whatever the situation, it was somehow connected to the woman in Toronto. Georgie Wells was the reason she had appeared at the meditation workshop. Her words came back loud and clear. *We will be together in times to come, when I will help and protect you.* Now was that time, she was certain of it. As Nancy remembered her words, she began to relax. Whatever the problem, she would get help. As her unease subsided, her curiosity heightened. What could possibly have happened to upset Georgie Wells and, even more baffling, Alan Jessop?

The doorbell rang and she jumped.

Nancy opened the door, then stepped back to let Alan enter. He held her hand and kissed her on the cheek.

'I can smell the coffee, so why don't you ask me if I would like one?' he said, smiling down at her.

'Coming up; make yourself comfortable, you know the way.' Nancy was reaching for the tray in the kitchen when she heard the door bell again.

'I'll get it,' called Alan.

As she carried the tray of coffee in Georgie Wells was standing by the sitting room door.

'Please take a seat. You look as if you could do with a coffee too.'

'I could at that, Miss Harnetty.'

'Oh please call me Nancy, everyone else does.' Nancy didn't hand him the coffee but placed it beside him, as Georgie's hands were visibly shaking, and she realised he was as apprehensive about this meeting as she was.

'Did you have any problems finding my flat?' she asked.

'No, I'm a cabbie so I know Barnes quite well.' Nancy chatted for a while, trying to put him at ease. Georgie was a small East End Cockney and, judging by his accent, had definitely been born within the sound of Bow Bells.

'Well, Georgie,' she asked at last. 'How can I help you?'

'I don't rightly know. I've been puzzled by something that happened recently, and I ain't slept since.'

'Tell me what happened,' she asked gently.

'It was three weeks ago, but I remember it like it was three hours ago. Just come home from work I had, and in the middle of getting me dinner, when I had a strange feeling I was being watched. I turned round - quick like, and blow me down, there was Elsie. God's truth Nancy, she was floating in the middle of me bloody kitchen. She was just *floating*. I'll tell you another thing, don't ask me how, but I just knew what she was thinking even though she never opened her bleedin' mouth.' He suddenly realised what he had said. 'Sorry, I didn't mean to swear and normally I would mind me P's and Q's, but I ain't thinking straight since this happened.'

'No offence taken, so you just tell me in your own words, okay.'

'Right' he replied but didn't continue immediately. He was looking uncomfortable; he obviously didn't like relating the experience.

'I could tell she was sort of confused and unhappy and.... lost. She kept pleading with me to help her. Now you'll probably think I'm bonkers, but as I tried to talk to her she just sort of faded and disappeared.' He looked totally bewildered. 'I don't know what happened to Elsie but I do know she ain't happy. You've got to help her.'

It was Nancy's turn to look confused and briefly looked at Alan; he was more than competent to have dealt with this.

'Look, Georgie, it sound to me like Elsie passed very suddenly and doesn't yet realise she is dead, but there are special groups of people who do what we call rescue work with these poor souls, to help them over to the other side.'

'But she ain't dead. Leastways that's what Mr Jessop here says.'

'Not dead?' She turned an enquiring glance to Alan.

'Tell her what else you saw,' said Alan.

'Oh, yeah, there was a silver cord connected to her and as she floated, it sort of floated with her.'

'Good Lord, are you sure?'

'Course I am. Never been more sure of anything in my life,' he replied firmly. As Nancy looked at him her sense of unease returned.

'Let's start at the beginning. Who is Elsie? Tell me everything you know about her, everything.'

'She's my cousin. But I ain't seen her for about eight or nine years, even though she's about my only relative. We never had a lot in common, if you know what I mean. Her mum and my mum were sisters, but they're both dead, including our dads. If we have any other family, I don't know where they are.'

'What kind of person is Elsie?'

'Well, if there is such a thing, I'd say she was a born spinster. Doesn't mix well and likes her own company. After I saw her, I couldn't get her out of me mind, I thought she must have died, and for some reason or other had come back to me. Perhaps there was something she wanted me to do? So I looked for her address and went round there to see if I could find out what had happened to her, but she'd left there four months before and done a bunk owing two weeks' rent which hadn't pleased her landlady. Anyway, I left none the wiser. That's when I went to see Mr Jessop here, to try to find out why she was so unhappy, and how I could help her. You could have knocked me down with a feather when he told me she wasn't dead.'

'Do you know if she ever had any interest in black magic?'

'Well as I said, we didn't keep in touch on a regular basis, but I would say no, she's a simple person and I don't think the likes of that would ever take her fancy.'

'Have you been to see the police?'

'Are you kidding? And say what, that I was worried 'cos I'd seen Elsie floating in my kitchen one evening and that when I went to visit her after eight years, she'd moved on, so do you think you could put out an APB on her? Look, I don't know how, but we got to help her, 'cos dead or alive, Elsie is .....
tormented.' He was pleading now.

Nancy was quiet for a moment. 'I think I have to agree with you. In fact I think we both do. Her last address obviously can't help, because if she planned to leave owing money, she would hardly have told anyone there where she was going. Do you know where she worked?'

'Yes, she worked at Barnet General Hospital, but she ain't there either. I phoned them, and all they would say was, they weren't at liberty to disclose information about former employees.'

'Did you explain that she was a close relative and that you were trying to trace her, because you were worried about her?'

'Yes, I did, but they said it wasn't their policy to give out information over the phone and said, if I was really worried, I should contact the police, so I was back to square one. That's when I rang Mr Jessop.'

'I suppose they have their rules and regulations like everyone else,' said Alan. 'So what do we do now'?

'Georgie, I know you're upset at the moment, but I would like to see if I can contact Elsie. Having said that, I have never tried to communicate with a person in distress like this before who, even more disturbing, is not dead. I'm not sure if I can do it, but I would like to try.'

'What do you mean? Have a séance round a table holding hands? I don't know whether I could handle that that.'

She smiled for the first time since he had arrived. 'You've been watching too many films. No, that's not what I had in mind at all; in fact, I don't want you to do anything but sit quietly, while I just close my eyes for a while.'

A look of total relief spread over his face. 'Oh, I think I can cope with that.'

'Make yourself comfortable then and just relax with me. You can close your eyes too, if it will make you feel more at ease.'

Georgie decided this might be a good idea; he didn't think he was ready for any weird noises or happenings. 'Right,' he replied.

'I could do this after you have left, if you would prefer?'

He suddenly realised that she knew how he felt and found it a little unnerving, but he didn't dwell on it. He could only think of Elsie and her pain.

'No, I'd rather stay.' He wanted answers tonight, if there were any.

Nancy made herself comfortable in the large armchair and closed her eyes. She mentally said the Lords prayer and then sat very still. Georgie watched her with interest and a little apprehension. As he studied her, he began to feel the peace that seemed to surround her and he slowly began to relax too. He wanted to close his eyes, but now decided to remain alert for Elsie's sake.

Nancy's breathing gently began to slow. At first she could see nothing as she projected her thoughts to Elsie, asking her to tell her where she was and that she wanted to help her if she could. Nothing... only a grey mist, which swirled and danced threateningly before her. She had to get rid of this mist; it was so dense. Nancy knew instinctively that if she was to communicate with Elsie, this fog must be cleared.

She began to concentrate and focus her thoughts on the distortion that had formed a dense barrier. She looked at the mist and mentally flooded it with a brilliant white light. At first, nothing happened. The mist would be highlighted and lifted temporarily, but as she briefly rested her mind from the effort, it would return as dense as ever. She wasn't even making a slight chink in the density.

She had to keep trying. She opened her mind again, but this time put all her mental effort into holding and flooding the mist with light for as long as she could. She thought of nothing else, only the light. How long she held and pushed the concentration of light into the mist, she did not know, but thought the bombardment must have continued for at least five minutes. If it did not hold now, it never would. Nancy looked for the mist. It had gone. A sense of elation overcame her, as she looked at the bright white comforting light. As the tension eased, it allowed her mind some rest; the whole experience had taken much more stamina and effort than she had expected.

Her success was short lived. The mist came swirling back denser and darker than ever, with a menacing force that stunned her. Then despair set in. It was stronger than her, much stronger. She could not send it away. Wherever Elsie was, it was a dark and unhappy place and she could not match the power of this dark force.

Suddenly, she felt a loving and protecting force behind her. Nancy turned slowly and faced the presence she had encountered in Toronto. She was greatly comforted by her and sent out her thoughts on the problem that was troubling her most. *'If I cannot disperse the mist that surrounds her, then I cannot reach her.'*

'You have to travel through the mist, not push it away, Nancy.'

Nancy returned her eyes to the moving mass and realised for the first time that it made her uneasy. Instinct had made her try to clear it rather than face it.

'I'm afraid of it, but I don't know why.'

'I know, but part of the answer you seek is there. I will protect you, Nancy, never doubt me.'

She nodded. It was a while before she could summon the courage to mentally draw herself towards it, as the presence waited patiently. She drew near; then entered the swirling dark mass. It enveloped her so swiftly that she was unprepared for the sudden jolt that shook her body, but knew it would have been far more severe if it had not been cushioned by the protective presence immediately behind her.

She heard her thoughts. *'You must go deeper, Nancy, but do not be afraid. I will stay close to you. No harm will come to you.'*

As she projected herself deeper into the mist, she experienced and saw things that would have touched and damaged her psyche forever, had the power of the presence

25

not stayed close. She was able to understand the pain and torment, but somehow detach her emotion from it. By understanding but not feeling, she was protected. Like reading in a newspaper an account of some terrible experience, which though upsetting, would not have the same effect as experiencing it first hand.

She turned to look at the presence that was now so close that their faces slightly intermingled.

'Just a little further, Nancy.' She turned and pushed deeper into the mist.

Suddenly she could hear a blurred beep and a distorted voice in the distance, but she had no power to answer, or see who spoke. Then it hit her. She was hearing and experiencing what Elsie could hear. Hearing and feeling only that, which Elsie could feel and hear, Nancy realised that Elsie had no control over her thoughts or actions - a sort of detached brain wave, that was unable to make others aware of her pain or feelings of total panic, only receiving, as if in the distance, barely audible sound waves as someone spoke. All thought process seemed delayed, as if in slow motion.

Nancy now realised that Elsie's attachment to the living world was tenuous, but her mind registered total surprise when she saw that Elsie was also touching, but could not enter, the haven that death would grant her, if only she could reach it. She was somehow connected to both worlds. Her spirit was held in a sort of no-mans land, without the freedom to enter or become part of either. She realised, with sheer amazement, that Elsie's soul was trapped between the living and the dead. Nancy's personal despair returned. She had no understanding or experience of this nightmare, nor the knowledge or power to release her from this void.

Suddenly, she felt the gentle presence behind her and realised they now shared the same knowledge. That was why they were here.

'Now, do what I cannot Nancy. Give her some comfort.'

Nancy was touching Elsie's psyche and knew she could reach her.

'I don't know how I can end your pain, Elsie, but I want you to know I will not rest until I have found a way, however long it takes. Can you hear me?'

The answer was delayed, but answer she did. *'Yes.'*

Nancy felt a tear run slowly down her cheek, but did not try to wipe it away. She knew it was not hers.

Georgie couldn't take his eyes off Nancy. He watched with interest now, not fear, the different expressions that crossed her face from time to time. He wasn't sure how long she remained like this, but he thought it was about twenty minutes. Suddenly, she opened her eyes and took a sip of the water beside her. She leaned back and closed them again for a moment. The experience had drained her. Alan motioned to Georgie to remain quiet.

'I think she must be in a coma or semi-conscious,' she said at last. 'There's a mist that surrounds her, that does not allow me to see her, but I know she can hear blurred distant voices.'

Nancy saw no good reason to explain everything to him - she just couldn't. He would never understand; she didn't understand. Anyway, he would draw no peace from knowing, so she gave him the only comfort she could.

'I was able to communicate with her briefly, to tell her I will do everything I can to help her, and you have my word, Georgie, that I will.'

'God bless you', he replied, 'and at least we know she's alive. If she can hear voices in the distance, then someone must be looking after her. Perhaps now the police will help us try to find Elsie?'

'I'm not so sure' said Alan. 'I hate to say this, but nothing has changed as far as the police are concerned. The only difference now, apart from you telling them how you encountered Elsie, is that a psychic (and we are not top of their reliability list) tried to communicate with her, and thinks she's in a coma.'

'Oh gawd,' exclaimed Georgie.

'We are trying to help you,' said Alan, 'we really are, and I'm not suggesting for one moment that you shouldn't go and see them. I just don't want you to raise your hopes too high, so please, think it through before you contact them.'

'Georgie's right,' said Nancy, 'the only logical way forward is for the police to become involved, but I have to agree with you, Alan, there's not much chance of that happening under the circumstances.'

She was thoughtful for a moment, then, as if to herself, said, 'not unless we know someone who is, or was connected to the police force and has received help from us in the past. They might well lend a more sympathetic ear.' She looked at them. 'I think I know a man who might fit the bill. Why don't I call him tomorrow and sound him out?'

There was no opposition to this suggestion and, as there was nothing further they could accomplish that night, they decided to call it a day. They saw Georgie to the door and promised to keep him informed of any progress.

'How much do I owe you both? You didn't charge me last time, Alan.'

'Nor will we today, Georgie,' answered Nancy. 'This wasn't a normal sitting. Elsie is in distress so we feel honour-bound to try and help her, but you must understand, this is new to us. We can give no guarantees, only a promise we will try.'

He nodded. Georgie's face looked considerably happier as he left Nancy Harnetty's home. He felt that, at last, he would get help with a problem that, to him, had been insurmountable.

Nancy walked to the drinks cabinet. 'I think we could do with one, don't you?' She poured two whiskies and handed one to Alan.

'What happened, Nance? You don't look too good.'

'I don't feel too good. I've never had an experience like it.' She told him, as clearly as she could, all that had happened.

28

He listened in disbelief. 'Nance, what in God's name is happening?'

'I wish I knew, but I wish more that it had never happened.' They sat quietly for a while as they drank their whisky.

'Well,' he said. 'What's the next step?'

'We have to find Elsie as quickly as possible. Only then can we understand why her spirit was in such torment that it left her body. Not only left her body, but sought out Georgie to ask for his help. Time is of the essence. No one should have to suffer like she is. The problem is, I'm not confident my police friend will want to help.'

'Typical.' said Alan. 'People ask for and expect our help when it suits them, but are at the back of the queue when things are reversed.'

'We can't blame them for that, or expect it. After all we charge a fee for our service and it's on a one-to-one basis with no one else involved. I have a choice as to whether or not I do a sitting and they have a choice as to whether or not they want one. This is totally different. I will be asking for his expertise and help, that I won't expect to pay for but the taxpayer will. It might also entail the manpower of other policemen, who more than likely have never asked for, or received any help from people like us. They would, understandably, examine our evidence under the same basis as any other. And, let's face it, you have already given your thoughts on that, which if I'm not mistaken, were not positive.'

'You're right, so try not to rub it in, okay,' he answered with a rueful smile.

She smiled back. 'I think this situation is getting to us, and it's only the beginning. We'll have to watch that.'

He nodded, then, on a more serious note, added, 'I have never heard of anything like this. Oh I know the spirit will leave the body in the case of an accident or serious illness, because the spirit gains peace by leaving its physical body and getting away from the pain and stress it's suffering. But what you are describing seems as though the spirit has been ejected from the body and is in great distress – not peace. I cannot understand it. It defies the knowledge I have of this phenomenon.'

'Yes, it does, which is why we must find Elsie, not only for her sake, but to find answers to our questions.'

Alan finished his drink and stood up to leave.

'I'll contact my friend tomorrow and see if he'll agree help us,' said Nancy. 'Then I'll call you.'

She closed the door, locked up for the night, and returned to her chair to finish her whisky. She took hold of the small writing pad on the table beside her chair and studied the details she had taken from Georgie Wells:

Elsie Turnbull: age, 33 years; height, 5ft 6"
Weight: approx. eight and a half stone
Hair colour: light brown; complexion, fair
Occupation: hospital cleaner (last known job)
Georgie will try to supply photo; last saw her in
1974, just before Christmas
Last known address, 4 Rudleigh Street, Barnet
No history of mental illness, in fact, enjoyed
good health.

Not a lot to go on, but as she really couldn't do any more this evening, she decided to read a book she had bought in the States, which so far, she had not found time to look at.

FOUR

Isabel Jennings looked for her front door keys in her large, disorganised handbag. She hadn't put them in the side flap as normal when she had hurriedly left for work that morning, which of course was a mistake. Because, to coin a phrase, she carried everything in it but "the kitchen sink". A look of relief spread across her face as her fingers found the Yale key.

'Thank you,' she said to no-one but herself as she put the key in the door and entered. Her relief increased as she kicked off her shoes and sent them hurtling down the hall. Her feet had felt like raw meat since at least lunchtime.

Isabel was a pretty girl, with a bubbly personality that most people found endearing. She had come over from Canberra, Australia, when she was 20 years old, to work and tour the country for one year. That had been five years ago and she was still here. Every year she planned to make it her last in England and go back to her roots, but as the years went by she was finding it harder and harder to book that plane home, for the simple fact was, she was happy here.

She loved London, the people and indeed the way of life she now had. 'One day,' she would say to herself, 'I'll go home', but as each year passed, she knew this to be less and less likely. Isabel worked as a nurse at the local hospital, and today had been a long duty so she was tired. She quickly made herself a small snack and slumped onto the old but comfy sofa. She was thinking she ought to get down to writing a letter to her mother and father, which was well overdue. Her eyes closed as she dozed after her hectic day. There was always plenty to do at work, but today had been never ending.

Suddenly, she felt a prickling at the back of her neck and automatically tensed herself.

What was wrong? She hadn't heard any strange noises yet felt she was not alone, that she was being watched. A sense of

31

fear gripped her and her heartbeat increased as she slowly opened her eyes and looked straight ahead.

She was totally unprepared for the sight that met her eyes, which widened dramatically as she gasped in total surprise and terror. Her heartbeat increased so rapidly that she became light- headed and felt she would faint. Her forehead and hands began to perspire as she felt the scream, which she was unable to release, gurgle in her throat.

She had no recollection of how long it was before she spoke. She heard her own voice as if in the distance.

'John!' she exclaimed, stunned. She tried to stand up, but found she could not move a muscle. John Harris was no more than four feet away from her, hovering in mid-air in the middle of her sitting-room. She stayed mesmerised, looking at this totally unbelievable sight, before her reason began to tell her this could not be, and if she closed her eyes and prayed, he would disappear and all would be well again. She closed her eyes tightly and began to pray. Suddenly, he began to plead with her.

'*Please – don't shut – me – out.*'

It was at this point that she felt herself going into shock; he had communicated with her but not in the normal way. She had no understanding of how, but knew she was hearing him telepathically. Without warning, his heart-rending plea turned her shock and fear into compassion. There was something so piteous in his cry that her thoughts now were totally filled with concern for him. As she stared at him, she suddenly noticed a thin silver cord that seemed to be attached to him in some way - it certainly floated and moved with him. She looked more closely now, trying to take in every detail, but it was his look of torment that held her astonished gaze.

'John, whatever is the matter?' She whispered, hardly daring to breathe.

John's thoughts were projected to her loud and clear, but spasmodically.

'Must – help me Isabel – trapped in – a void, can't get – back. Can't get – to the light – must help me – no one – else; no one.'

His last communication became much louder, almost a shout. At this point, he slowly began to fade before her eyes. She could not move; she was too distressed. Her eyes were still wide and her mouth slightly open. He was no longer there, but she could still see him in her mind's eye. So vivid was the image that she knew she would never forget it. Never.

Isabel was not sure how long she remained on the sofa; she lost all track of time. Suddenly, the phone rang. It seemed so loud, and was such a jolt to her system, that she hurried across the room to pick it up quickly.

'Hi, it's Gina. Where have you been? You really must get yourself an answer-machine, so you can call back people like me. This is my third attempt.'

'That's exactly why I don't have one, Gina; my phone bill would go up dramatically. Anyway, I'm sorry you couldn't catch me, but I've had to cover two extra long shifts due to holidays and sickness, you know what it's like, but you've got me now so what's up?' She tried to sound light-hearted. She didn't want to talk about what had just happened.

'A few of us are meeting in the local tomorrow night and hoped you could make it too?'

'I'd like to, but I can't make it tomorrow. Can I take a rain check?'

'Are you alright' asked Gina. 'You don't sound too well?'

'Nothing that a good nights sleep won't cure' she replied. 'I promise I'll call you in a couple of days.' As Isabel replaced the receiver, her thoughts were still in turmoil. She knew she had to do something to help John, but in heaven's name, what?

She stood still while her mind raced. How had John's body appeared and then disappeared in her home? Was he dead? If so, what had he meant when he had said he was "trapped in a void?" Perhaps he was lying dead somewhere, undiscovered. If that was the case, she should call the police. The police: what could she say to them? She recalled the events of the night in her mind and then shook her head despairingly. They would think she was a fruitcake. No, that was definitely not the answer, but she had to do something.

It was then she remembered an article she had read recently in one of the magazines, about a woman who was supposed to be an exceptional clairvoyant. As the thought occurred to her, she was already moving in the direction of the magazines, which she usually kept after she had read them. The patients' waiting room at the hospital made good use of them, so she knew she would not have thrown it away. She quickly flicked through them.

'Here it is. Nancy Harnetty,' she said, heaving a sigh of relief, 'and she lives in Barnes.' Isabel had a habit of talking to herself when she was agitated or distressed.

She picked up the phone again and rang directory enquiries to ask for the number, carefully writing it down on the pad beside the phone. As she replaced the receiver, she glanced at Nancy Harnetty's telephone number and then at the clock. It was 10.45 pm. No, it was probably too late to call, so she folded the slip of paper carefully and put it in her purse. She couldn't take the chance of putting it in her unruly handbag - just in case. Things placed there had a tendency to disappear.

Isabel made her way to her bedroom, as if in a dream, and undressed. She had a leisurely bath, put on a clean nightie and crawled into bed. Her body was tired but her mind was wide awake. As she lay in the dark, she remembered John and their time together. They had met not long after she had arrived from Australia. He was a very serious young man, who did not mix well with people. Basically, he preferred his own company. That was, until he met Isabel.

They were total opposites, which was probably why they were so attracted to one another. She loved to talk and he loved to listen. They had been together for two years before

Isabel had ended their relationship. Whereas, in the beginning, she was happy just to be with him, to the exclusion of others, after a year she had begun to miss the company of her old friends. He, however, was adamant that he was happy just being with her and didn't need the company of others; so they had slowly drifted apart.

It had been at least a year since she had last seen him. They exchanged the odd birthday or Christmas card, but that had been it. He had gone back to being a loner and she rejoined her large circle of friends and, until tonight, had hardly thought about him in the last year.

As Isabel closed her eyes and tried to block out the sight of his tormented face, she knew it would be a long night.

FIVE

Nancy woke early the next morning, feeling she was nearly back to normal. She no longer had the deep fatigue, which had invaded her body for at least ten days before she'd returned home. She opened the bedroom curtains, yawned and stretched as the gentle sun touched her body.

In higher spirits, she made her tea and even hummed a tune. She espied one of the little grey squirrels scampering around the garden, looking for nuts in the ground where it had previously buried them. They could be quite a nuisance, as they loved to bury them in her potted plants, digging them out regularly, leaving the plants in disarray. However, as she'd known she was going to be away for a few months, she hadn't planted any, but they still checked out the empty pots; force of habit, she guessed.

Nancy showered, enjoyed a leisurely breakfast, and then glanced at the clock. It was still a little too early to call Alex Moorland, her police contact, so decided to leave it for another half-hour or so. She picked up the newspaper that had just been delivered, and was on her way to the sitting room when the phone rang. Nancy was totally unprepared for what transpired next.

The voice was hurried. 'Hello, my name is Isabel Jennings, and I'm really sorry to call you so early, but I have to get to work. I was so worried about something that happened last night; I just couldn't wait till I got back tonight to call you.' Barely pausing for breath, Isabel continued.

'It's my ex-fiancé. Something awful has happened to him. He's obviously dead, but not at peace, in fact, it's as though he…. oh, how can I explain it….tormented. Yes that's it, tormented.'

Nancy felt the hairs begin to stand up on the back of her neck. She'd heard those words before. Isabel's voice became louder and quicker, as she remembered the terror of the night before.

'He says he's in a void, and can't get back to the light. I don't know what it means, what is happening, or what I should do. Please, Miss Harnetty, can you help? I'm desperate and don't know who else to ask.' She was almost hysterical now.

As Nancy listened, the feeling of foreboding that was never far away these days, returned. 'Calm down,' she said, 'and just tell me how and where you saw him?'

'You're not going to believe this, Miss Harnetty, but if *you* don't, who will.' There was more than a note of despair in her voice.

'Before I can help you, you *must* answer my question. Where did you see him and why do you think he's unhappy?' She asked firmly.

'I hope you don't think I'm one of those odd people, who get some kind of kick out of calling with time-wasting nonsense, but you must believe me when I tell you what I saw. John, my ex-fiancé, was in the middle of my sitting-room, just sort of hovering in mid air, and I know that it sounds as if I was hallucinating, but there was a thin, wispy cord attached to him.'

Nancy was too stunned to reply.

'Are you still there, Miss Harnetty? Please don't put the phone down.'

'Yes... yes, I'm still here. I think we should meet Isabel. Can you come to see me tomorrow at about eight?'

'I'd have seen you tonight if you had asked me, but eight tomorrow night will be fine. Give me your address and I'll be there. I can't tell you how grateful I am.'

Nancy sat down slowly. What was happening? No-one had ever described this phenomenon to her in all the years she had been a practising medium, yet, within the space of twenty-four hours, there had been two incidents. She put her head in her hands as she tried to understand, but it was not helping. As she clutched her head, she suddenly heard a voice say.

'There are others, my dear.'

Nancy knew, before she opened her eyes, that the presence was there. Just knowing she was near made her feel calmer.

'Who are you?'

'Who I am is not important at this time, but one day you will know. In the meantime, because I have chosen to help you, just think of me as your guardian angel, albeit temporarily.'

'Do you mind if I shorten that, and just call you Angel?'

'I have no objection to that, as long as you don't expect me to sprout wings.'

Nancy smiled for a brief moment, and then her doubts came crashing back.

'Angel, I really think I'm the wrong person to help Elsie, especially as you are now telling me there are more people suffering like her.'

'I had no part in choosing you, Nancy, but those who did chose well. You have compassion for others and a fear that makes you cautious of that which you do not understand and, although you are not yet aware of it, courage. You are the one, Nancy.'

She smiled gently at her; then she was gone.

Nancy's head returned to her hands. How on earth was she going to find the other trapped souls? If this was Angel's way of helping, then she was not impressed. Why give her this information and then leave? Suddenly, she realised she must already have the answer to that question or Angel would not have left, but what was it? Of course: Alan and Mabel. She could not, and was not expected to do it all; she must delegate some of the load. She rang Alan and was as brief as she could be in explaining all that had happened during the morning.

'I need you to call Mabel, and ask her to contact all the people she knows who give readings, and find out if any of them have heard similar stories. She's in contact with some of the best mediums in the country, so she's a good place to start.

Can I ask you to do the same, Alan? We'll need names and addresses and any other information they have, no matter how insignificant it may seem.'

'I'll get onto it as soon as I put the phone down, and I'm sure Mabel will be glad to help, but we should offer to pay for her telephone calls. She's in her eighties now and not a wealthy woman.'

'Of course, that's the least we can do. You know, Alan, the more I think about this case, I realise there are other details that I should have thought of at the time, but didn't. I guess the reason for that is because *these appearances* should not have happened the way they did.'

'In what way?' He asked.

'Well, the silver cord for a start. Have you ever seen it?'

'Never.'

'Exactly!' said Nancy. You're a very developed clairvoyant, but you have never witnessed it. It's referred to as a silver cord, but I saw it as a very thin shimmer of light. We know that people who travel astrally, are still connected to their body via this silver cord, which only separates from the body when we die. So, obviously, Elsie is alive. Now, I have only met a handful of people who have the ability to either sense, or see, an astral body, but usually they cannot see the cord, only sense it. In other words, as far as I'm aware, there are only a few people in the world who can actually *see* the silver cord.'

Alan didn't like what he was hearing.

'Yet now we have two people, who, never having shown any psychic ability, not only sensed, but saw Elsie and John. What is even more surprising is that they communicated with each other. Now comes the most amazing part. They both clearly saw the silver cord. I, myself, have only seen the cord on one occasion, many years ago, and then just for a brief moment. I am convinced I was shown the cord as confirmation that it does indeed exist, and that some higher power was called in to allow me to witness it. In other words, even I do not have the ability to see the silver cord naturally; I needed help. This brings us back to Georgie and Isabel. With no developed psychic ability, they could only have seen and heard what they did with a massive intervention of power from the other side.'

'Nance, I can't take all this in, even though I know what you're saying makes sense.'

'That's not the only thing I find extraordinary. From time to time, those who have passed on before us will try to help us when we are truly desperate, and answer our prayers if they can. But this is different. Georgie and Isabel were not aware of Elsie's and John's plight, so they certainly were not seeking any help. No, this time they were shown the problem; otherwise, to this day, they would never have been aware of it. They needed to see the silver cord so that when they contacted someone like us, we would immediately understand the significance of it.'

'Good lord!' exclaimed Alan. 'You're right.'

Nancy remained silent for a minute. 'I can only draw one conclusion from this, which I find even more frightening.'

'Which is?'

'That whatever is happening not only has us worried, because we can't understand it, but has offended and angered those in the next world too. There is an unwritten law that they do not interfere with our lives. We have total responsibility for our lives, and create our own heaven or hell; not that there is a hell, as depicted by the devil. So then I ask myself why? And of course, the answer is very simple.'

'Well, you've lost me,' said Alan.

'Whatever is happening has those in the next world as worried as we are. So worried, that they decided they had no alternative but to join forces with those who have the natural gift of communication with them. Angel has told us there are more, so we can only assume the problem is increasing. Those in *this* world must have created this phenomenon: why else would they send Angel? Had this problem originated from the

40

other side, it would have been dealt with there, and they would not have needed our help.'

'Nancy, if that's the case, why don't they just tell us what is happening, so that we can try and stop it from source?'

'You know the answer to that. They have no given rights over our world, or we over theirs. We can communicate and join forces in extreme circumstances; but there are no shortcuts. We will have to labour here, as they will labour there to help us. As the mystery unfolds, it will still be our decision, every step of the way, whether we want to continue or not. We will still retain our free will and they, theirs. To be honest, Alan, I'm afraid of the fight we have ahead. Neither of us has ever had to contend with anything like this, but we must try. We have no choice. The police would never believe these people. Even I needed convincing.'

Both had heavy hearts as they said goodbye.

There was no time to lose. She rang Alex Moorland.

'Morning, Alex. Its Nancy Harnetty here, how are you?'

'Couldn't be better, What about you, did the tour go well?'

'It went very well, except it was too long and tiring, and I'm really glad to be home.'

'Well, we're glad to have you home, and you've saved me a phone call, I was going to contact you in a few days and ask you over for dinner.'

'That would be nice, but I really need to see you sooner. I need your help.'

'That's a new one - you needing my help; it's usually the other way round.'

'I know. I need to call on your experience, Alex, but only if you're agreeable, and I will understand if you decide you can't help.'

His voice now held a more serious note. 'When do you want to meet?'

'It's very short notice, but I'm hoping you can be at my flat before eight tomorrow evening? I have a young woman coming to see me and I would like you present when she tells her story.'

There was silence for a moment. 'Are we talking about police business here?'

'I'm not sure, but I think that it may well be, and, if so, we'll need some help tracing a missing person unofficially, possibly two.'

'Why unofficially?' Alex was slightly baffled now.

'Because, at this point in time, the police would never believe, or understand, what has happened, and the two people who have contacted me so far, know this.'

'I'll be there before eight, Nancy. See you then.'

She replaced the receiver with relief. Alex had become a good friend over the years, but he was no fool, and he had not been one for bending the rules in his favour before he had retired as a Detective Chief Superintendent, so she had not been sure he would even consider helping. She was not out of the woods yet, either. He might find Georgie Well's and Isabel Jennings's experiences too unbelievable to accept.

Oh well, she would cross that bridge when she came to it.

SIX

Alex Moorland was fifty-eight years of age, and looked it. His lined face was more rugged than handsome, which made him attractive to women and accepted as "one of the boys" by the men. His tall body was still slim, muscular and agile and he wasn't afraid to walk the streets at night. He could still take care of himself if need be.

His eyes were the most striking thing about his face, and were the feature people noticed and remembered most. Dark brown eyes that were alert and, you knew, missed nothing. Some criminals he had interviewed in the past had described them as piercing; piercing eyes that could see into their minds, almost as though he knew what they were thinking. Alex was well aware of this effect and had never failed to take advantage of his natural talent.

He walked to the bedroom, opened the closet door and picked up his gym-bag. He worked-out at least three times a week at the local gym, and had been about to leave when Nancy had called. He put the bag on the bed and sat down. He looked at the picture of Lillian on the bedside table and his face softened.

It was five years ago, when his daughter Leila had persuaded him to see Nancy. He had no experience of psychics, through choice. He'd always considered them to be strange people. Most were probably harmless, but strange people nevertheless, who were at odds with what most people considered the norm. But it was a free country and, as long as their beliefs did not interfere with anyone else, it was their business.

He had always dealt in hard facts; someone staring into a crystal ball, spouting off information that only *they* could allegedly see and hear, did not amount to hard facts in his book. No, psychics did not produce hard facts; or so he had thought, until he met Nancy.

Six years ago his wife Lillian had died, leaving him devastated. Then, slowly and systematically, he had lost his zest for life. It had been a terrible shock. Lillian had not been unwell; a little tired perhaps, but not really unwell, so when she had a massive heart attack and died within a few hours, it had seemed to Alex that his life had come to an end too.

He recalled that telephone call from the hospital with pain, and re-lived the panic getting to the emergency unit. He was rushed in a squad car with flashing lights and loud sirens, but had hardly been aware of them. By the time he had arrived, she was unconscious.

He had clutched her hand and gently implored her to open her eyes, as he called her name. Lillian had not heard him. He had watched her, with growing despair and desperation, as she had slipped quietly and slowly away.

That he had not been able to say goodbye, still hurt, even though he had now come to terms with her death. If only she had regained consciousness long enough for him to tell her how much he loved her. They had pronounced her dead two hours later, and he could not believe or understand it. For a year after her death, it was as though he was on automatic pilot. He existed, but it wasn't living, not living as he had lived with Lillian for the last thirty years.

The light had gone out of his life.

When Leila had first asked him to see Nancy, for a month or so he had refused.

'She's dead. You know it and I know it,' he had shouted at her.

But somehow the suggestion had stayed with him until, in the end, he felt like a drowning man, clutching at straws, and he had finally gone to see Nancy Harnetty in desperation.

When he called Nancy to make an appointment, he was curious to see if she would try to pump him for any information prior to their meeting. She didn't, apart from

44

asking his name and telephone number, in case she should have to cancel due to unforeseen circumstances, because she had a two-month waiting list. He remembered, with some embarrassment, how rude he had been when told she could not see him sooner.

It was ridiculous. It had taken a great deal of soul-searching on his part to contact her in the first place, but to wait a further two months to know whether or not he was wasting his time had upset him more than he could ever have imagined. He was adamant. He was sure she could fit him in before, and asked her to recheck her diary.

Nancy had been quiet, but firm, in stating that she could not. She had then suggested other mediums that might be able to see him sooner. He had decided to wait.

From the time he had walked into Nancy's small flat, he had felt as if a great black cloud had been lifted from over his head. When he arrived, Nancy had told him that his wife was already waiting for him, and that this sometimes happened when there was a strong love bond between two people.

Lillian had so many memories to share with him, that Nancy (and indeed most people) could not have known; he was convinced she was somehow communicating with Lillian, and, for the first time in a year a sort of peace returned to his heart and mind.

Alex learned that Lillian's spirit now existed on another level. He also discovered, to his surprise, that she had been as unhappy as he was, because she'd had no respite from his grief. Lillian said she would always stay close to him and Leila, but he had to accept that they would not be together until it was his time. It was important for the sake of their daughter, who had borne an intolerable strain, not only coping with the loss of her mother, but also with her father's grief. Lillian's message had been simple but enlightening.

'Tell him I love him and I always will. My passing has not diminished my love for him or Leila. Tell him to remember the

good times, and learn to live his life as it is now, so I will not feel his pain: then we can both be at peace.'

He sighed as he picked up the gym-bag and left. As he drove, he recalled his conversation with Nancy and wondered about their meeting tomorrow night. He could not imagine how people could disappear and the police not be interested. He also had some concern that getting involved might, in some way, compromise his past reputation. He had always done everything by the book, and he didn't like the "unofficial" implications of it.

Although he had retired three years ago, Alex could still pick up the phone to any number of contacts if he needed information, but he would still need a bloody good reason; he wasn't sure that a good reason to Nancy, would necessarily be so to him. In fact, under the circumstances, he was sure of it.

He pulled into the car park of the gym and turned the car engine off.

Damn! This was going to be very difficult. Nancy had helped him get his life back together and he was very grateful, but being grateful and police business were two different things. He was very probably going to have to refuse, and that was truly upsetting for him. Why couldn't she just stick with what she knew and understood? He would go tomorrow evening and give her the benefit of the doubt, he owed her that much at least. He and Lillian owed her that.

* * *

Alex arrived early at Nancy's flat. He had worried about this meeting most of the night, because she might misinterpret his agreeing to be there as an assurance that, whatever the situation, he would help. He needed to talk to her beforehand and explain that this was not the case, but he wasn't looking forward to it. No matter how he tried to reason with himself, he still felt he was letting her down in some way.

46

Nancy opened the door and welcomed him in. If she was surprised that he was so early, she certainly gave no indication of it.

'Would you like some coffee, or shall we talk first?'

He smiled at her and immediately relaxed. He should have known she might well have anticipated his unease. Alex didn't know how she did it, only that her knowing and understanding how he felt, made what he had to say much easier.

'No coffee thanks, but I do need to talk.' He made his way into the sitting-room and waited for Nancy to be seated. He stood with his back to the fire-place, his legs apart and his hands firmly lodged in his pockets. He became a little uncomfortable, as he realised this was the sort of stance he normally adopted in his official capacity, but it had been instinctive. He was undecided, for a brief moment, as to whether he should sit down, or not. No, he would remain as he was, because, rightly or wrongly, he felt more at ease reverting to a former habit.

'You have become a good friend and your friendship is important. I hope you know that?'

'Of course I do, Alex.'

'There's not much I wouldn't do for you and I hope you know that, too?' She nodded.

'I just want to say that I cannot promise to help you with this situation, but I will stay and listen to whatever is worrying you and give advice if I can, but that's it, okay?'

Alex was not one for long drawn out speeches, so it flashed through Nancy's mind that had he arrived ten minutes early, and not half an hour, it would have been more than adequate.

'Of course it is' she replied. 'Now shall we have some coffee?'

'Why not.' A broad grin spread over his face. 'I can't tell you how relieved I am to have got that out of the way.'

'I know,' said Nancy. 'I know.'

Isabel arrived early, too, and it wasn't long before they were all seated.

'Isabel, this is Alex Moorland and he's a retired police officer. If you don't mind, I would like him to sit in on our discussion?'

'I'm not sure he can help me, Miss Harnetty, otherwise I would have gone to the police in the first place. In fact, to be perfectly honest, I would have preferred to talk to them about this matter.' She quickly raised one hand, aghast.

'I shouldn't have said that. I didn't mean to offend you, really I didn't.'

Nancy smiled, to put her at ease. 'Call me Nancy, and, don't worry, no offence taken.'

Isabel glanced uncertainly in Alex's direction. 'I just don't think the police would have believed me. I find it hard to believe myself, even though I know it happened. They would just have decided I was a bit of a nutter.'

Isabel had Alex's full attention now. Interesting; if Nancy was her second choice, then, in his estimation, she was more believable.

'I would still like Alex to stay, Isabel.'

Alex decided he wanted to stay, too.

Tears appeared in her eyes. 'I need help' she said quietly, 'so if you think it's necessary, then, yes, he can stay.' Isabel searched her handbag for some tissues and wiped her eyes.

'I came home from work two nights ago, and something happened which at first terrified me, and then filled me with nothing but pity.'

Isabel looked at them uncertainly, as she realised the implication of what she had said. 'I know I am contradicting myself, but that is truly how I felt.'

The tissue caught another stray tear.

'I was engaged to a man called John Harris, for a couple of years, but I have not seen him for quite some time. The other night I was very tired. I'm a nurse, and the hospital where I work is very short-staffed at the moment. When I got home, all I wanted to do was crash out on the sofa, which I did, and then I must have dozed off. Anyway, suddenly I was awake, but I still had my eyes closed. I had a really strong feeling I was being watched, yet I knew no sound had woken me. I was afraid, but didn't know why. I wanted to open my eyes, but couldn't. I kept telling myself I was being really stupid, and if I opened my eyes, I would see how silly I was. In the end, I forced myself to open my eyes.'

At this point, they could feel and see the terror in her face, as she recounted what had happened.

Nancy moved quickly and sat down beside her on the settee. She put her arms around Isabel and tried to comfort her.

'I know it's hard for you, but you have nothing to fear now. Just hold onto me. It's very important that you tell me exactly what happened, before I can help you.'

Alex noticed the 'I' rather than the 'we'. She was keeping her word.

Isabel drew comfort from the nearness of Nancy, as she continued.

'I opened my eyes and could not believe what I was seeing, nor can I describe the sheer terror I felt. I thought I was going to pass out.' Her eyes were wide and staring, as she remembered.

'John was in the middle of my sitting-room, just sort of hovering, suspended a few feet off the ground. He looked as terrified as I was. I couldn't move a muscle. My natural reaction was to run, but it was as though I was paralysed. I wanted to scream, and I kept opening my mouth, but nothing came out. I don't know how long I remained like that; it was as if time stood still. I had no control over anything. I was terrified, but instinctively knew I had to try and think clearly. I told myself that if I closed my eyes, the sight before me would disappear. I began to reason that this could not be happening, and that I was having some kind of nightmare, because I was so tired, so I started to pray to God to stop this vision and send it away.'

Isabel began to sob.

Nancy held her closer and stroked her head. 'Take your time Isabel, there's no rush.'

'I'm sorry to keep crying, I don't normally. I guess it has affected me more than I realised.'

She didn't speak for a while, as she tried to calm herself. 'As I began to pray, I heard John say, please don't shut me out. His words were intermittent; laboured, as though it was as difficult for him to communicate with me, as it was for me to understand what he was trying to say, or what he wanted. He begged for my help. He said there was no one else who could help him. He said he was trapped in a void and couldn't get back to the light. I could feel his pain and how unhappy he was. No, it was more than unhappy; it was as if he was *demented*.'

Isabel was quiet for a while. She became more peaceful and the tears stopped. Her eyes had been firmly fixed on the ground, as she struggled to tell her tale. She found it hard to meet their eyes, in case she saw the disbelief she expected. She knew how unreal it must sound.

'I know it sounds strange, he didn't actually speak to me. But somehow I knew what he wanted to say, and could feel his pain. There was a silver cord, attached to his body, which sort of floated and moved with him. I remember everything, as though it had just happened; every little detail, yet the vision seemed so unreal that, even now, I keep asking myself, was I dreaming? How is this possible, Nancy? What happened?'

'It's only possible under extreme circumstances, and only if there is no other way. You were the link John chose because he trusted you.'

'Will it happen again?' she asked.

'No, I don't think it will. I believe he now knows that others are aware, even though, to be honest, I'm not sure what is happening. I can't say it will end his misery, but I'm sure he will draw some comfort from it.'

Nancy stood up. 'I think you could do with something a little stronger than coffee, Isabel. In fact, I think we all could. What can I get you?'

'Vodka and tonic, if you have it.'

'Coming up,' she smiled.

Nancy returned with a tray and passed Isabel her drink.

Alex had not spoken at all during Isabel's story, but he'd missed nothing. His face gave no indication as to what he was thinking, but she knew he was moved by her story.

'I know this is will be a shock for you, Isabel,' said Nancy, 'and I wish I didn't have to say what I am about to, but I have no choice, especially as I will need more information about John if I am to try and help you.' For the first time, Nancy looked a little uneasy.

'Isabel, there is no easy way to say this, but John is not dead.'

Alex's eyes narrowed as he watched her, but her total attention was directed at Isabel.

This was the last thing Isabel expected to hear. She was too amazed to reply for a moment; then disbelief made her react.

'He must be dead. Why else would he appear like he did? He would have just telephoned or come round to see me if he needed my help; it doesn't make sense.' She took another tissue from her bag, as the tears returned.

'How can he be alive when he was floating like that? No, it's not possible? I can't bear to think of him suffering and still be alive.'

'It doesn't make sense to me either, but there must be some reason things are happening as they are, even though I don't understand what it is.' She sighed. 'I know how hard this is for you, but John is not dead.'

'How do you know he's not dead?' asked Alex.

'The only way the spirit can leave the body, and return, is via the silver cord; it's the living body's lifeline, and its only source of re-entry. The silver cord only separates from the body when it dies, so, you see, John must be alive.'

Nancy turned her attention back to Isabel. 'Is there any chance that you could have made a mistake about seeing the cord?'

'No, I saw it very clearly all the time I could see John I did not make a mistake about that.'

'Then John is most definitely alive.' They were both looking at Nancy expectantly, as though she would now reveal how she could end his hell. Neither Alex nor Isabel moved.

'I'll try to explain as simply as I can. When you saw John, you clearly saw a cord of light attached to him that moved as he did, so you knew, without a doubt, that somehow it was part of him?'

'Yes,' said Isabel.

'Going back to Egyptian times, they referred to this apparition as the Ka, meaning the "spirit that resides within". In other words, the spirit that resides within a living body. The Egyptians even believed that some statues had Ka's, which is why they worshiped some effigies as Gods. So the knowledge that we possess a spirit or soul (whatever you prefer to call it) is not new. Every religion teaches this. Whether you choose to believe it, or not, is personal choice. On this occasion, you will have to accept my word that the Ka exists, if you are to understand how it happened. What I cannot explain is, why.' Nancy picked up her whisky - she needed it.

'The body is a complex and wonderful thing. It's made up of muscle, tissue, blood, bones, a nervous system, and vital organs and so on. It also has energy. Every time you decide to do something, a message is sent to your brain, via this energy, to enact it. I believe this energy source is an integral part of the spirit within us, and retains the knowledge we acquire during our life-time. It's a scientific fact that you cannot destroy energy. It can be changed, but you cannot destroy it. So when our body dies, this energy leaves it in spirit form, because it can no longer function within it.

'Now, there are a few people who have the ability to make their Ka leave their body at will. In some countries, such as America and Russia, experiments have been conducted with people who have this gift, but usually for a dubious purpose. The advantage, they envisaged, was mainly for spying. Imagine sending an agents Ka anywhere in the world to listen in on secret meetings, without anyone realising they had an uninvited guest who defied detection.

'Sometimes a person's Ka is ejected from their bodies by accident, usually through trauma, such as a car crash, or near-death experience. Many such experiences have occurred during surgery, but the body *always* experiences a feeling of peace and tranquility, losing all sense of pain and fear. Some do experience confusion and find it hard to understand, when it's an involuntary action. Others are just very curious and intrigued by the experience. But I say again, the body is at peace and free from pain. This is not the case with John. What you have described is the total opposite.

'What is even more worrying, Isabel, is that John is not the only one. This is the second time in forty-eight hours that I have heard a similar story, but in all the years I have been a clairvoyant, I have never had anyone come to me with such a problem. The only difference is that the other person is a woman. Her name is Elsie Turnbull.'

'Could it be some kind of black magic?' asked Alex.

'As I have no idea what we're dealing with, I cannot rule that out.'

Alex turned his attention to Isabel. 'Do you feel up to answering a few questions?'

She could only nod; she could not take in all Nancy had said.

'Since this happened, have you tried to contact John at all.'

'Oh yes, I called his work yesterday. He's worked for the same company for several years and they remembered me. Evidently, he left for home as usual one Friday after work, and did not return the following Monday morning. When they didn't hear from him after a few days, they telephoned him and left a message on his answer-machine, because it was so out of character for him not to let the company know if he was sick. When he still didn't call, they became quite worried and sent someone down to his home on two occasions, but there was no answer and his neighbours said they hadn't seen him either. By this time, they were really concerned and reported his disappearance to Croydon police station.'

'What did they find out?' Alex asked with interest.

'They gained entry to his flat and found all his clothes had gone, so the police decided he had left voluntarily for some reason or other. He's not been seen since.'

Alex's eyes narrowed. 'What kind of person is he?'

'Oh, very much a loner,' she replied. 'He didn't have any real friends, just a few acquaintances, but he never sees any of them on a regular basis. He might have changed. I haven't seen him for a couple of years, but I wouldn't have thought so.'

A warning bell rang in Nancy's head. 'I don't know whether it's relevant or not, but Elsie Turnbull was also described as a loner.'

'Sometimes loners have psychiatric problems.' He directed his suggestion to Isabel.

'Definitely not,' she replied, 'he's just one of those people who is happy with his own company, and he has so many interests, he isn't the type to get bored.'

'Nancy, did you get the impression from Elsie's relative that she may have had psychiatric problems, no matter how small?'

'No; just the opposite.'

'Then it may well be relevant,' Alex replied.

* * *

Isabel had just left, and Nancy wasn't sure whether she had made her feel a whole lot better, which under the circumstances, was understandable. Nancy was feeling just as low, because of the responsibility that had been placed on her shoulders. What was it that Angel had said? They would help and protect her. She was glad of their support, but the "protection" bit worried her. Initially, she hadn't interpreted this to mean it could be dangerous, now she was not so sure. If this was some kind of black magic, then she was right out of her depth. Her knowledge of black magic was zero, so why had they chosen her? It should have been someone who had the ability to fight on the same level. Nancy had never been interested in the black arts, and didn't want to have to start now.

'A penny for them?' said Alex.

She decided not to share her thoughts with him. If he decided to help, Nancy did not want him to do so because he felt some responsibility to protect her.

'It's just a lot to think about and I'm wondering where to start.'

'We could start with me picking up the pieces from where John and Elsie disappeared.'

She could not hide the relief in her face. 'What made you change your mind?'

'Isabel. She didn't strike me as being fanciful or silly, and the cockney taxi driver sounds like he has both feet well and truly on the ground, so I find it hard to believe he would have just thought this up, and for what reason? Then there's the coincidence of two people, who do not know each other, having a similar experience. Two, in my book, is not enough, but if there are indeed other cases out there, then my gut is telling me I should make some enquiries; having said that, it's going to be one hell of a job. The longer a person is missing, the harder it is to trace them, so I can only do my best with the little information we have at the moment, and without police resources, it will be even tougher. If there really is anything in this, then I wouldn't be a good ex-copper if I didn't try and investigate it, but, I have to be honest, I have never liked unofficial investigations.'

He thought for a moment. 'I'll make this a private investigation; I prefer the sound of that.'

Nancy laughed.

'But if I discover anything to substantiate these disappearances, I pass all relevant information over to the proper authorities. Agreed?'

'Agreed.'

'You know what, Nancy, I don't like the circumstances of this case, but I'd be lying if I said I wasn't looking forward to getting my teeth into a really interesting investigation. I guess the excitement never really goes away.'

SEVEN

Alex picked up the phone and rang Bilston Police Station, where he had been stationed for the last10 years before he had retired at the age of 56.

'Put me through to Sergeant Bill Palmer, if he's on duty, please.'

'Yes, he is. Who's calling? Hold on please.'

Bill Palmer and he had worked well together. They had never been true buddies, but they had a lot of respect for each other. Bill was not what he would call a "forward thinker", but he was first-class when given direction and tasks to do and was very methodical. He rarely missed a thing.

'Hello, Alex. It's been a while since we last spoke. How's the world treating you?'

'I've no complaints Bill. What about you?'

'Well, I'm still overworked – nothing's changed there - but that goes with the territory, so I have to "put up or shut up".'

Alex laughed. 'As you said, it goes with the territory.'

'Now, what can I do for you? Not looking for tickets to the police ball are you?' He could have bitten his tongue off as he said it. Alex used to enjoy them, but only because Lillian did. 'That was a stupid thing to say, Alex, I'm sorry.'

'No offence taken, but I do need your help.'

'Fire away.'

'I want you to check with Croydon station and get any details you can on a John Harris, who was reported missing, and on any progress they may have made.'

'Okay, but why do you want to know? Have you information you think can help Croydon?'

'Not at the moment. I'm making a few enquiries on behalf of a good friend, but my investigation will be from a totally different angle; one they wouldn't even consider. There's an outside chance his disappearance is connected to another, so you'll just have to trust me on this one, Bill. But you have my word that when, and if, I turn up anything Croydon should be aware of, I'll pass everything over to you.'

'Fair enough leave it with me and I'll see what I can do. I'll get back to you later today if there is anything to report.'

'I'm going out now and not sure what time I'll be back, so just leave a message on my answer-machine. No specific details, mind you: just that you called.'

Alex checked his watch and noted it was 9.40am; time to leave. It would take him a while to get there, but the traffic should be lighter now. He decided he would start with Barnet General Hospital, Elsie Turnbull's last known employer.

The journey was not a good one and took longer than anticipated, but the one thing he had plenty of these days, was time. He drove past the hospital looking for the car park and discovered it was situated at the rear. He switched off the engine, picked up the folder he had placed on the seat beside him and read the brief details Nancy had taken from Georgie Wells. It didn't say how long she had worked at the hospital, just a "long time" as far as Georgie could remember.

He walked briskly to the stepped entrance at Barnet Hospital and leapt up them, two at a time. Inside, he paused to get his bearings before approaching the enquiry desk.

'I would like to speak to someone in the Personnel Department please.'

'Do you have an appointment?'

'No, I do not.'

The enquiry clerk studied him. He certainly wasn't applying for a porter's or cleaner's job. Had he been, it would have been easy to refer him to someone else, even without an appointment. They were crying out for porters and cleaners. He looked the official type.

'The Personnel Department doesn't usually see people without an appointment. They prefer to see a CV first. Do you have one with you that you can leave, with an indication of the position you're looking for?'

'I'm not looking for a job, thank you, so please just get onto Personnel and tell them that Alex Moorland would like to see whoever is in charge.'

The enquiry clerk looked a little uneasy. The man had an air of authority about him, which was intimidating and made her reticent to question him further. She rang through to Personnel and spoke to Mrs. Roberts, the Senior Personnel Officer.

'Mrs. Roberts would like to know why you wish to see her.'

'I'm making enquiries about an ex-employee, who we have reason to believe is missing.'

A look of interest crossed the enquiry clerk's face as she relayed the message.

'Mrs. Roberts will see you in five minutes, if you don't mind waiting?'

'I'll wait, thank you.' She directed him through what seemed a maze of corridors, but eventually he found himself inside a small waiting-room off a long narrow corridor.

He was not a patient man, mainly because he was not used to being kept waiting. She had said five minutes. He checked his watch; it was now nearer twenty. He decided enough was.....

'Mrs. Roberts will see you now. Her office is the second door on the right, down the corridor.'

He was already walking in that direction as he called over his shoulder. 'Thanks.'

Mrs. Roberts was a plump lady with a pleasant manner. He guessed her to be in her mid-forties.

'Please sit down', she said indicating a chair. 'Now, how can I help you?'

'I'm trying to trace a woman who used to work here, called Elsie Turnbull. She was employed as a cleaner, I believe.'

'Yes, Elsie worked here for about fifteen years, and a very good worker she was too - always punctual and very reliable. Are you a private investigator?'

'No, Mrs. Roberts, I'm a retired Detective Chief Superintendent and I have been asked to make enquiries on behalf of her cousin, Georgie Wells.'

'Oh yes, that was the gentleman who rang recently, but I am afraid it's not our policy to divulge details over the phone. It could be anyone, you see.'

'Did Elsie contact Barnet Hospital to say she was ill, or anything, prior to her leaving?'

'No she didn't. In fact it was quite strange the way she left. She just didn't report in for duty on Monday, although she was at work on the previous Friday and didn't appear to be unwell or worried in any way. I was a little concerned when we heard nothing from her, as she was always so reliable, and it was totally out of character, so I rang her lodgings. Her landlady checked her room and we were both shocked to discover she had, in fact, moved out.' She lowered her voice, 'evidently, she left owing rent. Her landlady was livid.'

'Have you had any enquiries for a reference from any prospective employer?'

'No, this surprises me as she has an excellent work record. She was also dependent on the money she earned, so I cannot see how she could survive without a job.'

'Did anyone contact the police to report her missing?'

'I certainly did not, Mr. Moorland, but there was a very good reason for that. Elsie had taken all her clothes and the few possessions she had, before she left, so, wherever she went, it was obviously planned.'

'Before she left, did she take any holiday entitlement?'

'Not as far as I can remember, but I'll check.' Mrs. Roberts left the room for a while.

Alex sighed. He was beginning to have a really bad feeling about Elsie Turnbull, and felt annoyed that people who had known her for so long had not been more suspicious. He didn't know Elsie at all, but his gut was telling him something was wrong.

Mrs. Roberts bustled back into the office. 'How strange,' she said. 'We still owe her three weeks' holiday money.'

'For someone who was so dependent on her wages, I find that strange too. Why not just give in her notice or take three weeks' holiday before leaving her lodgings? After all, she could still have left her lodgings without advising her landlady, if that was her intention, and she would have been a few weeks' wages richer to help her on her way.'

A frown appeared, 'Yes, I see what you mean.'

'Did Elsie have any problems at work, such as disputes with any of the other staff?'

'No, not that I am aware of, but I wouldn't have thought so. Elsie was the type that came in and got on with her work and didn't waste time gossiping with others, which is why she was such a gem. I was very sorry to lose her.'

'Is there anyone she worked with, who she might have confided in, that I could speak to? Perhaps they could give me some indication as to her state of mind before she left.' asked Alex hopefully.

'The only person I can think of is Mavis, another cleaner, who has worked here even longer than Elsie; nearly twenty years, if my memory serves me right.'

'Mrs. Roberts, it's very important that I speak to her now. Time is of the essence here, the longer a person is missing, the more difficult it is to find them.'

Mrs. Roberts did not answer immediately; she needed to think about his request for a moment. She hadn't come up against a situation like this before.

'Alright, but only if I'm present and Mavis is agreeable.'

'I have no problem with that.'

'I'll send for her. Would you like a coffee while we wait?'

'I thought you'd never ask.' he smiled.

She returned his smile.

As Mavis entered the room, out of sheer habit he tried to assess the type of person she was. He noted with interest that she was doing exactly the same with him. There's not much she misses, he thought.

'Mavis, I'm a retired Detective Chief Superintendent making enquiries about Elsie Turnbull on behalf of a relative,' he was about to continue when she interrupted.

'About time someone did.'

'Why do you say that, Mavis?'

'Because she wouldn't just go off like that without a word, no, she never would. She was a creature of habit and not the adventurous type at all.' She was becoming a little agitated.

'No, she liked to do the same things at the same time everyday. That's what made her feel secure, knowing that she had her little job and her little room. She wouldn't have taken off like that without a word to no one, nor a by your leave. She was too conscientious and would have worried that her work wasn't being done. She would have called, I know she would.'

Alex did not believe his next question was relevant, but he had to cover all angles.

'Do you think it conceivable that she'd met a man and not told anyone about him, especially if he was married? If she decided to go away with him, she wouldn't have mentioned it for obvious reasons.'

'Look here, Mr. Moorland, or whatever you're bloody name is, I ain't stupid. I know I would have sensed a change in Elsie if she had met a man, especially as she hadn't had a boyfriend in the fifteen years that I knew her, and I would guess never had a regular boyfriend. No,' she said emphatically, 'I'm sure I would have known.'

He studied her for a moment. 'I'm sure you're right, Mavis. So if there was no involvement with a man, do you think she could have got into debt?'

'No, I don't. Why would she suddenly need money? Clothes weren't important to her. Most times she bought them from charity shops. She wasn't a smoker or drinker and she told me she saved, regular like, for her retirement.'

'So what do you think happened to her?'

'I ain't got no answer for that, but I do know something's wrong, and it's about bloody time someone tried to find her.'

'Mavis, you have been a great help to me and I appreciate your honesty.'

Alex returned to his car, swung himself into the front seat and reviewed the events of the morning in his mind. He picked up his notebook and jotted down the details, while they were still fresh in his memory. Now, he had a good idea of the type of person Elsie was, and instinct told him she was in trouble.

He now supported Nancy's concern for her, although they had both come to their conclusions for different reasons. He was no expert when it came to the unknown, but he did understand basic facts as they were given to him and in Elsie's case, they did not tally. He'd wager she did not leave of her own free will, and there could only be one logical reason for removing her belongings. Someone did not want an official investigation, no matter how small.

But why? It didn't make sense. She wasn't a wealthy woman, or likely to inherit a substantial amount of money or property. He was sure Georgie Wells would have mentioned it if she had. No, it did not add up. He decided to go straight to her last known address and speak to her landlady. Perhaps he would find some of the answers there. He checked the notes Nancy had given him for her address and the name of the landlady. Yes, there it was, Rudleigh Street, and the landlady's name was Dodds.

Alex wasn't familiar with the Barnet area, so looked up the A-Z before moving off in a southerly direction. Twenty minutes later, he drew up outside No 4 and walked up to the door of a shabby house that looked sadly in need of a coat of paint. He knocked and waited.

He thought he saw a slight movement of a side-window curtain, and a few minutes later the front door opened.

'Good morning, are you Mrs. Dodds?' He asked politely.

'Who wants to know.' she replied suspiciously.

He introduced himself and asked if he might have a few words concerning Elsie Turnbull.

An undisguised look of interest now showed on her face as she stepped back and ushered him in.

'Have you found the cow?' She called over her shoulder.

He followed her into a small sitting-room, noting the furniture was as shabby as the exterior.

Mrs. Dodds had a definite limp. He noticed her fingers were deformed, so he guessed she suffered from arthritis. He suspected she had been a bit of a looker in her younger days - she still showed traces of a delicate, oval face and bone structure - but the years had not been kind to her.

'No, I have not found Elsie as yet. That's why I need to talk to you.'

'I don't see why. She certainly left no forwarding address with me, nor would she, seeing as she left owing me two weeks' rent.' She paused. 'Mind you, her relative Mr. Wells paid it when I told him. I thought that was very decent of him, I did, very decent, especially as he hadn't seen her for a few years.'

'To be honest Mrs. Dodds, we're not sure what has happened to Elsie. But her cousin seems to think she would not have just gone off like that and, I have to admit, neither do I. So if I could ask you a few questions, you may be able to throw some light on the situation?'

'Like what?'

'I understand that all Elsie's clothes and belongings had been removed from her room. Do you have any idea when this might have happened?'

'I heard and saw nothing, but if she was going to do a runner owing me rent, I wouldn't would I?'

'Are you in most of the time?'

'Yes, so if you're asking me when I think she took them, it was probably on a Friday afternoon. My daughter always picks me up in the car and then takes me shopping.' Her face softened.

'I look forward to Friday afternoons; we have lunch out and it makes a nice break for me. I can't get around as well as I used to.' Her face hardened, 'That would be the only time Elsie could guarantee I was out.'

'When did you first realise Elsie had left?'

'A lady from Barnet Hospital rang, asking where she was. Said she hadn't been to work and they hadn't heard from her. I became concerned for her then, because I realised I hadn't heard her either for a few days. I thought she might be ill in bed, so I went up and knocked on her door. I kept calling her but when I didn't get a reply, I fetched the spare key and let myself in. You could have knocked me down with a feather when I realised she had taken all her bits and pieces, and her owing me rent.' The memory of it brought a touch of anger again to Mrs. Dodds voice.

'Did she pay her rent weekly?'

'No, fortnightly. She got paid every two weeks, you see, so she was due to pay the rent that week.'

'Had she always paid her rent on time?'

'Regular as clockwork. That's why I was so surprised. Ten years she had rented that room and I never once had to chase her.'

'Then why didn't you think there might be something wrong?'

'Because she took all her belongings. I've had lodgers on and off for the last thirty years and, I can tell you, if they take all their bits and pieces, it's because they've done a runner.'

He was silent for a moment before he asked. 'Have you asked any of your neighbours if they saw Elsie moving her things out?'

'No, Mr. Moorland, I keep's me-self to me-self, and I don't want others thinking it's easy to leave owing me rent, if you know what I mean?'

65

'Mrs. Dodds, I'm sorry but I will have to ask your neighbours if they saw anything, because I am now more convinced than ever that Elsie did not intend to leave as she did. In fact I would say we have a missing person.'

'Why did all her belongings go then? They weren't worth stealing.'

'I won't be able to answer that until I find someone who saw her property being moved. Now, I can systematically knock on everyone's door, or you can give me some indication as to who might have been the most likely person to have noticed something?'

'No,' she replied quickly, 'don't do that; try old Mrs. Bates opposite at number 5. If anyone saw anything, she did. Nosey old bat, always watching out her window. Can't sneeze without her knowing it.'

Alex thanked her and proceeded to cross the road and knocked at the door of Mrs. Bates. A voice from behind the door said, 'I ain't buying anything. If Mrs. Dodds sent you here, I can tell you now, I don't need nothing.'

A look of amusement crossed his face. So she had watched him enter and leave number 4. That was an encouraging sign.

'Mrs. Bates.' He raised his voice so he could be heard through the closed door.

'My name is Moorland and I am making enquiries about a woman who used to lodge at Mrs. Dodds. I just want to ask you a few questions, because it's important that we trace her.'

Mrs. Bates opened the door slightly, but left the security chain engaged as she peered out at him.

'I can talk to you here, Mrs. Bates. I understand you being careful about letting strange people in your home.'

She released the security chain and stood back as she opened the door.

'Are you a policeman? You look like one.'

'I was in the police force, but I'm retired now. This is a private investigation, Mrs. Bates, on behalf of a relative.'

'Well, don't stand on the doorstep like that, come in.' He followed as she shuffled into a room that still showed some evidence of its former elegance.

'Enquiries about what?' she asked.

'A Miss ElsieTurnbull had a room over the road at number 4. She lived there for quite a few years and I'd like to ask you a few questions about her, if I may?'

'Such as?'

Alex had found, during the course of his career that "watchers" were not usually "talkers", and Mrs. Bates was no exception.

'Did you know Elsie Turnbull by sight?'

'Yes, she's a nice woman, unlike that landlady of hers.'

'She was last seen on Friday June 19th at her place of work. At some time on or around this date, her personal belongings were removed from that address. I know it's a while back, but did you see Elsie leaving with any luggage?'

'No' she answered.

So far so good, he thought. 'Did you notice anything unusual round about that time at the house opposite?'

'No, how can I remember that long ago?'

He had a sudden thought, he wondered if she was in the habit of watching Mrs. Dodds' daughter fetch her on a Friday afternoon.

'We think it was a Friday afternoon when her personal belongings were removed, because it's the only time Mrs. Dodds is not at home. That's the day her daughter calls to take her shopping.'

'I know.'

She stared at the wall opposite for a while with her eyes slightly closed as she tried to remember, and then a look of recognition suddenly appeared on her face.

'Now I remember. Yes, there *was* something I thought was strange, nearly forgot it. Mrs. Dodd's daughter called for her, so I know it was a Friday. Some ten minutes after they had left, a man I'd never seen before goes up to the front door and lets himself in. I remember thinking she must have a new lodger. Anyway, about twenty minutes later, he came out carrying two suitcases and off he went. Not long after that, another man let himself in and did exactly the same thing, only this time he was carrying two large bags, you know, those hold-all things. When he went in he was carrying one large bag, but came out carrying two.'

'Was one bag smaller than the other?'

'It could have been, I can't remember, but why would it matter? '

'I was just thinking, whoever it was could have placed a smaller bag inside the other.'

'I suppose.'

'The first man - was he carrying any suitcases when he went in?'

'No.'

'Are you quite sure about that?'

'I may be old, but I'm not senile.'

He smiled. 'Of that I have no doubt, Mrs. Bates.'

She studied him. He could be a bit of a charmer when necessary.

'Have you seen them since, or did you see them together at any time?'

'I haven't seen either of them since, but I don't think they were together.'

'Why?'

'Well, the first man walked down the street and round the corner, but the second man got into a parked car down the road and drove off.'

'Did he drive off in the same direction as the first man?'

She thought for a moment. 'Yes, he did.'

'Did you mention this to Mrs. Dodds at all?'

'Not on your life, she would just have called me a nosey old bugger. She's done that before now.'

'Can you remember at all when this was, Mrs. Bates, apart from the fact it was a Friday?'

68

He didn't rush her, as she struggled to remember. He guessed her age to be in the mid-seventies; a small frail woman with gray, straight hair tied severely back in a small knot.

'Must have been sometime in June, because the young couple next door left on their holidays the following day, and I remember thinking about the two men carrying luggage from number 4, and how everyone was going on holiday except me. But I don't remember the date. Why don't you ask the couple next door when they went on holiday? They're at work now, but I can give you their home telephone number.'

'I would appreciate that, Mrs. Bates. You have been very helpful and I cannot thank you enough.'

Her face lit up as she received his praise. 'You're very welcome, I'm sure.'

He waited while she searched for the telephone number; she obviously had a much better relationship with the young couple next door, and was probably a great asset to them if they were out working all day. Having another pair of eyes watching your home is very advantageous in an area not classified as salubrious.

He made his way back to number 4 and rang the bell. Mrs. Dodds must have been waiting for him because the door was opened immediately. As he sat in her sitting-room and related what Mrs. Bates had seen, her mouth fell open with surprise.

'I gather from your expression you have no idea who these two men are?'

'None at all, Mr. Moorland. I'm really worried. If they have keys, suppose they come back while I'm here on my own.' She thought for a brief moment. 'How can they have keys, its not possible?'

'Oh, I'm sure they did, but please don't alarm yourself. They will never come back; they have what they came for - Elsie's belongings. If they wanted to steal anything of value, they certainly would not have emptied her room so meticulously. No, they would have taken only things they could sell, not just concentrated on her room. They'd have searched the whole house but, as far as I am aware, only *her* things were taken.'

'Nothing else is missing, but why? It doesn't make sense.'

'It makes perfect sense. They did not want Elsie to be reported as a missing person, and as you and the Personnel Officer at Barnet Hospital said, no-one takes all their belongings unless they voluntarily *want* to disappear. That's what they wanted you to believe, and that's exactly what you did believe.'

'Why didn't they take it all in one go; why pick it up in two lots?'

'I suspect it was to attract less attention. If a van arrived and a couple of men had let themselves in and cleared the flat, someone would probably have enquired who had moved out. A man on his own attracts much less attention, especially carrying suitcases. Anyone carrying suitcases or bags in June is a natural sight; because that's the time people go on holiday. It has been five months since Elsie disappeared, and no one was any the wiser till now.'

'Dear God; poor Elsie' said Mrs. Dodds.

'Yes,' replied Alex, 'poor Elsie.'

EIGHT

Alex took his time driving home; he had a lot on his mind. The more he learned about this case, the more puzzled he became. It didn't make sense. He needed to speak to Bill Palmer; he had the bit between his teeth now. As soon as he arrived home, he went straight to check the answer phone. Bill's brief message just said, "call me when you can," so he did.

'Hi Alex, I checked with Croydon and they confirmed John Harris had been reported missing, but they were not pursuing it at the moment because, on making enquiries, they found his home had been cleared out.'

'When you say his flat had been cleared, do you mean his clothes?

'Yes, everything personal, even down to his toothbrush and toothpaste. Wherever he went, it looks like he planned to stay for a while.'

'I find that a bit odd. I mean, if he was that serious, why not let his company or someone know he was taking off for a while?'

'Who knows, but lets be honest, Alex, wherever he went, it had to have been planned over some time.'

'Or, his abduction was planned over some time.'

'Now you're not making sense. If someone wanted to abduct him, why not just do it? I've never heard of an abduction case where they went back to collect the victims clothes and, I'd guess, neither have you. After all, this guy wasn't Paul Getty. Anyway, why stop at his gear. Why not take other bits and pieces they could sell?'

Alex was quiet for a moment. 'I've been speaking to his ex-fiancé Bill, and in view of what she said. I would prefer to make a few enquiries, just to confirm everything is kosher, if you don't mind. '

'Such as?'

'He was buying his flat, so if he moved, does he intend selling or renting? Is he still paying the mortgage? Does he have any money in the bank, or has any money been paid in or out of his account in the last few months? From the little I know of him, what's happened is totally out of character. I know it's hassle, Bill, but one way or another it has to be done. I've got a bad feeling about this.'

'You don't think Harris left of his own free will?'

'Well, let's just say, having checked out someone who disappeared in similar circumstances, no I don't.'

'I'm probably missing something here, but what's the point of going to all the trouble of moving his belongings? That carried a much greater risk of things going wrong.'

'The answer to your question is much easier than the reason for his disappearance. If I'm right, whoever was responsible wanted everyone to think he took off, of his own free will. You know, the longer a person is missing the harder it is to find them. The trail goes cold, and people's memories fade with time. In fact, I think that's the reason for their efforts. They didn't want the police investigating, and if that was their intention, they have been very successful.'

Bill didn't answer immediately. He still wasn't convinced. 'We're going to have to meet and discuss this Guv. I need to know more than I do now before I'm convinced I'm not wasting police time. The only reason I'm helping is because I worked with you for ten years, and there's not a man at the station who doesn't trust your judgement, but I could get severely reprimanded for this, especially by the DCS who took over from you. He's not known as a tolerant man.'

'You're right, we need to talk and we will. I don't want to make things difficult for you, but hold everything for the moment. Hopefully I can you save you some time.

Let me talk to his ex-fiancée first. She might be able to tell us who he banked with etc. By the way, Bill, I owe you for this and I won't forget it.'

'You're not wrong there, Guv, but I could come out smelling of roses if you're right.'

'Let's hope so.' Alex smiled as he replaced the receiver. It had been a long time since he had been called Guv, and it brought back a lot of fond memories. He picked up the phone again and rang the hospital where Isabel Jennings worked. They were not happy about private calls, but because he said it was urgent, they promised to get a message through to her. She rang back within ten minutes.

'How are you feeling today, Isabel? I guess last night was tough on you.'

'You will never know how tough and, believe it or not, how uncomfortable the situation was for me. But I hope you didn't call just to commiserate, Mr. Moorland? I'm terribly busy.'

She sounded harassed, and she was. Knowing she had felt uncomfortable, only confirmed his conviction that she had been sincere when telling her story. He still couldn't quite lose his original opinion of people who were connected, even in the remotest way, with the hereafter.

'No, I need to ask you a few questions that are important; otherwise I would not have called you at work. John's current flat - was he living there when you were together?'

'Yes.'

'Do you remember the name of his mortgage lender, who he banked with and which branch?'

'His mortgage is with Direct Line in Croydon and he banks with a local Barclays, but I'm not sure which one.'

'Sixty-four dollar question, do you still have a key to his flat?'

'Yes, but only because he wouldn't take it back.' Her voice broke slightly. 'He said if I ever I changed my mind, just to come back and he'd be waiting.'

'I don't know what your shift time is this week, Isabel, but the sooner we get down there, check out the flat, and speak to some of his neighbours, the better. I'm hoping you can make it some time tomorrow?'

'I finish at three, so I could meet you outside John's flat at about four-thirty.'

'Perfect, see you there.'

'Mr. Moorland, I just want you to know how grateful I am for your help.'

'Isabel, I'm not promising anything, so don't get your hopes too high. It isn't going to be easy because of the time gap. Oh, and by the way, call me Alex. As I'm not working in an official capacity, I would prefer it.'

'Thanks I will, and I know you'll do your best.'

'You can bet on it. See you tomorrow.'

He picked up the phone again. Some people had said in the past how interesting and exciting his job had been, but he knew better. It entailed a lot of boring job functions, such as continual telephone calls, like now. It only became exciting when they led somewhere, but most times they did not. They just eliminated a possible area of enquiry.

He rang Bill back with the details Isabel had supplied, and then took stock of his next move. Suddenly, he remembered he had invited Nancy for dinner. He looked at the clock - 5pm. He'd better get cracking.

Alex had never been a cook, as such; the odd boiled egg and toast when, on the rare occasion, Lillian had been sick, but that had been it. Now of course it was different. Lillian was no longer here, so he had been forced to learn the rudiments. Nothing fancy, mind you, but his culinary expertise had developed to what he now considered to be a fair standard. This usually amounted to the normal meat, potatoes and two veg, but it was adequate.

He had, in many ways, even relished learning to cook, because it had given him another interest and something to apply his mind to after his retirement. He thought about

Lillian and how efficient she had been in the kitchen; she was a wonderful cook and organiser. Whether cooking for two or twelve, it had made no difference to her. He missed her so much, even more so because he'd been forced to realise he hadn't developed any personal interests or hobbies outside his family or work.

His work hours had been long and demanding, so any time away from the job he had devoted to Lillian and Leila. No, there had been no time for anything else, but then he had never contemplated life without her. Perhaps if he had considered that she might go first, he would have made more of an effort to indulge in other pursuits.
He sat for a while thinking about that one. No. He would have devoted more time to her, not less; not been so keen to put in extra hours on difficult cases. He sighed as he got up. He was glad he hadn't known. Counting the days or months, even years, would have been intolerable.

* * *

Alan Jessop walked up the small garden path that was overgrown and sorely in need of drastic weeding. Some of the weeds had grown to at least two feet and then, flattened by wind and rain, had bowed onto the path making a little carpet as he walked. He decided to pull up a few, as he made his way to the quaint front door, just in case they were slippery when wet, flinging them to the side as he went. He didn't think Mabel would mind. Anyway, it was too late now. The door had a new coat of white paint, but instead of improving the appearance, it made it look a little sad. No preliminary work had been done to clean or rub down the paintwork before the intended facelift. He smiled to himself and knocked on the door.

He knew the front door opened straight onto the small sitting-room, and it wouldn't take Mabel long to answer it. Nevertheless, she still felt it necessary to call out that she was on her way.

As the door opened, he was surprised and taken off-guard for a brief moment to see how small and frail she had become since he had last seen her, two years earlier. She stood back from the door to let him pass, greeting him as she did so.

'Come in dear, come in. It's so nice to see you after all this time. How long is it? I'm afraid the memory's going but then I'm not getting any younger, am I?'

'If I'm as able as you, Mabel, when I'm your age, I won't have anything to complain about.'

She laughed heartily. 'It's a long time since anyone referred to me as "Able Mabel". They used to, you know, but it seems a lifetime ago now. Now, sit yourself down Alan. I'll make a nice cup of "Rosie Lee", then, we'll get down to business.'

Alan seated himself in one of the small armchairs and smiled to himself. If he'd had any doubts about calling an eighty-five year old for help, he need not have worried. Her movements were much slower, but her mind was as sharp as ever. If there was anything to find, she would find it.

Mabel bustled back in carrying a silver tray that had seen better days, and set it down carefully on the table. She put a cup beside him with a small plate of biscuits, and then sat down opposite - a little gingerly, he thought. Her body was slowing down, but her eyes were bright and alert.

'Now, dear, I've got everything ready for you. Names, addresses, telephone numbers and the dates they were last seen: when these very unnerving apparitions appeared. As I understand it, they were all dreadfully upset.'

'*All.* Mabel how many are there?'

'Eighteen, so far, and I'm still trying to confirm others. You know what it's like. People come to someone like us in desperation, but then get cold feet and back-track when you contact them for more details. They feel uncomfortable about it, and decide they don't want to get involved, and say perhaps it was just their imagination. Not a lot I can do about that, apart from leaving my name and number. I ask them to think about it for a few days, and have been surprised to find that at least six have reconsidered and faxed over the details. But there could be as many as thirty.'

'Faxed! You have a fax machine?'

'Oh yes, dear, a must these days when your hands are as arthritic as mine - so much easier for them to write it all down and just fax it over, and if there are any mistakes in the details, well, I can't be blamed, can I? So you see, Alan, a fax machine is an absolute necessity.'

He couldn't believe what he was hearing. 'How long have you had a fax machine?'

'Sad to say, dear: just a year. I wish I had been aware of the benefits earlier. They have been going for years, evidently. Still, better late than never.'

Alan was having trouble getting his head round the fact that eighty-five - sorry eighty-four year olds, bought fax machines, but then he rather suspected they did not. Mabel was probably a one-off. She handed him the printed details.

'You will have to photocopy those, dear, evidently they fade with time and we don't want to lose any information, do we?'

'Quite right,' he answered. She knew her stuff. He read as he drank his tea.

'They're all over the country. I cannot believe what I'm reading, but it must be right; they couldn't all have dreamt this up. What's happening for God's sake? I have never had to contend with anything like this before.'

'Nor I, Alan, but sure as eggs are eggs, it's not right. It's unholy, something terrible must have happened, something I have no experience of and suspect neither has anyone else.'

'I hate to say this and I know she doesn't relish it, but thank goodness Nancy Harnetty has been chosen to try and fight this evil, because evil it is, I'm sure of that.'

Mabel was thoughtful for a moment. 'Yes, you're right, it could only be Nancy, but you say she was chosen?'

He told her all he knew; she did not move an inch or speak until he had finished.

'Alan, I hope I live long enough to know the outcome of this matter, because it is unprecedented for someone on this earth plane to be called by those above for help like this.'

'Don't worry about that, Mabel; you're not ready to meet your maker yet.' He was smiling.

She knew he was telling her the truth. Her face relaxed as she said. 'Shall we have another cup of tea?'

'Why not.' As she turned to go to the kitchen, he called her back. Alan had always joked with Mabel, and she usually gave as good as she got. It was one of the things he found endearing about her.

'Why are you so worried about not knowing the outcome, Mabel? If it isn't resolved here before your time, then you could have made enquiries about it when you got upstairs.'

'Ah, but I can't guarantee I will be privy to such information in Heaven, because I have a feeling it's being dealt with at the highest level, and you know, dear, I have never had delusions of grandeur.'

He chuckled. 'What are you like Mabel?'

'I'm like me, dear,' she answered, with a slight frown on her face. Sometimes she returned as good as she got, without realising it.

* * *

Nancy picked up her bag from the seat next to her in the car, and then made her way to the Pay and Display machine. As she returned to her car she glanced at her watch. She was about fifteen minutes late meeting Alan for lunch and it would take her another good five minutes to get to her destination. She quickly placed the ticket on the dashboard, and then walked briskly in the direction of the café where they had agreed to meet. Nancy was a little breathless as she pushed open the door of the small eatery, and looked around for Alan. She spotted his raised hand at a table in the corner, and made her way over to him.

'I'm really sorry. I guess I didn't leave enough time for the traffic. Every man and his dog was out there today. I don't know where they all came from.'

'Sit yourself down, Nance, and let me order you a coffee while you unwind.'

'You always say the right things. I could murder a coffee right now.'

They had been friends long enough to be totally relaxed in each other's company, without any awkward gaps in conversation. While they ate, they chatted for a while about general topics of interest, but did not touch on the subject that was the purpose of their meeting until they had finished their meal, and were waiting for their second coffee to arrive.

'So how was Mabel, and was she able to find out anything?'

'She is looking quite frail, but sharp as ever.' He sighed, 'Angel was quite right, there are others.'

'How many?'

'To date: eighteen. There are more, but some of them don't feel they want to put anything in writing, as it were; it could be as many as thirty.'

Nancy had been sitting forward in the chair with her elbows resting on the table, but slowly leaned back in what could only be described as a slump.

'Eighteen or more; it's inconceivable. What on earth can we do Alan? The problem's too big.'

'The answer to that is, of course, we can't do anything without Angel's guidance. Don't forget her. You're not on your own.'

'It's not her I doubt, it's me; am I up to it?'

'Only time will tell, Nance, you can only put one foot in front of the other and just keep going. Plus, you need faith.'

She looked at the names, addresses and details Alan had given her and read them again, but with more concentration this time.

'Anything strike you as relevant about these details?'

'All loners,' he replied, without hesitation.

'Exactly; all loners. So, whatever the reason for their disappearance, one of the benefits for whoever is behind this, is that they would not be missed for a while and, *if* they were, probably not by anyone who was close enough to make enquiries on their behalf, such as work-mates. This is why sightings of their Ka's began to appear. It was the only way they could alert others that they were in trouble.'

'I think that about sums it up, so what's the next move?'

'I'm having dinner with Alex Moorland tonight. I'll pass on all this information and see if he has any suggestions as to where we go from here. He was out and about this morning, seeing if he could find any leads. Let's hope he has.'

They sat for another half-hour or so, going over some of the details, then decided to call it a day.

***

Alex pottered around the kitchen, preparing the vegetables and meat. The menu this evening was roast chicken, roast potatoes and two veg. Hardly exotic, but tasty. It was very nearly ready so he hoped Nancy would be on time. He wasn't disappointed.

They were both hungry, so wasted no time in tucking into a meal Nancy had to admit was delicious, and she felt much better for it. She'd only picked at her food earlier when she had met Alan, even though she had ordered something very light. Food could be both sustenance and comfort, and that's how she felt now - comforted.

'You looked very tired, Nancy, when you arrived, but I must say you're looking a lot better now.'

'I feel better and my compliments to the chef.'

80

'I'll tell him,' he replied smiling. 'Are you too tired to discuss my progress regarding Elsie, or would you rather leave it till another evening?'

'Time is of the essence, Alex, tired or not. That goes for all of us.'

'Right you are.'

She listened with interest, but did not ask any questions until he had finished.

'So, at this point, you definitely think Elsie was abducted by professionals, but you're not sure about John Harris?'

'I'd need to check John's details the same as I did Elsie's, but I have a feeling they may well be connected. I want to know if anyone witnessed John removing his belongings. If he wasn't present, they were taking a bigger risk.'

'Why?'

'I'll answer that question with another. Who do you know who gets someone else to do their packing when they're going away for a while, or on a holiday?'

'I see what you mean - highly unlikely.'

'Exactly, so if Elsie's and John's disappearance are connected, then they would have crossed the "t's" and dotted as many "i's" as possible. Now, nothing is without risk, but organising the removal of John's gear carried a far greater risk than Elsie's.'

'I would have thought it was the other way round. After all, Mrs Dodds had boarders; far more bodies around, so far more likely to be seen.'

'Not true, Nancy. Her property was moved in a few suitcases over the holiday period; a normal sight in June. Elsie also owed rent, so everyone assumed she'd done a runner; even the "nosey" Mrs Bates wasn't alerted, even though she witnessed two strange men entering and leaving with suitcases.'

'Yes, I understand that, but not why moving John's possessions was more difficult. After all, he lived alone; there wasn't anyone else to worry about,'

Alex was smiling patiently now. 'You know, Nancy, I hadn't thought about it until now, but we make a great team. I'll never be able to compete when it comes to psychic detecting, but I'll beat you hands down when it comes to earthly detecting.'

She laughed. 'I won't argue with that.'

'The very fact that John not only lived alone, but was more than happy with his own company, made it twice as difficult. *Any* stranger seen entering or leaving with hold-alls or suitcases from his home would have raised more than a few eyebrows, and just as much gossip. Not so a house where it was well known Mrs. Dodd's had lodgers.'

'Oh, of course.'

'Add that to the strong possibility that John was very likely buying his flat, then the problem increases. Its one thing to make it look like someone's done a runner from a boarding house, but who would abandon a home they were buying? Their whole objective was to cover any loopholes which would necessitate any enquiries, and it worked like clockwork; even the initial police investigation was dropped. I'm meeting Isabel Jennings tomorrow at John's flat; evidently she still has the key. I'll also try and speak to his neighbours on the off-chance someone remembers something. How did you get on, Nancy?'

'These are the names, addresses and details of people who had similar experiences to Georgie and Isabel, and before you ask if this is a regular occurrence, no it is not. I have never known a situation like this, and nor have any of the clairvoyants who did the sittings. This is a totally new phenomenon.'

Alex left the table and returned with the coffee. As he placed the cups on the table, a thought occurred to him.

'What I don't understand, Nancy, is as this is of such great concern to you and the dead, sorry, for want of another word, why can't you use the power you have and just ask what's happening?'

What happened next took Alex Moorland completely by surprise, and was an experience he would never, ever forget, not if he lived to be a hundred. A voice answered him from behind. He spun round and saw a woman standing near the window. He knew instinctively that she fitted the description of the lady who had appeared to Nancy in Toronto. He looked at Nancy and was amazed to see her head slumped forward on her chest, and that she didn't appear to be aware of what was happening. A slight fear gripped his heart.

'What have you done to her? Stop this at once.' He demanded.

'Please don't be afraid for her. My reason for being here is to protect her, not harm her, so please just listen to me. I will answer your question, because you must understand if you are to help. Nancy has no right to ask such questions and she knows it, as I have no right to answer them, even though I have the knowledge she seeks.'

Alex wondered if he pinched himself, would she disappear. This could not be happening.

'We cannot interfere by giving you all the answers, otherwise you would become as robots, waiting to receive your next instruction in life, never making any mistakes or being in control of your own destiny. No, it would never be permitted. Everyone has free choice with the opportunities, tribulations and temptations they are born into. For some it will be easier than for others, but all will experience some pain on their pathway'.

'How we choose to develop our souls while we live will, in the end, be the choice of each individual, and we are not allowed to interfere, nor do we wish to. From time to time, we can give guidance when you truly need help and the circumstances are such that we may give it. Now is such a time, but you must labour to right the wrongs that are being committed. To overcome this evil, you will have to change

some of your views on how you work. Normal police work will not eradicate the wrongs we endeavour to stop.'

'There will be times when we ask that Nancy accompany you and others, even though she does not have the experience for such situations, but she is the one who has the ability to hear me. On occasions, it will be vital that I give you and others guidance. Guidance only Nancy can hear. It was not by choice Nancy asked for your help. You were chosen too. We know you have been considering private investigation work for a long time now. You want to be able to choose the cases you cover, not be assigned to them. We hope you will choose to help these poor souls.'

Perspiration had formed on his forehead. How on earth did she know what he had been considering for the last year? He had told no one, not even Leila.

'We are concerned for you. We know Nancy will hear and heed our warnings, but it is not the same for you. You cannot hear our warnings. There will be danger for all who seek the truth, so I hope you will put your faith in us and heed our advice, as this will be the only time I will be permitted to speak to you.'

Alex was feeling decidedly uncomfortable; out of his depth. The only sure thing he knew was, the impossible was somehow happening.

'I will, on that you have my word, but who are you?'

'Who I am is not important, but be warned, those who would thwart you, already know of your enquiries regarding John Harris. To be forewarned; is to be forearmed.'

Then she was gone. He didn't know how long he stayed transfixed; staring in the direction she had appeared, before he remembered Nancy. Her head was still slumped forward and she looked pale, but as he moved towards her, she began to slowly lift her head.

'Nancy, are you alright? You look so pale; can I get you a brandy?' He knelt before her and placed his hand on her shoulder.

'No, I'm okay, but I would like some cold water.'

Alex quickly returned with the water, and watched her with concern as she slowly drank. It was a while before she opened her eyes, and he was surprised at how steady her gaze was now.

'I hope we didn't frighten you, Alex? But there was no other way.'

He smiled weakly. 'I'm a big guy, Nancy, but there was a moment when I despaired of my water-works.'

She smiled back. 'I knew she would be here. She came to me first thing this morning and asked my permission to talk to you with my help; an earthly link if you will.' She seemed to gain strength with every passing minute.

'This is going to be much more dangerous than I realised, Alex, and I know this is all very new to you and goes against the norm, but we must take her advice. In fact I feel so strongly about this, I won't continue with your help unless you agree.'

'Nancy, I've already agreed to the conditions. You were here; you must have heard what I said?'

'Believe it or not, I didn't.'

'I'm trying to get my head around this, I really am,' he said. 'But one thing's for sure, I want to help with this case. I've had a lot to absorb and try to understand in this last hour, but, whether you like it or not, you need me as much as I need you.'

He grinned. 'Anyway, Angel said I was "chosen" to handle this enquiry, and I would say her vote probably carries more weight than yours.'

'Oh, I can't tell you how relieved I am to hear that Alex,' then she frowned. 'Is there something else worrying you?'

'It was something Angel said. She said they already knew about our enquiries regarding John Harris, and that there was danger for any who sought the truth. I've been thinking, she only mentioned John, why not Elsie? It must be because they are only aware of the enquiries concerning him, but how?'

Alex was silent for a moment, as he tried to understand why this should be. Then his face hardened. There could only be one explanation, and he didn't like it.

'Of course; the police computer. Bill Palmer would have checked the computer first, and then called Croydon to see if they had any off-the-record information; not everything gets logged on the system. But, here's the rub, Nancy, another department can keep a check on any person entered on the police computer who they wish to keep tabs on. It's a sort of fail-safe system, so that different departments don't screw up on each other, if they both have an interest in the same person. This way they can liaise with each other, so they must have a police informer. Someone installed a computer check on John Harris to monitor any developments. Or, they have an informer at Croydon. My money's on the computer check; too much of a coincidence the other way round. They don't have the same problem with Elsie, because she's not officially listed as missing.'

'Oh dear, we have to speak to Bill immediately and warn him.'

He looked at her in surprise.

'Remember what Angel said. *Any* who seek the truth will be in danger.'

Alex didn't need prompting; he was already walking in the direction of the phone. He rang Bilston Station first, just in case Bill was on night duty. They confirmed he had finished at four and was not expected back till 3pm the next day.

'I know where he lives. I think under the circumstances, I'd rather speak to him face to face. The quicker I see him, the better. I'm going to have to tell him to lay off John Harris, and rethink how we proceed. Do you mind if we cut dinner short, Nancy?'

'No of course…..' She stopped in mid sentence. 'Sorry Alex, but I have to come with you.'

'Why? I'm only going to tell him to discontinue any follow-ups on John. He'll want an explanation, and I think it will be easier telling him rather than telephoning.'

'I don't *know* why, only that I should go with you. There must be a reason, just don't ask me what it is, because I haven't a clue.'

She sighed. 'We have already been through this one, Alex; I can't keep explaining, nor will I,' her anger was beginning to show now. 'We will have to work on trust with Angel, and that's it. No more, no less.'

He smiled. 'Do you think Angel will object if we take my car?'

'Well, I can't answer for Angel at the moment, but I certainly would prefer you.... Sorry, Alex, we have to take mine.'

He sighed. 'Hang on a sec' while I call Bill to let him know I'm on my way. I'll explain about you later.'

'Call him on the mobile while I drive.'

NINE

The night was chilly and blustery as they made their way over to Bill Palmer's house. They didn't speak as Nancy negotiated the traffic which, considering the time of night, was heavy. They both had a lot to think about. Things had moved quickly in the last few days and she was surprised at how much had come to light that no one had been aware of until now. Because her mind was elsewhere, she wasn't immediately aware that Alex had spoken. 'Sorry, say again?'

'I said I might have a little difficulty explaining about you, Nancy. He still thinks the way I used to regarding clairvoyants, but we really do need him on our side. I, er, don't suppose you could give him a little message?'

'What do you mean, little message?' She knew exactly what he meant. Trying to excuse and explain herself to other people was a new problem for her. Until now, she'd only had to contend with people who sought her help; some, because they believed, others as a last resort, or the "just curious". Friends accepted her for who she was. He had the good grace to look embarrassed as he answered.

'He refers to psychics as spooks.'

She sighed. 'This is not a subject we have ever discussed, Alex, but I'm more than aware of how some people view psychics and, believe it or not, I don't have a problem with it. Everyone has a right to think and feel as they choose, as long as they don't try and interfere with those who, for whatever reason, do not share their way of thinking. This goes both ways, so I have never tried to convert others to what, for me, is an undeniable truth, but that's exactly what you're asking me to do.'

Alex sensed her anger and he understood, but he had no time to pussyfoot around with her. 'It's important he's on our side, Nancy, so if your psychic intervention can help sway him in any way, then you bloody well ought to try, because he's the only inside police help we have and, whether we like it or not, we damn well need him.'

He was getting hot under the collar now. 'In fact, I don't give much for our chances without him.'

She stopped at the traffic lights and turned to face him. 'All right, Alex, you've made your point. I can't guarantee anything, but I will try, all right?'

He raised his hands in front of him as he answered. 'Fair enough. That's all I ask.'

She returned her eyes back to the road. 'We should be there in a few minutes but I'm not sure where I turn off from here.'

'Take the second on the left and then it's the first street on the right. We want number 35 Winton Street.' Nancy took the second left, then continued past Winton Street and took the next right. As she turned the corner, Alex was already telling her she had missed the turning, but although irked, he decided to try patience instead of annoyance.

'Don't worry, Nancy, take a left at the bottom into the one way system and double back.'

Nancy pulled over and parked the car. 'Now I know why Angel asked me come this evening. Bill's house is being watched.'

'What! Nancy, that is ridiculous.'

'Ridiculous or not, that's what Angel says. Are we to start doubting her so soon?'

He didn't answer her immediately, instead he turned and stared out of the front window frowning. 'If she's right, I don't want him to lead them to us.' He searched his pocket for his mobile and called Bill.

* * *

Bill Palmer had been watching the late-night movie, but had dozed off in the middle as usual. He jumped when the phone rang, and nearly dropped it in his haste to pick it up quickly, so as not to wake his wife and son who had gone to

89

bed earlier. He checked his watch and wrongly guessed it would be the station calling him this late. He was surprised to discover it was Alex, and even more surprised to discover he wanted to come over right away to see him. Bill didn't ask too many questions over the phone. It must be important. He was curious, very curious.

As he made his way to the kitchen, he stopped at the bottom of the stairs to listen, to see if the ringing had disturbed his wife or son, but heard nothing. He decided he needed a coffee; he wanted to be wide-awake when Alex arrived. He tried to anticipate the reason for his visit; surely it couldn't have anything to do with John Harris. Oh well, he would know soon enough.

He returned to his chair, placing his coffee beside him, and tried to follow the tail-end of the film, which wasn't easy, but he had nothing better to do while he waited.

The phone rang and he was much quicker picking it up this time. It was Alex again.

'There's no easy way to say this, Bill, but I think your house is being watched; I'm round the corner in Abbot Street, is there any way you can get out without being seen?'

'Is this April Fool's day, Alex? You can't be serious.' He was incredulous.

'I've never been more serious in my life.'

'Who would possibly want to watch *me*?'

'If I knew that I'd be a lot wiser, but we won't find out with you sitting there instead of us discussing it here.' Alex had raised his voice a smidgeon. It was almost as though he was still the "Gov'nor." Bill recognised the slight authority in his voice.

'I'm on my way. I'll go out the back door, but you'll have to hang on. I'll have to get over two garden fences, so this better be worth it.'

'I'll wait, but careful how you go. I'm in a red Vauxhall parked on the left, the opposite end of the one-way system. I'll watch out for you.'

90

Bill left the light on in the sitting-room, which was situated at the back of the house, made his way to the stairs and climbed, two at a-time. He left the light off as he moved to the window in the bathroom that was situated to the front of the house, and slowly moved the net curtain. It took his eyes a minute to adjust to the dark as he looked out.

Cars were parked sporadically either side of the road, but if he was being watched, they wouldn't have parked directly outside - too obvious. They would probably be parked a few cars down where they still had a good view of anyone arriving or leaving. He didn't move for at least five minutes, but saw nothing suspicious. This was crazy. He let the curtain fall gently back, and then hurriedly opened it again.

Someone had lit a match inside one of the cars parked on the opposite side of the road, but it had gone out very quickly. Whoever it was had probably lit a cigarette, but he couldn't see any glow, so they must have put it quickly under the dashboard so as not to draw attention to themselves. He strained his eyes; it looked like a dark saloon, possibly a Ford. He counted the number of cars back from Jim Reed's car, which was parked opposite his house, then gently replaced the curtain.

He went down the stairs as quickly as he had mounted them, took the keys for the back door which hung nearby, and locked it behind him as he left. He waited a few seconds but nothing moved. It was a long time since he'd had to climb a garden fence and he wasn't relishing the idea, but Alex was right: someone was watching his house.

He was cursing under his breath now. He wasn't tall for a copper, five foot nine and of slim build. Fortunately, he was fairly agile, but this first fence was not doing him any favours. He found an old bucket at the end of his garden, and this just gave him the little extra height he needed to haul himself over.

Once he'd cleared the fence, he crouched and waited. He hadn't disturbed anyone - so far, so good. It wouldn't do for a Police Sergeant to be caught lurking in other peoples' back gardens; it would be difficult to explain. He slowly made his way to the last obstacle, hoping it would prove to be easier to negotiate, and was relieved to find it was. Before he hoisted himself up, he peered over the fence to make sure the street was clear. He already had his bearings as he landed and marched in the direction of Abbot Street.

Abbot was not a long street and it didn't take him long to find Alex, who was already out of the car and beckoning to him. It had been a night of surprises for Bill, and another awaited him as he climbed into the back seat.

'Who's this, then? You didn't say you would have anyone with you.'

'It was a last-minute decision, but I think it's just as well you meet Nancy Harnetty. It was Nancy who drew my attention to John Harris in the first place.'

'Is John Harris a relative or friend of yours?' She looked a little too old to be the ex- fiancée.

'No, I've never met him,' she answered honestly.

He directed his attention back to Alex. 'Then why is she here and what's her interest?'

This was the part Alex was dreading, and it wasn't how he had planned to deal with it.

'She's here because I will need her help in areas I have no expertise in. Likewise, she will need our expertise and experience.'

'Is she an informer?'

Alex sighed. He had not been looking forward to this, but it was time for the truth; no pussy-footing or half-truths.

'No, she's not an informer.'

'Then you had better tell me what you both know, so I'm as wise as you are. Especially, why I'm being watched, *and* how you knew?'

'Fair enough, Bill. All I ask is, you listen first and ask questions later.' He told him everything. Nancy's involvement, his enquiries regarding Elsie, and the strong possibility that there were many others.

Bill kept his word and said nothing while he spoke, but Alex could see and feel the rage mounting within him. What he hadn't expected was the calm that enveloped him, as the fury mounted in Bill.

Bill could no longer contain himself. He exploded.

'You got us involved in this shit, on the word of a fucking mental psychic?'

Nancy had slowly been shrinking in her seat while Alex was explaining to Bill. She knew she was in for the brunt of his fury but, when it came, she was unprepared for such a personal and stinging assault. Anger now invaded her, as thoughts raced through her mind in split seconds. Alex's stupidity in thinking she could open Bill's mind with a few honest messages, and her original feelings that it wouldn't work, were obviously right.

Alex opened his mouth to defend her, but it was too late. Nancy had already taken the bait, her voice raised to the point of shouting.

'Your Grandmother has only one thing to say to you – GERONIMO! And if you're wondering which one, because they're both dead, she's on your mother's side.'

She was stunned. That was not what she had intended to say at all. It had just come out in her anger.

If she was stunned, the effect on him was astonishing. His fury had gone and shock had set in. Oh dear, what had she done. That was not what she had meant to say, so why had she said it? The answer was obvious, of course; it must have been Angel. Her anger turned to concern.

'Bill, I'm really, sorry, I never meant to say that, really I didn't. That's not how I work. Please forgive me.' His answer was slow in coming.

'No, it's me who should be forgiven. I'm sorry for what I said, but this was the last thing I expected to hear. I wasn't ready for it.' His body slumped and his eyes looked wet.

Neither of them knew what to say, so they said nothing.

'My parents didn't have much time for me, and that's something kids become aware of very quickly. No-one ever says it, or mentions it, so you think it's normal, but somehow you know it's not; not when you see how other parents treat their kids. It wasn't till my father died that my mother explained why. She couldn't understand that, by then, it was too late for us to have a true mother-and-son relationship. I guess she didn't think it through, but I knew that if my father had lived, she would still have treated me the same way. Nothing would have changed.'

'She just thought she could transfer her love at a later date, as though it's some kind of commodity passed down to the next of kin after death. My father could never sire children, you see, so he knew I wasn't his. Mum compensated by showing he came first in everything, including love.'

His face softened. 'If it hadn't been for my Gran, well I don't think I would have survived as well as I have. She was the one who loved and looked after me, enough for three people. When she died, it was like losing my right arm, but I'll never forget what she said to me just before she passed away. *"I don't want you thinking you're alone now. As long as I'm in your thoughts, I'll always be around."* She smiled at me then; she'd always had a wicked sense of humour. *"I don't know if there is life after death, and I don't hold with calling spooks back, but if there is, I'll let you know. I'll just yell GERONIMO."*

Bill looked sad as he said, 'and that's exactly what she did. Thank you for that, Nancy.'

She nodded and patted his shoulder.

He turned his attention back to Alex. 'This surveillance - has it got anything to do with Harris and, if so, how did they get onto me? I didn't advertise it in the local paper, and I kept it close to my chest, like you said, Alex.'

'Did you run his name on the computer files?' he asked.

'Yes, you know that's normal. There wasn't much there so, as I said, I rang and spoke to the duty sergeant.'

'If that's the case, it doesn't make sense.' Alex ran his hand over his chin while he stared out of the front window, then turned his attention back to Bill.

'You must have said something that worried them. What exactly did you say?'

Bill frowned, 'I'll have to think, I didn't give it much thought at the time. I was just doing you a favour, Alex. Let's see; I asked him if he had any off-the-cuff details, not logged on the computer; sometimes there are. That's when he told me they were not actively making any more enquiries, but had left it on file for reference.'

'There must have been something else, Bill. Think.'

Slowly it dawned on him, and he looked a bit sheepish. 'I think I mentioned there was an outside chance it was linked to another missing person. You know how it works, Alex. If they give you something and you have anything to add that might be connected - but I told him it was unofficial, there was nothing definite.'

'That's it, Bill. That's the answer. Whoever you spoke to at Croydon, added that information to the computer, and the source - you. Now they need to know the name of the person reported missing to you at Bilston, just in case, by sheer chance, you have made a connection to one of the other missing people. They want to double-check they haven't overlooked anything. They can't afford to take any chances. The problem was, nothing had been officially reported at Bilston, so the only link they have is you.'

He was thoughtful for a moment. 'If it worried them that much and they have these resources available to them, then it must be a fairly big operation, so I am inclined to think "supposition" must be fact.'

'Which is?' asked Bill.

'The other eighteen missing people must be linked.' Nancy answered for him.

95

'What eighteen missing people?' Bill was looking to Alex for the answer.

'I don't have time now, Bill, I really don't, but I'll fill you in on everything once we've dealt with the guy who's keeping tabs on you.' Alex raised his hand and rubbed the back of his neck.

'We're not dealing with amateurs,' he continued, 'so we're going to have to start covering our tracks. Thank God Angel's on our side; otherwise we would have blown it tonight. Finding out they were already on to Bill's enquiry, then being made aware they had organised surveillance was pure gold. Now, there are a number of things we have to do immediately to get them off Bill's back and ours. We have to make them feel safe again.'

They both waited. He was in charge and neither of them questioned it. There was no doubt in Nancy's mind that he more than deserved the position he had achieved in life. He looked at neither of them as he spoke. Nancy could almost feel the thoughts and ideas racing through his head as he diagnosed the situation and formed a plan of action. He turned to Bill.

'I think, under the circumstances, you'd agree we can't hand this case over to the police yet?'

'Not unless I want to be retired early, no.'

'Right, then the first thing we need is to establish where your surveillance is and get the number of the car. He may well have used false number plates, but he can't possibly know we're on to him, so he may have been a little careless.'

'No, you can't check his number plates,' said Nancy hurriedly.

They both realised the implication as she said it, and Bill was beginning to feel a certain amount of respect for her.

'She's right,' said Alex. 'It's probably safe to assume that if they're checking Harris and any related connections, they would also monitor any interest in their own people.'

'Now what,' Bill was exasperated. 'It's like fighting our own men.'

'That it is,' concurred Alex, thoughtfully. He stared out of the window, frowning, and the frown increased the lines on his brow, etching them even deeper. He'd never had to work like this and he didn't like it, but if he was serious about his intention to try private investigation work, then he had to retrain his way of thinking. He was beginning to acquire a new respect for the 'private' investigator. He dragged his thoughts back to the situation in hand.

'We need that car number because it's the only lead we have to whoever's involved in this. How we check the registered owner will have to wait, but it's the only direct lead we have to them at the moment so we must get it. Our next move is going to be very tricky but, again, we have no choice. At some time or other, he'll get a replacement. When that happens, we'll follow him, hopefully to his address, and then see if we can access the electoral roll for a name. That will be easier said than done because we're dealing with professionals, so he'll be watching his back out of sheer habit. I can't think of any other way. Anyone got any better suggestions?'

They both shook their heads

'Right then, we're all agreed?' He looked at Nancy hopefully. 'No direction from Angel?'

'Not even a twinkling light,'

'Bill, if I were you I would climb back the way you came, and stay out of this altogether. They have your name and address, not ours, so it could be dangerous for you. I don't want you making them aware of our involvement, either; the less they know the better.'

'No chance. I take great exception to anyone watching me, and I don't like bent coppers, so whatever's happening, I want in.'

'I can understand that and, to be honest, I'm glad you decided to stay with us. It would have been nigh on impossible without someone on the inside, but I had to give you the opportunity to opt out.' Alex sighed.

'It's not going to be easy tonight and we'll need all the help we can get, but you can't stay, Bill. He knows your face, so we can't risk him recognising you.'

Bill didn't like what he was hearing, but he knew Alex was right.

'Okay, I'm on my way.' He turned to Nancy, 'I was out of order, Nancy.'

'Were you? I've forgotten.'

He looked at her thankfully. 'Well, I won't remind you.'

'I've just had another thought,' said Alex. 'If their surveillance doesn't identify the link to Harris, they may decide to make direct contact with you to cover all angles. If that's the case, you'll need a ready answer that will satisfy them enough to call them off, but what?'

'Isabel,' replied Nancy without hesitation. 'Bill could say one of her friends had asked him to make enquiries about her because she hadn't seen or heard from Isabel for a while. You could truthfully say that, as John Harris was a known boyfriend, he had tried to contact him in respect of his enquiries; hence his initial interest in John Harris, and the possibility that they might have gone off together. This way, Isabel will be the missing person connection. Bill had since discovered she had unexpectedly returned to Australia, because there were a few problems back home, so Harris was no longer of interest.'

'Nice one, Nancy, it could work,' replied Bill.

'Well I can't think of a better idea,' said Alex, 'but we will have to assume they will follow it through and double check it, so I'll call Isabel early tomorrow and see what I can arrange with her. I'll get back to you, Bill, before you start work at three.'

'Right, I'll wait for your call.' He opened the car door and disappeared in the direction he had come from.

'Nancy, it's best you drive and I concentrate on getting the number of the car. Don't drive too fast so that it's difficult to get his number, or too slow to make him suspicious. There's not a lot of room with these parked cars, but you're going to have to turn round so that we enter Bill's road, making sure the Ford has its back to us as we pass. That way he'll only get a back view of us, too. Can't be too careful. Can you manage that?'

'There's only one way to find out.'

She switched on the engine and drove forward until the cars were a little more spaced, and then turned the car in the direction of Bill's street. As she turned into Winton Street, she had one repetitive thought: not too fast - not too slow; it was beginning to sound like a dance step. She looked at the speedometer; it read twenty miles an hour. The speed had to be about right, otherwise Alex would have said something by now. She would have continued at that pace, but was forced to slow down even further because a large black cat decided to saunter out in front and cross the road; they couldn't believe their luck.

'I've got it,' said Alex.

'Brilliant,' said Nancy. 'What do I do now?'

'Drive down to the high street and I'll get a couple of coffees. He won't be relieved yet-a-while, and I think we'll be in need of a hot drink before the night's out.' They found one of those late-night, fast-food outlets. It wasn't the best coffee they had ever tasted, but it was hot, and they felt a certain amount of relief that someone had invented the throwaway cup, as the proprietor did not appear to be too bothered about his rather grubby working gear.

They drove back to Winton Street and parked about five cars back from the surveillance car, drank their coffee and waited. It was a cold night and, had they known in advance of their predicament, they would have put on warmer clothes. Alex checked his watch. It was half-past twelve; it would be a long night.

99

'Why don't you close your eyes and rest for a while. You probably won't sleep but it helps.'

'Not for the moment.' The coffee was bad but it wasn't lacking in caffeine. 'I'll try later.' They sat and waited, and talked in low voices.

Nancy did eventually close her eyes for a while and Alex was right, she didn't sleep, but it gave her some respite as they waited. She hadn't offered him the same courtesy because she knew he would refuse. She could sense his alertness, and wondered how he managed to remain calm at the same time. She wondered if she would learn to be as capable in this kind of situation as he was, but decided it was an experience she would prefer not to relive. She was cold, tired and becoming increasingly stiff after the hours of waiting.

Suddenly she became aware that Angel was close, and opened her eyes.

Alex was leaning forward in his seat and staring straight ahead. He looked at her and said. 'Get ready to go. A car just passed him slowly and flashed his lights, so it's probably his replacement. He's continued down the road towards the one-way system, so he'll probably go round and come back on himself. Parking is tight here, so he obviously wants his accomplice to move so he can park in the same spot.'

They were parked a couple of cars down from the end. 'Quick, Nancy, reverse out of this road, then take a first right back into Abbot Street. Drive down to the end and wait for the car to enter the one-way system. We're the next entrance down from him, so be ready to fall in behind him. He'll be watching his rear end, not who's in front of him, so it will be to our advantage'

She was already reversing, when she said, 'of course you know it's illegal to reverse into a main road.'

'Let's hope there's enough room to turn at the end, so we don't have to.'

There wasn't, so she had no choice. The car she had forced to stop, was now behind her, and the driver was already rolling down his window and shouting the odds about "bloody female drivers" but it fell on deaf ears. She indicated to turn right immediately, which infuriated him even more, and they heard his horn blast as they disappeared down Abbot Street. She drove quickly to join the one-way system at the end of the road.

They both looked at the oncoming traffic and waited for the dark coloured Ford to appear.

It was now six-fifteen in the morning and fortunately no-one was waiting behind them.

'There he is. He's just joined the one way system behind that bus, but he's crossed immediately onto the outside lane, which means he's going to double back on himself, so you'll have to get out fairly quickly. Be ready as the bus passes.'

She was ready – too ready. She shot out from the side turning and entered the one way system as the bus passed, but, in her haste, accelerated to the point where the car careered slightly and veered into the outside lane too soon. Her heart sank and her pulse raced as she just caught the tail-end of the Ford Sierra. There was the sound of breaking glass, as the blow shattered the front lights on the passenger side of Nancy's car, and the offside rear lights of the Sierra.

Unfortunately, in her effort to enter the one-way system and fall in behind the Sierra, she had forgotten to fasten her seat belt. Nancy braked hard and was propelled forward, so that she caught the side of her eye on the steering wheel. It had been instinctive to lower herself in the seat in the split second when she realised she would hit the car. She felt the trickle of blood slowly ease its way down her face. The Ford accelerated and was gone.

'Oh dear, what have I done. How could I have been so stupid?' Nancy couldn't hide the despair in her voice; her eyes already welling up with tears, which was partly due to shock.

Alex got out of the car and walked round to Nancy's side.

'Come on, it's all right. Lets get you into the passenger seat and I'll drive.'

It always amazed Alex how little time it took, after a minor accident, to cause chaos. The traffic virtually came to a stand-still as he helped her into the passenger seat, so he lost no time in moving the car.

'I'm so sorry Alex; I don't know what came over me. I really don't. I was a little on edge but not to enough to make me shoot out like a banshee.'

She hadn't been able to face Alex until now, and was surprised to see he wasn't in the least perturbed.

'I'm taking you to casualty to get that eye looked at and you checked out.'

'I'm a little shaken, Alex, but I'm all right. I don't want to go to the hospital. Just take me home.'

Alex pulled the car over and parked as soon as he could. 'Yes you do, Nancy.' He was smiling as he said. 'I'm sorry you hurt yourself and I'm sure, as you say, you're just shaken but, believe it or not, the situation now is just perfect.'

She looked at him in amazement and wondered if she wasn't the only one who had banged their head.

'Our intention was to follow him but we were probably on to a loser, because he would very likely have made a few detours on his way home to make sure he wasn't being followed if he's the professional I think he is. Everything they have done so far has been very professional, so you can understand why I had my doubts about tonight. Now, thanks to you, Nancy, it's a whole new ball-game.'

'What on earth are you talking about?'

'He's a driver who did not stop at the scene of an accident, so if you have to go to hospital because you're injured, we can ask the local police to trace the name of the driver.

That's what I'm talking about - a foolproof way of checking his details. The Sierra driver won't be happy about it, but he won't necessarily be alerted either.'

'Brilliant.' She felt like hugging him. 'I can't tell you how bad I was feeling about bodging the whole issue, especially as it was the first time we had worked together.'

'Right, no arguments then, we go to the hospital.'

'No arguments. The hospital it is.'

He studied her for a moment. 'I know it will probably go against the grain, but could you say you feel worse than you do, like add a headache and back pain – whip-lash even? It's dishonest, I know, but they have shown no mercy to Elsie or John.'

She smiled. 'You had better get me to the hospital. I can't tell you how poorly I'm feeling.'

He returned the smile as he pointed the car in the direction of the nearest hospital.

As he drove, his thoughts returned to what Nancy had said after the accident. She was a little on edge, but *not* enough to make her accelerate like she had. Then he thought about Angel.... and wondered.

TEN

It had been a long time since Nancy could remember feeling
so tired, and it was a new experience to feel elated at the
same time. She had not felt comfortable taking up valuable
hospital time, pretending she felt much worse than she did,
but, as Alex had said, it was for a good cause. Surprisingly,
it wasn't the lying - that came more easily than she would
have thought possible because all she could think of was
Elsie and John - it was the kindness and consideration she
received from the hospital staff, who had been very
thorough in their efforts to determine the extent of her
injuries, that had made her feel guilty, and she deeply
regretted taking up their time. Time that should have spent
on someone more deserving, but there had been no
alternative.

They had x-rayed her back and neck and, as she had
known, had found nothing untoward, but, as a precaution,
had suggested that she might have sustained slight whip-
lash, so had fitted her with a neck-brace to give some
support and asked her to come back for a check-up in a
week's time.

Alex had been delighted with the neck-brace. He said it
was much more visible than an Elastoplast and would add
credence to her request when she asked the police to check
the driver's details.

Nancy put the key in the front door with relief, and an
immediate feeling of comfort enveloped her with the sight
of familiar things. It was good to be home. She made her
way to the kitchen for a much-needed cup of tea while she
ran a hot bath. She was very cold and made a mental note to
leave an old thick coat in the boot of the car to cover any
such emergencies in the future. As she lay soaking in the
bath with her eyes closed and the tea beside her, tired as she

was, she couldn't help thinking about last night's events. She tried to block them temporarily from her thoughts and just enjoy the warm comforting soapy water that embraced her body, but couldn't.

Something was nagging at her. Something.... she had somehow missed. Such a lot had happened the night before, all of which was new territory to her, making it difficult to recognise immediately any small detail that could be important. She sipped her tea and, in spite of the nagging doubt, began to unwind and feel more peaceful.

Later, she realised "unwinding" was the answer to unlocking, and remembering that "little" detail which would eventually answer a lot more of the jigsaw puzzle. That was how she was now beginning to think of it; bits and pieces coming together which would eventually tell a picture or story. Suddenly, it hit her.

Nancy almost leapt out of the bath and was only half-dry as she opened the bottom cupboard in the sitting-room and grabbed her sketch pad and pencil. *She had seen his face;* it had only been for a brief moment but her headlight had caught him full face. He had obviously realised before she had that, at the speed she was travelling there would be a collision, and had turned to face her oncoming car; and in that split second she had *seen his face*.

He must have sensed her car coming at him from the left rather than seen it, because his view had been blocked to a certain extent by the bus he was following, and his concentration was engaged on manoeuvring to the outside lane.

She sat down and stared directly ahead, not focusing on anything in particular but just reliving that split second over and over again in her mind to recall as much detail of his face as she could. She remembered his wide-eyed surprise, then the almost instant hardening of the jaw, as he returned his vision to the road just before he accelerated and was gone.

She started to draw slowly at first, trying to get the shape of his face as near perfect as possible, because she knew that making it too wide or too narrow could change the features quite a lot. If it was too wide then the eyes and brows would be spaced further apart, perhaps the mouth would appear wider and so on until it altered the picture to a "perhaps" rather than a definite. She instinctively knew that the shape of the face could also influence the perceived character of a person; such as, if a person had a fuller or fatter face, they were considered to be jolly and that wasn't necessarily the case. A long serious face conjured up a dour personality, when, in fact, it might hide a wonderful sense of humour. What you saw was not always what you got – so she tried hard just to draw the face without adding any imagined character.

She lost track of time as she worked, but eventually held the drawing out in front of her and smiled.

Yes, it was him. She had only seen him for a brief moment, but she knew the likeness was good. She would call Alex, but not now. Now, all she could think of was bed and she couldn't delay it any longer.

***

Alex had been glad of a few hours' sleep before he met Isabel Jennings outside John Harris's flat. He was already waiting in his car when he saw her approaching on foot. She still carried her large handbag that housed more than she would ever need, but "be prepared" was her motto, and she was.

She smiled at him as he greeted her. 'Let's hope John hasn't changed the lock since I last saw him,' she said.

'It would complicate things,' he agreed.

They made their way up to the first floor and Alex noticed Isabel had her fingers crossed as she tried the key in the lock. Her relief was evident as the door swung open and they stepped inside. 'Now what?' she asked.

106

'Just look around and go through everything. I have no idea what we are looking for, or if there's anything to find. These guys have been very thorough so far. It's standard police procedure to check a missing person's home, but it won't have been carried out in this case because he's not regarded as missing. You take the bedroom; I'll take the sitting room.'

They moved furniture, checked under and in the bed; looked in cupboards and drawers, behind pictures, and any nook and cranny that looked interesting including those that didn't. They searched for nearly half-an-hour - nothing.

They sat on the sofa and looked around, trying to decide if they could have missed anything. Isabel suddenly sat up straight and a look of inspiration lit her face. She turned to face Alex.

'He used to keep a diary; I found it by chance one day and was sorely tempted to read it.'

'Did you?'

'No, the mere fact that he had hidden it, told me it was very private, so I just put it back and never mentioned it.'

'Why haven't we found it? We've virtually taken this place apart.'

'Because it was in a hidden drawer. I only found it by chance when I was cleaning the flat for John, when he had a particularly heavy work load on.'

She rose and made her way to a little antique-style desk in the corner of the room. It had two front drawers positioned over elegant bowed legs. Immediately above the drawers there were two decorative panel inserts about one-and-a-half inches in height. Isabel pressed the right insert and released a narrow hidden drawer. It was still there. She held the diary to her for a moment, before turning and handing it to Alex.

As Alex took the diary he asked if there was still any coffee in the kitchen and suggested they make a black one while they went through it.

'It would be quicker if one of us reads the diary out loud, then we can stop and discuss any points that seem unusual, plus you might well recognise inconsistencies that would not be immediately recognisable to me, and vice versa.

He suddenly realised how difficult this was. 'I hope it won't be too upsetting for you?'

'I hope not too, but it has to be done.'

Isabel had opted to read as it was decided she would have less problem with his writing. As Alex listened, it occurred to him that John Harris was a very sensitive young man. His thoughts and feelings were gentle, with a seemingly incredible sense of strength and understanding behind each written sentence. Some people naturally distance themselves from others, either because they find it hard to communicate or bond with them, or because childhood or later experiences have made them wary of people.

Alex was no analyst, but he was convinced that John had none of these hang-ups; he just didn't need as much human contact as lesser mortals. He was surprised at the effect the diary was having on him and the way his train of thought was moving. He would never have used the phrase "lesser mortals" before. That was the sort of terminology he associated with mythology books and was foreign to his vocabulary, yet it had entered his thoughts quite naturally as he listened to Isabel read.

He became slightly uncomfortable hearing John's inner-most thoughts. He wrote about every-day work, people and ordinary events with an almost philosophical mind which Alex knew was natural to him, not sought or conjured.

He didn't want to hear anymore. It was all right for Isabel to read his diary, but not him; what he was hearing at the moment bore no relevance to the crime. It was his way of showing respect for this man he had never met but felt some admiration for. Anyway, Isabel was astute; he knew she wouldn't miss anything.

'You read it, Isabel, I'll check his books. Let me know if there's anything that concerns you.'

As she continued to read, he walked over to look at the large number of books that were displayed on recessed shelving. He expected to find Socrates, Plato and other philosophers on the over-crowded bookshelves, and was not disappointed. John Harris obviously had a love of reading, and his interest covered many subjects: popular classics, technical and teach-yourself manuals, autobiographies and many others. Anything and everything interested him.

He started to lift out some of the books and skim quickly through them. This was an unusual man; one who was somehow on another plane of thought from his fellow man, but not with a feeling of arrogance; more an understanding, tolerance, concern and kindness towards the world in general.

Alex was deep in thought as he browsed along the bookshelves and he started when Isabel suddenly called him.

'He was being followed; well, he thinks he was being followed. He's listed quite a few instances about six weeks before he disappeared, but says he was never really sure because it wasn't always the same man, and his logic was telling him it didn't make sense.'

'Did he describe any of them?'

'Yes, you can check their descriptions in a minute. Evidently, they just seemed to follow him everywhere: work, home, library, the gym. He said there was no rhyme or reason to it. He couldn't understand if they were interested in where he went, why they never approached him. He was on the point of going to the police, even though he thought they would ridicule him, but because no one had ever threatened him, he knew, technically, no crime had been committed'

Alex sat down beside her and slowly read through the later part of the diary.

'We should give this to the police; they couldn't ignore this evidence could they?' Isabel sounded much brighter now.

Alex put the diary down and just stared ahead for a second or two.

'No, they couldn't, but they would not investigate in the same area as us, for obvious reasons, and they would not believe the connection between John's and Elsie's disappearance and, although I hesitate to say it, Isabel, many others.'

'Not just Elsie and John?'

'No. Nancy made some enquiries on the grapevine. So far there have been twenty-four incidents, and a further six as yet unconfirmed.' He finished his coffee and frowned, pushing the lines ever deeper into his forehead.

'You're not going to like what I have to say, so I hope you trust me enough to bear with me on this. There's more than an outside chance that they have a police informer, who will update whoever's responsible, of any progress we make. Once you make Croydon Station aware of this information, whoever is holding John will know too, and if I was in their shoes I'd close ranks and cover my tracks even further. If you really want to help, then I'm asking you to leave this diary with me, and let us continue as we are. I'll decide when we go to the police, but it will only be when we have either discovered the informer's identity, or can find a way round them.'

'I'm afraid for him, Alex.'

'So am I, and it will be even harder for me, as I will be answerable for any wrong decisions I make, and that's not sitting lightly on my shoulders.'

'I'm too confused to know what I should do, I'm only sure of one thing, and that is you wouldn't lie to me, so I'll just pray every night that you find John and Elsie soon.'

* * *

110

Bill Palmer put the phone down and tried to act and look as if a bombshell hadn't hit him; he was finding it very difficult. Disbelief, mixed with surprise, agitation, excitement and many other emotions were racing through his mind. He looked at his watch. It was eight p.m.; he had two full hours before he finished his shift and he didn't want to be here.

'Digby,' he called. He always addressed other officers by their surnames while on duty.

Peter Digby looked up from what he was doing. They were both working on the front desk at the time.

'Yes Sarg.'

'I'll be back in a few minutes.'

'Right Sarg.'

Bill Palmer could barely contain himself as he made himself walk calmly and at a normal pace to the yard at the back of the station. He looked around to see that he wasn't within earshot of anyone, took his mobile out of his pocket and dialled Alex's number. He was never more grateful than when he answered.

'Alex, its Bill, we have to meet.'

'When?'

'As soon as possible, I finish at ten, so could we meet somewhere later, perhaps in a pub?'

Alex didn't answer immediately. 'Let's meet at the local near the station. I'll be at The Pig and Whistle before ten and I'll bring Nancy if I can. I was going to suggest we all meet tomorrow anyway, as it seems she has a few things to report as well.'

'I don't think I am, but what if I'm still being watched?'

'We'll make it look like a chance meeting, and having Nancy with me will help.'

'I've got to go,' said Bill. 'I'll see you there.'

Alex picked up the phone to Nancy and arranged to pick her up at nine.

111

Alex and Nancy were lucky to find a table in the far corner. Alex looked around to see if there was anyone there he recognised and was relieved to find there wasn't. He bought a couple of drinks and sat down to wait for Bill.

'Were the police able to help you with the number plates you gave them, Nancy?'

'Unfortunately, it was just as you suspected; he was using false number plates.'

Alex face fell. 'Wonderful,'

'Because the plates were false, they asked me if I could give a description of him, but I said no. I thought it better to lie until I'd spoken to you first.'

Alex replaced his poised pint on the table. 'What do you mean?'

'I did see his face, but I was in shock at the time, so didn't realise it.'

Hope re-appeared on Alex's face. 'You can give a description of him?'

'I can do better than that. I've drawn his face.' She explained how she had eventually remembered the full, if brief, memory of his face from the car headlights.

'I didn't know you could draw?'

'Oh yes, when I was a little girl I would try and draw the children that I could see in the spirit world. My first efforts were not good, but, as they say, practice makes perfect. Well, perhaps not perfect in my case, but enough, I think, for us to recognise him if we ever saw him again.'

'You're a bloody marvel, Nancy, and no mistake. Let's have a look at him.'

The more he worked with her, the more he appreciated her.

At that moment, he heard Bill call his name. 'Fancy seeing you here, Alex; long time, no-see. How are you?'

Nancy stood up and kissed Bill on the cheek. 'What a surprise, Bill, must be at least two years since we last saw you.'

If Bill was being followed, Alex knew their chance meeting looked convincing. Both Alex and Bill watched the door to see if anyone else walked in; they didn't. Not that it confirmed anything, because if he was being tailed, they could just as easily watch the door or check on him through the window. He bought Bill a drink and sat down.

'So far, so good,' said Alex smiling. 'While we talk, if we smile now and again and not look too serious, I think we'll be more convincing. I don't want us to give the impression this is anything other than a social meeting.'

'I think they've called the surveillance off,' said Bill, 'but better safe than sorry. I had that phone call today, Alex,' he continued. 'The one you said I might get, and you will never in a million years guess who made it.'

'So I won't try, who was it?' He had never appreciated guessing games; it just wasted time.

'Jean Elliman.'

Alex did not reply and Nancy realised he was totally stunned.

'She must have known I would be surprised and question why someone of her calibre would call me on such a minor incident. I didn't have to ask; she had all the answers ready. She said one of her team had obviously made a mistake and probably entered the wrong John Harris on the computer, it was a common name. She was sorry to have bothered me, and said something about having to do to do everything herself if she wanted it done properly. Of course, I was very sympathetic and said I often had the same problem.'

'Did you believe her?'

Bill noted the effect Jean Ellimans's name had on Alex, and felt important being the bearer of such extraordinary information.

'Not for a minute. I'm pretty sure the surveillance has been called off me and someone had to give the order for that. We were expecting a phone call and only Jean Elliman rang. Since that phone call I'm fairly certain I haven't been followed, so she must have given the order.'

'I'm bloody staggered; I just cannot see what Jean Elliman has to do with the likes of John and Elsie. It's too ridiculous for words.' Alex was obviously struggling with this last piece of information.

Nancy could contain herself no longer. 'Who is Jean Elliman?' She directed her question to Bill.

'You know more about her than I do, Alex.'

He picked up his pint and drank before he answered. 'I first heard about her from Ted Mundy. He's involved with training procedure for all police recruits, and, as such, gets to hear about any real potentials during training. Jean Elliman shone right from the start. She came from a working-class background, but had many natural attributes, such as being able to mix very easily with people from all walks of life, including the very wealthy, which is unusual. Mind you, she is a very good-looking lady, probably in her mid-thirties now, if my memory serves me correctly. But good looks alone will not suffice. She was highly intelligent and was promoted quite early in her career; a pattern of promotion which repeated itself from one squad to another; drugs, prostitution and the Fraud Squad, until her eventual transfer to the terrorist department, and you don't get transferred there because you have a pretty face. No, Jean Elliman is considered the cream of the crop.'

'Do you think it was a coincidence then?' asked Bill, 'I mean, just a coincidence, and a genuine mistake that the wrong info was fed into the computer?'

'I'm not sure, so let's hang fire on this at the moment and get onto the next thing. Nancy, let's have a look at your drawing and fill Bill in on your developments.'

She related the events quickly and then passed the drawing to them. It seemed the night for surprises had not yet ended.

'It *can't* be,' said Alex.

'Well, if it isn't, he has a double,' replied Bill.

'You know him?' asked Nancy.

'Are you sure about this drawing, Nancy; I mean, no nagging little doubts that it's not quite right?' Alex was looking at her intently.

'Absolutely none: that's him. Who is he?'

'His name is Luigi Spinnetti. He came to live in England about twenty years ago and he's one Italian we could well do without. We know him, but he has no record apart from the odd parking ticket. I knew of Spinner (that's our nickname for him) but never had the misfortune of him crossing my tracks. He's been pulled in for questioning from time to time over the years, but nothing ever stuck. He's clever, not your average villain, so we have never had the pleasure of charging him with anything.

'He used to dabble in anything: drugs, prostitution, theft and protection rackets. This guy wasn't fussy as long as he made money. He went from one racket to another. The last I heard, he had progressed to a Mr. fix-it, but an expensive Mr. fix-it; someone wants to pull off a big art job - Spinner could always obtain plans of the security system and the security guards' roster, even find the best people for the job. Now he specialises in setting up and totally organising any criminal venture and running the business for people who wish to be anonymous, but still retain control of the outfit. No-one gets to know who they are, except Spinner. Now do you see, Nancy, why I find it difficult to believe your drawing, identifying Spinner as the driver?'

He held up his hand as she started to protest.

'I said difficult, not impossible. One of the reasons Spinner has been able to stay the right side of the law, is because he never takes chances, so what happened last night would make some sense. *If* he received a call about Bill's

115

investigation and decided he needed to put a man on it right away, he would only have used one he could trust. If there was no one available at that precise moment, I think he would have covered it himself, rather than use an outsider.'

'What I can't understand is,' said Bill, 'the few people we have uncovered as being possibly connected, are all top people.'

'That's why I'm beginning to think we might be on the right track. Jean Elliman and Spinner are too much of a coincidence. One or t'other, but not both' replied Alex. 'We just haven't uncovered any motive yet, which is why it's so hard to swallow.'

Bill looked at the empty glasses and decided it was time for another round. He certainly needed one.

'Haven't seen you in a while, Bill,' said the guy behind the bar.

'Not as young as I used to be, Reg, and most of my drinking cronies have opted for the easy way out and retired. Give it another couple of years and I'll be joining them.'

'And I won't be far behind you,' replied Reg. 'I'm looking forward to putting my feet up in the evenings, instead of pulling pints.'

'How long have you been in the pub trade?'

'Thirty years. I enjoyed it for the first twenty, but each year since has got a little harder, so I'll happily take the gold watch and go.'

'Well, I hope it is a gold one. Problem is, plastic is so popular these days.' They laughed as Reg set the drinks down and took the money.

Alex had been carrying a large brown envelope with him and, as Bill set his pint down, he took out two copies of stapled sheets and gave one to each to them.

'These are photocopies of a section of John Harris's diary that Isabel found when we visited his flat. Take it home and read it; don't take any chances, Bill, by taking yours to work.'

He nodded.

'Evidently, he was being followed for about six weeks before he disappeared. He wanted to go to the police but was afraid they wouldn't believe him, which, sad to say, is probably true. He's written down very accurate details and I'm surprised at the amount of time they devoted to him. Now, is that because he really is in some way connected to terrorism, or the other thirty disappearances, and, if so, are the two connected? Personally I don't think they are, for one very good reason - John couldn't understand why he was being followed.'

'If he had been connected with anything remotely dubious, let alone terrorism, he would have known it highly likely that at some stage someone might become interested in him, and I'd stake my reputation he was genuine when he wrote that he couldn't understand why he was being followed.' He looked at Nancy.

'Got any idea or inspiration on this one?'

'Not really, no.'

'Can't you ask Angel?'

Nancy raised her eyebrows. 'You still don't get it do you, Alex? We labour to find the truth, and when the time is right she helps, like she did today.'

'How did she help today?'

'Someone other than a hypnotist had to help me retain that split-second image of Spinner.'

'I hadn't thought about it, but now you mention it, it was pretty amazing.'

'You know, for someone who was totally alien to the idea of help from the other side, you seem to be swinging about-face.' Nancy looked a little smug.

'She ain't wrong, Alex,' Bill was smiling.

ELEVEN

Nancy had a sick feeling in her stomach, coupled with a sense of unease that had grown in the last few hours. She tried to read to take her mind off it by keeping busy, but it wasn't helping. She stood up and walked over to the window and looked out at her garden, seeking some solace. She usually gained a sense of peace, looking out onto this quiet area of her home. This time she didn't attain the peace she sought, but her mind became a little calmer.

It was the same feeling she remembered so well on the plane back from Toronto. The feeling that something bad was about to happen. A sense of foreboding was engulfing her body and mind and becoming stronger with every hour that passed.

Nancy wondered how long she had been there before she felt her presence. She turned and faced Angel. *'I'm sorry you're sensing my coming has caused you so much pain, Nancy. Should I come another time?'*

'No, don't go. This feeling I have will not go away until we have spoken. I know that.'
Nancy looked and sounded tired. 'I can't help my failings Angel. I told you, you would be better off with someone stronger than me.'

'I know, but only those who feel pain as we do, are chosen.'

The *"we"* was not lost on her. Nancy suddenly realised Angel was coping with her own pain, but for a different reason.

'Elsie has been with us since yesterday.'
'Oh no! She's dead?'

'She is at peace now. Her horror has ended, but you must be strong. I want you to see Elsie as she was before her torment, and how she changed before her spirit joined us.'

She held her breath. The moment that had held such fear for her in the last few hours had arrived. She wasn't ready; she would never be ready. Her throat felt constricted, making it difficult to speak.

The next minute Elsie appeared before her, smiling and happy and Nancy's taught body began to relax; then it tightened again as Elsie seemed to disappear before her eyes, slowly losing weight and becoming gaunt. Nancy looked on in an almost trance-like state.

Elsie's gentle eyes closed; her skull seemed to pull the skin tighter, and Nancy watched in horror as Elsie's shrunken head became shaven on one side and large scar marks began to appear, running from the side of her head to the back. Slowly, Elsie opened her eyes. Two empty sockets screamed at Nancy, or was it her own silent scream she was hearing? It was too much for her. Nancy shut her eyes, trying to block out the terrible sight just a few feet from her, but to no avail. She could still see in her mind's eye the awful continuation of Elsie's demise, because it isn't only the eyes that receive these visions. These pictures are communicated to us, via the part of us that is the same as theirs, and is an integral part of our body: our spirit mind. It is like seeing an enactment on closed- circuit television.

Somehow, it helped closing her eyes, even though it was a perceived comfort rather than a true one. Probably because shock was now over-ruling what she was seeing, the appearance of more scars over Elsie's now naked body did not hold as much revulsion. It was as if the initial witnessing of the change was somehow desensitising her to what was happening. Suddenly, the terrible sight that had invaded every nerve and part of her being, now mercifully disappeared.

She still had her back to the window. Her body felt weak and the need to sit down overcame her. Nancy had a strong desire to cry as she sat down and leant back in the chair. Her eyes closed automatically as she tried to breathe deeply and slowly, praying this would help calm her.

She felt Angel's gentle hands on her head and knew she was receiving healing. The warmth and peace that comes with healing slowly pervaded her body, and, with it, a lightness in her head. Gently, the black cloud that had surrounded her body and mind lifted as she drifted into sleep, releasing the tight spasm that held her.

Nancy wasn't sure how long she slept; only the acceptance of what she had seen helped carry the burden. She went to the cupboard and got out her sketch pad, placed it on her lap, and started to draw.

This time, her drawing was almost feverish; the vision was so clear and real. Not a fleeting glance, but a sustained slow evolving that was etched on her brain, so that recalling every minute detail was effortless, except for the unpleasant task of having to draw it. She made some alterations, not because her memory had failed in any way, but because of the limitations of her ability.

Twenty minutes later, she replaced her pencil on the pad and looked out of the window at the gentle evergreen shrubs and trees, looking for that feeling of comfort, before she picked up the pad again.

This time it was a lot easier. She drew Elsie as she had first appeared: smiling, healthy, and happy.

***

Alex paid for his coffee then looked around for a small table. He didn't want anyone joining him while he waited for Bill to arrive. He'd bought a paper, in case he had a few minutes grace to read, but it wasn't long before he heard the chair opposite him being pulled out, and he glanced up on hearing Bill's irate voice.

'Bloody women.' It was almost as though he was talking to himself; he neither looked at Alex nor acknowledged him.

'Because I said I was meeting you in the Mall for a coffee, the wife decided she wanted to come for the ride and have a look around. Which means I'll be hanging around here a few hours after we've finished. "Take your own car", I said. "No", she said. Doesn't like parking in the precinct's parking lot. Says the spaces are too narrow.'

Bill decided to repeat himself. 'Bloody women.'

Alex didn't answer him. He thought about Lillian. He would have given anything to have his "bloody woman" back.

'At least we won't have to rush,' said Alex.

'No, I guess there's always an advantage. You just have to look bloody hard to find it sometimes.'

Alex remembered Bill had favoured the word "bloody" to enhance most sentences in the past when he became agitated. He hadn't lost the habit.

'Right, let's get down to business. We have two major priorities. Number one, we need Spinner's address.'

'Do you reckon I should chance the computer?'

'No way; if Elliman is covering his back, we're finished before we even start.'

'I could put out a few feelers on the grapevine and see what comes back.'

'We can't risk that either. It's unlikely, but not impossible she'd get to know. We have to think like Spinner - no unnecessary risks.'

'Then I'm fresh out of idea's,' said Bill.

'Perhaps I could make a few suggestions then?' Bill knew when to shut up.

'I'm going back four years, but do you remember the Redmond case?'

Bill wrinkled his forehead. 'Diamonds?'

'That's the one. If you can find my case notes on it, I'm sure Spinner's address is in there. At the time, I was pretty sure Spinner was connected in some way, but I never even got close enough to call him in for questioning. Redmond went down, but not Spinner.'

'If it's still there, I'll find it.'

'Right, second priority will be much more difficult. We need to return the compliment and put a tail on Spinner. Difficult, because he's the type that's always looking over his shoulder (for good reason) and we can't call on police resources. It also warrants sustained surveillance of at least a month.'

'I've got some time owing to me, so I could manage a few weeks. With Nancy and you helping, I think we could just about manage,' said Bill.

'I think we'll have to leave Nancy out of this one. She's more inclined to hit him instead of following him.'

Bill chuckled, 'You could be right.'

'Anyway, he's too good; he'd spot us.'

'So how do we get round that problem?'

'We've got one option. I've racked my brains and can't think of any other: Georgie Wells.'

'Who's Georgie Wells?'

'He's Elsie Turnbull's cousin; the one that asked Nancy for help. He's been a cab driver for thirty years. I'm going to ask him to help us, and hope he can enlist some of his friends to track Spinner. Cabs are everywhere, which makes them much more difficult to spot.'

'You know, Alex, it might just work.'

'It's *got* to work, but we'll need Spinner's car number first. We might have to take turns in trying to get that. That's why we need his address.'

'Suppose he's moved?'

'He may well have, but we'll cross that bridge when and if we have to. What we need to do now is arrange to meet Georgie at Nancy's as soon as possible, because if he decides to help, he'll need to organise a few trusted friends.'

Alex left Bill sitting at the table, twiddling his thumbs and watching the clock.

* * *

Nancy looked at her watch as she got up to open the door. They were on time to the minute. She was glad about that. She wasn't looking forward to this meeting, so the sooner it started, the sooner it would finish.

'Hi guys.' She stood back as Alex and Bill entered.

'Has Georgie arrived yet?'

'No, should be here any minute now.'

She had been surprised when Alex had telephoned and asked her to arrange a meeting with Georgie Wells, because it seemed so opportune. She had been about to call him for the same reason. It was as though two separate things had occurred, which instigated the meeting at the right time. Two birds with one stone, as it were, although Nancy felt a sledgehammer was more appropriate in her case.

She had to show her drawings to Alex and Bill, as well as Georgie. They were all involved, and having them present she hoped would help make her task easier.

Goergie arrived not long after and the coffee was ready.

Alex looked at Nancy enquiringly. 'I think you have something to discuss with Georgie. Do you want to start first?'

The question took her off guard. God knows she wanted to get it over with, but had not considered the relevance of it, until now. No, Alex should go first. What she had to say and show Georgie would certainly upset him. Perhaps he would be too upset for Alex to continue, and this wouldn't help matters.

'No,' she replied a little too quickly. 'It's probably better you go first.'

Alex's eyes stayed with her a little longer before he returned his attention to Georgie.

'Right, we've made some progress since we last saw you, but I can't say we understand it as yet. This makes it difficult to pass anything over to the police, although, as you know, we are getting some unofficial help from Bill.'

Georgie's response was straight to the point. 'Yes, Guv.'

'The only way forward, as I see it, is to arrange to have a suspect's car followed. We need to know who he speaks to and where he goes; in other words, to try and identify anyone connected with him who might also be involved. He's not a stupid man, so he'd soon spot us if *we* tried. What we need are cars that don't stand out in the crowd. In other words: cabs. To be more precise, at least three cabs. Do you have a couple of friends you can trust, who could help us for at least a month?'

'I couldn't say for sure. I'd have to speak to a couple of pals first, but I think so. Is this really necessary? What's Elsie got herself into?'

'None of this is Elsie's doing, Georgie,' Nancy answered.

'Nancy's right, Georgie. Whatever's happening she's not a willing participant.'

'Oh Gawd, how does a little nobody like Elsie get caught up in anything like this. It don't make sense.'

'No it doesn't, and that's a fact,' said Alex, 'and its one of the reasons this case is proving so difficult,' he turned to Nancy. 'Perhaps you're ready now?'

Nancy nodded; she was resigned to her task ahead but very apprehensive. 'I have to show you a drawing, Georgie, and I want to know if you recognise the person?'

'Spinner?' Bill's first input so far to the gathering.

'No, it's not.' Nancy really wished it was Spinner's. All eyes were on her as she picked up a large brown envelope, took out the smiling picture of Elsie, and gave it to him.

'That's our Elsie. Where did you get this?' Georgie couldn't believe what he was seeing.

'I drew it yesterday.' She hesitated. 'There's no easy way to say this, Georgie, but I believe Elsie is now dead.'

The effect on all of them was immediate, and they all began to ask questions at once. She raised her hand and the barrage of questions stopped. Nancy only addressed Georgie, as she briefly explained about Angel and a little of what had happened.

'This must be very hard for you to understand, especially Angel, but I wouldn't lie to you about something like this. I couldn't tell you Elsie was dead if I didn't truly believe it.'

He slowly nodded his head. He couldn't answer.

'I have to show you another drawing. The one you hold in your hand is as she was. The one I will show you now is how she looked when she died. It's not like the first drawing; this one will undoubtedly upset you, as it did me. You don't have to look at it, and perhaps it's better you remember her as she was?'

Bill and Alex exchanged concerned glances. They wanted to know what they were up against, but wondered if the drawings would confuse them even more than they were now.

'Nancy, the only reason I'm here is because I want to *know* what happened to Elsie. I want to see it.' His jaw hardened as he spoke.

He took the paper that held the image of Elsie's horrific sightless stare; her last moments captured on this plain white paper for all to see and remember. He stared at it for a few moments before despair overcame him. He didn't cry. It was the long, low wail that escaped from his lips that took Alex and Bill completely by surprise. But not Nancy; she was ready.

He continued to wail as she moved to the back of the armchair and gently pulled him back until his head rested on the chair. Then sent up a silent prayer as she placed her hands on his head.

Dear God, let those who have the power of healing and love in their hearts be with me, and let Georgie feel the power of your compassion, love, and healing

* * *

It had been sometime before Georgie was composed enough to drive himself home. The three of them sat, each with a stiff drink in their hands, not speaking. They felt uncomfortable, waiting for someone else to speak first, but hoping they wouldn't. They needed time to come to terms with this new and disturbing development.

Alex broke the silence. He held his glass out and said, 'I need another one, Nancy.'

Bill cleared his glass in one gulp, held it out, but said nothing.

Nancy went to the kitchen for refills, but took her time. It helped just moving about; she had no desire to rush back and face them. She knew the responsibility of explaining the phenomenon fell on her shoulders. She had introduced them to the case; she had convinced them to get involved and help in a situation in which they were uneasy, mainly on trust. She knew they would be looking for definite guidance from her, to give some credibility and sense to what was happening, but she was floundering too. She understood *how* the phenomenon had occurred, the technicalities of it, but *why* was out of her experience and understanding. No - that wasn't quite true. She was beginning to see the light. She just didn't want to; it was too awful.

Nancy stood quietly for a moment, leaning on the kitchen worktop. This wasn't helping - she had to face them. She picked up the drinks and returned.

As she sat down, Bill said. 'Is this black magic, Nancy?'

'No, I'm sure it isn't.'

'How can you be so sure?' asked Alex.

She felt their unease as they looked at her. It always surprised her that people who totally ignored the possibility of black magic, when confronted with any abnormal happening, would seek the answer in the very area they chose to ignore. The two reactions contradicted each other, after all, how do you become apprehensive about something you don't believe in? Perhaps a dormant warning bell rings in their innate survival instinct, which, until then, they had been totally unaware of.

She sighed as she answered. 'Because if that was the case, they would have to be exceptionally powerful, and therefore I would have some knowledge of them. I would have come up against them at some time, or heard rumours. What we have here is some kind of criminal activity that is affecting and offending those good souls that have passed over to the other side, and I stress the word, criminal.'

Their shoulders visibly relaxed, and Alex's brow creased back into thinking mode, 'Right, then, we're going to have to start using the little grey cells and start coming up with some possible answers. What happened to Elsie to reduce her to this state?' He pointed to the grotesque drawing on the coffee table as he spoke. He couldn't bring himself to pick it up and look at it again. It was a sight he would have no problem remembering.

'Experiments; unauthorised experiments?' suggested Bill.

'Could be, what do you think, Nancy?'

She could barely bring herself to answer. 'Spare-part surgery.'

'Bloody hell,' exclaimed Bill. There was that word again.

Alex took a while to think before he answered. 'Makes sense, and fits the bill in some ways, but not in others. It would be much easier to carry out a human spare-part operation in a third-world country rather than England, much less risk of being detected. And why not use the locals from a third world country? I would think it was much easier to abduct bodies there, than here.'

'Your logical analysis holds far more water than mine, Alex, and Bill probably agrees with you, so if that's the case, we also have to rule out illegal experiments, because the same criterion applies. So we're back to square one, unless you have any other suggestions?'

'It's got to be something like black magic,' said Bill.

Nancy was emphatic. 'No, I know that, as sure as I know my name is Nancy Harnetty.'

'Then if we can't arrive at a logical answer, where do we go from here?' Alex directed his question at no one in particular.

'My gut still says spare-part surgery, and thinking about it, I can see one dent in your reasoning, Alex. I'm pretty sure that I read or heard somewhere that Asian organs, are far harder to match up with those of European descent; that makes the UK a far more likely target.'

'You could be making that assumption because of your drawing of Elsie,' Bill said quietly,' in the same way I assumed it could be black magic.'

'It's not just the drawing Bill; it goes deeper than that, but I don't know why.'

She was a little hesitant as she continued. 'So I'm going to break the golden rule and ask Angel. Whether she will help or not is another matter.'

Nancy knew Angel had been present for some time, so she wasted no time in closing her eyes, but before she could ask, Angel was already whispering in her ear.

Alex and Bill watched her with interest as her eyes closed, but were disappointed when she opened them almost immediately.

'No joy there, eh?' Bill said sympathetically.

'I got an answer of sorts. Well - more like a riddle really. Angel just whispered in my ear: secrets.'

'How does that help us?' asked Bill.

'I have no idea, but it must mean something.'

Alex rubbed his chin and stared into the distance. 'Secrets', he said as if to himself.

Nancy raised her eyes to heaven as she asked, 'Coffee Bill?'

'Yes, I'll help you.' They left Alex staring into space.

When they returned, Alex was waiting impatiently with his hands firmly lodged in his pockets. Bill acknowledged his attitude with interest.

'Don't tell me you've made any sense out of Angel's sparse contribution?'

'Actually it makes total sense, and was in fact the answer to Nancy's question. In future, if you would both spend less time worrying about your creature comforts and apply more time to the problem in hand, I would appreciate it.'

They gave a duly submissive response; no point in aggravating him any more than he already was.

'Initially, I found Angel's response odd; secrets, secrets about what? It must apply to their operation, so the answer there was simple enough; they wanted the operation a tightly kept secret. Then I began weighing up the pros and cons of keeping an illegal operation secret, and then the answers came.'

'1/ the fewer people involved the better.

'2/ engage only those you knew from experience you could trust.

'3/ those running the operation would be top calibre professionals.

'Now using these criteria, I weighed the pros and cons against Nancy's hypothesis. The alleged professionals so far identified are Spinner and Elliman. They definitely qualify as top calibre professionals and we know Spinner only uses the "tried and trusted"; he never takes chances. We also think the people who were abducted are kept in a drugged, comatose state, so you wouldn't need an army of medics to keep them sedated, and we have evidence Spinner uses no more than two people to remove personal effects, and possibly for the abduction itself. As far as I can see, the UK would pose less of a threat operating in such a way, using the likes of Elliman and Spinner. It has remained totally secret, and would have continued to do so if these unusual sightings hadn't occurred.'

129

'Now, let's weigh the need for secrecy against a third-world operation. Could the organisers find the equivalent expertise, as offered by Spinner and Elliman, in a third-world country? Could they identify and employ totally trustworthy kidnappers and medics? I doubt it. The very fact that it was a third-world country makes it much more likely their employees would be more open to bribes or kickbacks; therefore, my initial diagnosis was flawed, making Nancy's "gut feeling" much more of a reality. What do you think, Bill?'

'I honestly don't know. I'd never really considered illegal donor body parts before, but when I think about it, it could be very lucrative.'

'If Spinner and Elliman are involved, we're talking big bucks, and where there's a long waiting list in a life and death situation money can talk if you're desperate to jump that list,' said Alex.

'Yes,' Nancy agreed. 'In this country when you're placed on a priority list, your financial status is not taken into consideration; otherwise, there'd be hell to pay. Having money doesn't put you at the bottom of the list, but it won't escalate you to the top either. So what if you were discretely offered a quick solution for your dying husband, wife, child or mother. Would you take it? Especially if you could more than afford it.'

'I'd have helped my Gran if I could, no question about it, but not if I knew how they were obtaining their body parts,' said Bill.

'Then I think we may have the answer. It fits, and I would say we can confidently assume they don't advertise how they are able to supply spare body parts, when the National Health Service can't.' Alex's brow was still furrowed. 'But that doesn't answer *how* these abducted donors return and communicate in the way they do.'

'I think it has to do with the drugs they use,' said Nancy, 'which somehow puts them in a state of limbo till they're ready to use them, or they are of no further use. I think the drugs eject their spirit from their body, holding it prisoner between this world and the next, but I'm certain this is a side-effect which they are totally unaware of; otherwise they would not have continued with it at this stage. They would have tried to eradicate this defect for obvious reasons.'

'Bastards,' said Bill. 'That's why they targeted loners.'

'Exactly,' replied Alex.

Nancy was surprised that the explanation she had put forward to two very reticent men had been accepted with little argument. Her thoughts went back to the very beginning and the uphill effort, and on occasion, insults she had endured in trying to engage their help, and inwardly felt great relief. This case was painful, tormenting and hard to fight. She needed them by her side, not standing apart.

TWELVE

All eyes were on him and he had their total attention. It was like stepping back in time. Times remembered when it was almost an every-day occurrence heading and instructing meetings. But today it was different. He had no real jurisdiction over this meeting, but it was very important that it had a successful outcome. Lives depended on it.

Of the people attending tonight, two he knew well, one hardly at all, while two were total strangers.

It had seemed logical at the time to arrange the meeting in his own home, but he now regretted it. It somehow put him at a disadvantage and he felt it invaded his privacy. His home was where he unwound, had familiar things around him, was part of his and Lillian's extended personality; not the right sort of atmosphere to put him at his ease for a meeting such as this. Perhaps not them either.

He wondered if Nancy felt the same when they met in her home, but, if so, she had never shown it. On reflection, she probably didn't. She was used to giving readings on her home ground. It was how she operated and it may well have worked to her advantage. Too late now, so he'd better get on with it, but he wouldn't make the same mistake twice. Time was of the essence and the good news was that Bill had found his notes on the Redmond case and Spinner's address, which meant they could get on with the next step of identifying Spinner's car fairly quickly.

This was the reason for the meeting; he wanted everything in place and the surveillance team ready to operate, so any problems in setting up the team needed to be sorted in advance.

'First I would like to thank you all for coming here today, especially your friends, Georgie, so perhaps you could introduce them to us?'

132

'Right Guv.' He looked a little nervous but seemed to get into his stride as he went along. Georgie wasn't used to meetings like this in which he was expected to participate, nor, for that matter, any meetings. He was used to working and thinking on his own. He coughed slightly through nerves.

'They're both long-term cabbies and what they don't know about cabbing ain't worth knowing. This is Ben Connor.' Ben Connor held out his hand to Alex and they shook hands. He was a burly, dark-haired man with a strong northern accent who looked decidedly intimidating until he smiled. The smile had an almost magical effect on his features, transforming them from a stern, no-nonsense hard face, by highlighting the kindness that had previously been hidden.

'Oh, and this is Fred Bagnall.' Fred Bagnall was tall and thin with a pale, easily forgettable face, but he had an awareness about him that Alex interpreted as being astute and street-wise. Alex smiled as he shook his hand. Georgie had chosen well. First hurdle over.

After Nancy and Bill were introduced, he wasted no time in getting the meeting started.

'Georgie has probably filled you in on some of the details concerning Elsie Turnbull?' They nodded.

'Right, gentlemen, what we need now is to organise a period of surveillance on the only person we have a definite lead on so far, but I have to be honest up front and say he's a very dangerous man. So I don't want him approached in any way, no matter how much you think it may help. This particularly applies to you, Georgie, because I know you have very strong feelings about this. I want it understood and accepted from the outset, otherwise we'll have to come up with something else, because it could ruin what little we've achieved so far.' He waited for Georgie to answer.

'Understood, Guv.'

'I only want him followed without any of us being spotted, which is easier said than done, so if one of you thinks he's on to you, then abort the exercise straight away. This decision won't fall solely on your shoulders because you'll each carry one of us. But you're the driver up front and in a better position to know whether or not he's been alerted, so the final say will be yours. Are you all happy with that?'

They agreed by either nodding or with a verbal response.

He looked at Bill and Nancy. 'Understood?' They had.

Nancy noted he hadn't asked them if they agreed with this decision, but if Bill wasn't prepared to question it, she certainly wasn't.

'We'll make notes on where he goes, the time he stays and, if at all possible, take a few photos. I want to know who he meets and see if we can link any more likely suspects, Okay? Now, let me explain how surveillance works. Do you all have mobile phones? Good, because it's imperative we all keep in close contact with each other. No one cab stays behind him permanently, otherwise your face will begin to register with him, then he'll start looking for you. We keep changing the cab immediately following; in other words, you tail behind him for a while then fall back and let someone else take over. Now you all work and know the West End like the back of your hand, so if you can take any short-cuts and come in from behind again, having been out of his sight for a while, it will increase our chances of a successful surveillance. Any other tricks you think will help, I'll be happy to listen to. Any questions, gentlemen, or has anyone decided this is not for him?'

'I'm in,' said Georgie.

'Perhaps you should take more time out to consider?'

'I have; I've been considering it since we last met.'

'Fair enough. What about Ben and Fred?'

Ben Connor spoke to Georgie. 'You know, in all the years I've known you, you never once asked me for a favour, but you've done me plenty. I'm just glad I've got the chance to return one of them.'

'What about you, Fred?'

'I have no problem tailing someone, especially as Georgie needs help. But that's it. I've got a family to look after, and this guy doesn't sound like the kind you should mess with, so if I get bad vibes, for whatever reason, I'll pull out.'

'I'm glad I got that message through loud and clear.' Alex's instinct about the man had been right. The "street-wise" don't jump, they think.

'Now, let's continue. I won't tell you the name of our man, because the less you know the better, but I will tell you something about him, because if you know the kind of person you're up against, you'll remember to stay out of his way. He lives and plays in the West End. We have to check his address is still current, but even if he's moved, he'll still socialise up town. He dines frequently in the best restaurants and then goes on to clubs, in most of which he's a very welcome member. He's known as a spender, but then he can afford it. He's been mixed up in most rackets but has no prison record. In fact, technically, he's as clean as a whistle. He's a clever man, so don't underestimate him. Any questions, gentlemen?'

There were, but not what he was expecting. Their attention and interest was directed at Nancy. It seemed they knew of her reputation and found it too good an opportunity to miss to ask the sort of questions they had always been curious about, but had no answers for. Under the circumstances, Alex remained patient, but eventually decided it was time to call the meeting to a halt as far as Georgie and company were concerned.

'I want to thank you, gentlemen, for coming along and agreeing to help. You'll never know how grateful we are, or how important this is.'

* * *

Nancy and Alex came out of Green Park Station and turned right. Spinner lived in Shepherd Street, which was part of the once infamous Shepherd Market area, the most salubrious address for the up-market call girl.

'It's not necessary for you to be here, Nancy; this kind of work is not only boring and tedious but can be tiring too. All I need to do is get Spinner's car registration number and model. I don't need to follow him or get too close. Where's the problem in that?'

Alex didn't suffer fools gladly or tolerate any interference and, as far as he was concerned, that's exactly what she was doing. He was exasperated and it showed.

Under the circumstances, Nancy was showing much more restraint. She knew he didn't want her along; he'd made it blatantly obvious. Nevertheless she knew she had to be there.

'We've had this sort of conversation before, Alex, and I thought you had accepted there would be times when Angel would ask me to tag along. This is one of them. Don't ask me why, because at the moment I just don't know.'

'This is not a dangerous exercise; I am not looking to apprehend him. I just want his damn car number.'

She stopped just as they turned into Whitehorse Street and faced him. 'I know that. You have mentioned it on several occasions since yesterday, and it is both repetitive and exceedingly boring, and if I had a fiver for every time you'd said it, I'd be well in pocket by now.'

A broad smile creased his well-lined face. 'Point taken.' It was the boring bit that clinched it.

Nancy turned and walked determinedly down Whitehorse Street.

She was right, of course, but old habits were hard to lose. The strange thing was Bill's total acceptance of Nancy's roll. He never questioned it, just accepted it, and he didn't do it to appease her, or out of respect. No, somehow Alex knew his acceptance went deeper than that. So why couldn't he accept in the same way? He'd had a whole hour's experience of Nancy's genuine guidance and help; Bill, only one short, sharp angry word. Alex thrust his hand in his pockets and followed one step behind. It seemed safer, less likely to aggravate.

Whitehorse Street bears left straight into Shepherd Street. Nancy had reached this point and stopped dead.

'What's the matter?'

'I don't know. I'm not hearing anything but I'm beginning to see funny things I don't understand.' She looked around and saw a little Bistro immediately opposite. 'Let's get a coffee. I need to sit and think for a minute. Alex took her arm and led her over the road.

It was happening. This was the reason she was needed here. He ordered two coffees and didn't speak as she sat and stared ahead, not seeing her surroundings but seeing something. She suddenly turned her attention to him.

'I'm sorry, Alex, I can't fathom it out at all, so I'll just tell you what I'm seeing.

I keep getting quick, distorted flashes of either end of a street. Sometimes I see it clear and bright, another time it's sort of in a red haze. Both images are so fleeting I can't clearly identify the buildings or the people. Oh, and I know it sounds silly, but for some reason I get the impression we are sitting in a safe area.' She briefly raised her hands apologetically in the air. 'I don't know what it all means.'

The coffee arrived. Nancy put sugar in hers and stirred as she waited for a response.

Alex neither looked at her nor acknowledged his coffee. It was his turn to stare into space as he tried to make sense of what she'd seen. It didn't take long. Almost immediately his eyes lit up and hardened at the same time.

'He's got security cameras set up to monitor both ends of the street. It's only a small street so it wouldn't be too difficult, and they operate day and night. That's why you were sometimes seeing the vision in red.'

'Why bother to cover both ends of the street? There's only one entry and the other's a dead-end.'

'How many times do I have to say this, Nancy; Spinner never takes chances. I'm sure there are a few back walls at the lower end giving access that way. This way there are no surprises if he needs to do a runner. It would buy him precious time. I wouldn't mind wagering he's also got his back entrance monitored. Thank goodness you were with me.'

'And how many times do I have to remind you it's not goodness we have to thank, it's Angel.' She was smiling.

'Touché.'

'Why is it safe here I wonder?'

'Good point.' Alex looked around. 'This Bistro is slightly on a bend, which probably puts the camera at a disadvantage, but from where I'm sitting I would have no problem seeing Spinner's car turning out of his road.'

He grinned wickedly. 'It's like old times, Nancy, he'll have to slow to get out, to allow for any oncoming traffic, and it's his lucky night – you're not driving.'

She opened her mouth to reply, then thought better of it. She checked her watch, it was 6.30pm. 'Do you think we should have got here a little earlier? We might have missed him.'

'Saturday night was always a social night out for him. He usually has dinner first, then onto a night club so he shouldn't leave before at least seven to seven-thirty. Of course, there are always exceptions to the rules, but that's one of the unknowns with this, Nancy, and there's no way round it. Patience is a virtue. We could order a glass of wine and something to eat if you'd like?'

'That sounds very civilised. I could get used to this surveillance work.'

He laughed. 'Take the advice of a veteran; this is the exception, not the rule.' While Alex ordered, his eyes hardly left the window and a note-pad and pen was within easy reach on the table. They had ordered something light and asked to pay in advance just in case they had to make a quick exit.

138

They had eaten their meal and were lingering over a glass of wine when Alex suddenly stood, up speaking as he did. 'Right, he's on the move. Stay here! I'll be back.'

Spinner was indicating right, which meant he would drive down White Horse Street and then out into Piccadilly. Nancy had wondered why Alex had worn a tracksuit, now she knew. He took a woolly cap out of his back pocket, pulled it down over his head as far as possible and left. He began to jog fairly slowly and easily towards Piccadilly and didn't have to wait long for Spinner's car to pass him. He increased his pace, repeating the car number in his head making sure he got it right, then gently turned and jogged back in the direction he came.

Nancy was surprised at how quickly he returned. She wasn't sure how long he'd be. He picked up the note-pad, wrote down the number and sat down.

'You got it,' said Nancy.

'I sure have. Now let's enjoy the wine.' Alex felt elated and yet, at the same time, humbled. Had he walked down Shepherd Street tonight and studied Spinner's home which had been his intention, albeit discreetly, he would have blown it. He raised his glass.

'Let's drink to Angel.'

* * *

It was raining heavily the first evening they started their surveillance and Nancy had come prepared with a brolly and stout walking shoes. She remembered sitting all night outside Bill's home waiting for Spinner to move, and how unprepared she had been for that episode. Better too much than too little.

Two cabs were parked in Green Park, one either side of the road facing in opposite directions, so as to be ready to follow either way without them both having to turn quickly and perhaps attract his attention. They had decided Nancy should be in the taxi watching the Sheperd Street exit, because she had the advantage being able to communicate with Angel just in case he did something totally unexpected. Angel was proving to be a great asset and they hoped it would continue if the unforeseen should happen. It didn't.

Spinner's car appeared, drove towards Green Park, and then turned left into Piccadilly, eventually making his way to a quiet little Italian restaurant in North London, but not before collecting a female friend on the way. They waited patiently for an hour and a half before Spinner reappeared and continued on to a club. Alex was relieved that Spinner hadn't changed his habits. Dining then clubbing: usually with a pretty girl attached to his arm.

They followed, watched, took discreet photographs and waited. They documented his every move for a month, with times and dates, covering as many days and nights as they could, before Alex decided to call a halt. Not because they had enough evidence, but because of the lack of it. They were not getting anywhere and he knew it. Spinner as always was too smart. He was probably very aware that from time to time he would come under surveillance if the police suspected his involvement in a case they were investigating. It was every copper's dream to nail Spinner.

Spinner probably operated from his mobile, never having direct contact but calling over his instructions, or receiving them on it. Alex still had nothing concrete he could pass on to the police, so he was back to square one. Thinking logically, he had known all along it had been an outside chance but one he knew they had to take. What other alternative did they have?

Alex had photocopied all their notes and given Nancy and Bill copies of the information to study individually, to see if some small detail registered, which would warrant further investigation, which collectively they might have missed. Alex had studied it over and over again - nothing.

He was on his way to meet Bill and Nancy and hoped one of them had spotted something he'd missed, but he didn't believe in miracles.

It was no good; they were not getting anywhere, so Nancy would just have to ask Angel to give them something they could go on. They were at a standstill, but he wasn't relishing having to ask her; he knew how strongly she felt about it. He could hear her response in his head. "We have to labour this side and they will help when warranted." Surely this impasse was such a time?

Alex parked his car in the large ASDA Superstore car park and walked quickly to the coffee shop. He spotted Bill seated at one of the window tables, bought a coffee and made his way over.

'Hello, Bill, what time are you on duty today?'

'Not till three, so I'm not in a rush.'

'Good.' Alex picked up his coffee, but not before he had checked his watch for the second time. Alex didn't like being kept waiting.

Bill smiled inside. He knew better than to let it show. Bill found it strange how Alex accepted that nothing would have happened without Nancy, and yet he found it hard to work with her. He knew she was never trained for any investigative work, so he shouldn't expect her to operate as they did, but somehow he did. That was Alex's one mistake.

They were only aware of this nightmare, and Spinner and Jean Elliman's possible involvement, because Nancy thought, acted and responded in a way that was foreign to both their ways of thinking, and the only chance they had of succeeding was to pool their differences. Bill suddenly realised Alex had stood up and was on his way to greet Nancy. She made her way to the table while Alex got her a coffee. Nancy noted Alex was a bit off-keel but chose to ignore it. It wasn't lost on Bill, who considered this a shrewd move.

'Well, I've read and reread these notes till I'm blue in the face, but nothing. What about you Bill?'

'Ditto.'

'Nancy?'

'Well something struck me as a little odd.'

'Angel?' asked Alex hopefully.

'No: common sense. I noticed there was one pattern to his movements which might need extra scrutiny.'

A look of interest crept into Alex eyes. 'The only pattern I could see was he liked to wine and dine a lot, but he didn't meet anyone regularly. Even his women changed at a rate of knots. What pattern are we talking about?'

'Let's look at his outings for the last month. The only place he visited regularly was his doctor; four times in fact.'

'I already checked out the clinic. It's run by a man called Philip Menet and he's a Diabetic Specialist. It's on record that Spinner's been a diabetic for at least fifteen years, and he's not short of money. It makes sense he would look after himself and get the best medical treatment he could, and I wouldn't mind betting that Menet is one of the best.'

'That's why we missed it, because it was so obvious. But that was the *only* pattern I could see, so I also checked what kind of doctor or specialist he was, which is how I learned that Spinner must be diabetic. Like you, Alex, I initially dismissed it as irrelevant, but somehow it stayed with me. It just would not go away. In the end, I picked up the phone and called a friend, who not only suffers from diabetes but works for the NHS. Basically she said she would never be asked to visit a specialist that many times in one month but would be checked out periodically by her local GP, who would only send her to a specialist if she developed a problem, or in other words, unless her diabetes took a turn for the worse. Now, one thing we can be sure of, Spinner is many things, but sick he ain't. You don't boogie every other night like he does if you're ailing.'

'She's bloody right, Alex.'

Alex's eyes narrowed. He was thinking.

Nancy looked at him with approval. That's what she liked about Alex. He thought things through, never accepting anything as gospel. If there was a flaw in her thinking, he'd find it, and she had a feeling he still had a few questions; not because he wanted to work against her; she instinctively knew that. There was always good reasoning behind his comments.

'Okay, I accept this is a pattern that doesn't make sense. We know he's not sick so why this need to keep seeing this Philip Menet? On the other hand, where's the logic? Diabetes is his field of expertise, not transplants. Elsie and John Harris were not diabetic, so how did they come to his attention?'

'I guess,' said Bill, 'we can only answer that question if we check him out. Perhaps that's where Spinner came in; *he's* the one who sourced the loners. Anyway, nothing in this case so far has been logical, and we don't have anything else do we?'

'Yes we do.' Nancy placed a clipping from one of the society magazines on the table and slid it across.'

To a man, they exclaimed, 'Good God!'

There was a picture of a smiling Philip Menet with his arm round Jean Elliman.'

'My friend knew of Philip Menet. Evidently he has a very good name in his field, which is why she remembered she had just seen his photo in one of the society magazines, and he has just got engaged. Guess who to?'

'Not Jean Elliman,' replied Bill.

'Exactly,' said Nancy.

'It's too much of a coincidence,' said Alex looking at neither and almost as though he was talking to himself. 'Whatever's happening, she's involved right up to her neck in it, and the answer must lie with Menet but, like everything else in this case, we shouldn't necessarily search or investigate the obvious connections to catch these bastards, because we probably won't find anything. We have to open our minds to any line of investigation and consider all areas, no matter how insignificant or remote they may seem.'

He looked at them. 'I had trouble believing Elliman was really involved in this mess, but not anymore. I'm gonna have her guts for garters.' Looking at him, neither of them doubted it.

'She really was a mine of information,' continued Nancy. 'Apparently, he only takes private patients, which is considered unusual. When I asked her why, she said because National Health treatment is so good in this area, it wasn't really necessary to pay for private treatment and most people don't, so most Diabetic Specialists worked within the NHS. She said of course he might be the exception to the rule and had been successful enough to attract a much higher level of private patients, which didn't necessitate him having to work within the NHS. Then she said something really interesting. She said it was rumoured that he had other business interests, but no one really knew what. Anyway, she was sure of one thing; he mixed with and entertained a lot of society people, so either he inherited a fortune, or he's making an awful lot of money, otherwise he couldn't maintain his very expensive lifestyle.'

'That's it. He fits the bill. So his other interest could be illegal transplants, especially as he needs a lot of money to fund a life-style to which he's obviously become accustomed,' said Bill.

'Well, it makes more sense than black-market insulin,' replied Alex, 'but it's still all supposition, so we're going to have to either prove or disprove it.'

'Right, so where do we go from here?' said Bill.

'Good point,' replied Alex.

He turned his attention to Nancy. 'Over the years, you've probably met a lot of people from all walks of life. Know any that have good connections in the finance business?'

'Yes, Why?'

'We need to make discreet enquiries about Menet's business interests and find out exactly what they are.'

'I'll try, but I don't know if he will help. He may well feel like you and Bill did and I'm getting a little tired of trying to convince people they should help.'

Bill grinned; Alex frowned.

'Well, just do your best, okay?' No sympathy there.

'Right,' she replied irritably.

THIRTEEN

Nancy knelt in front of the large cupboard in the hall and moved a number of things until she found the old shoe-box she was looking for. If she had kept the card Sir Alexander Wheeler had given her, then it would be in here, but it had been a few years since the one and only time they had met, so she was not sure if she still had it. She got up from her crouching position, carried the box through to the kitchen and dumped the contents onto the kitchen table.

She surveyed the small mountain and decided a cup of tea would help fortify her for the task ahead. Placing her tea beside her, she started to check the names, putting them back in the box as she searched. Every so often she would pause as the names brought back memories of the sittings she had given and the people she had met. Most were good memories.

Oh dear, where was it? Perhaps she hadn't kept it. She picked up her tea and cupped it in her hands. Even if she did find it, she was very apprehensive about phoning him; he wasn't your average Joe Bloggs, but if he could help, there really wasn't anyone better qualified. Now where was the damn card?

Ah, there it was. She felt a little daunted as she read his name and position. Alexander Wheeler was the head of one of the most prestigious financial companies in the city, and a very busy man to boot. Would he have the time, or even consider making the enquiries to which she needed the answers? On occasions, when nervous, she was in the habit of talking to herself.

'Pick up the phone, Nancy and find out.' She rang Sir Wheeler's direct line and was quickly answered by a very efficient and slightly intimidating voice. Nancy hesitated, then decided now was not the time to be intimidated. 'Sir Alexander Wheeler please.'

The intimidating voice belonged to Mrs Braithwaite, his personal assistant.

'He's not in and will not be back in the office today. Can I help you at all?'

'No, I need to speak to him personally. When will he be back?'

'I'm expecting him back in the office tomorrow, but I don't recognise your name, Miss Harnetty. Does he know you?'

'Yes, so if you could tell him I called and that I need to speak to him fairly urgently, I would appreciate it.'

Mrs Braithwaite took her number and said she would pass on her message.

* * *

Alex wasn't letting the grass grow under his feet either; he was perched on the end of his sofa, phone in hand, as he waited to be put through to Professor Stannick. This was his second call to Stannick and he had been asked to call back after 11am when he might catch him between lectures.

'Alex, old boy, how are you?'

'I'm very well, Stannick. Hope you're likewise.'

'Feeling a bit tired; I think it's about time I thought about retiring. I don't feel as dedicated as I did a couple of years ago, which I would say is telling me something.'

'Then you're probably right, but not yet, Stannick, I need to pick your brains and ask you to be very discreet.'

Stannick was considered to be one of the best pathologists in the country and they had worked together a few times over the years. They had a mutual respect with the added advantage that they liked each other. 'Fire away, dear boy. This conversation never happened.'

'Do you know anything about a diabetic specialist called Philip Menet? He's got a clinic in Harley Street; it doesn't have to be specific information, although that would help. I'll accept hearsay and gossip?'

'Goodness, I'm not usually intrigued but must confess you've got me wondering. What's he done? Anyway, I thought you'd retired. Did you get bored and go back to work? I hope I don't miss all the blood and gore when I decide to jack it in. That would make me a very sad person.'

Alex laughed out loud. The professor had always had a wry sense of humour. It was one of the reasons they had worked so well together.

'I don't know that he's done anything, Stannick, so indulge me. He's connected to someone else I'm very interested in and, as always, I prefer to cover all angles. And to answer your last question, no, I'm not back with the police. The enquiries I'm making are on behalf of a friend.'

'Right, then I'll indulge you. For a start, that's not the only practice he has. He has an equally expensive clinic in Belgium, although the exact town escapes me for the minute. His mother was English and his father was Belgian. He has in fact studied in both countries which is probably why he practises in both. A very gifted man. I seem to recall he worked in Africa at one time in some field of research or other, but don't ask me what. Anyway, old boy, you can scrub him off your list, you're definitely barking up the wrong tree with him.'

Alex didn't think so. 'You're probably right, Stannick, but thanks for taking the time to chat all the same.'

'Anytime Alex; got to rush now, but keep in touch. We should have lunch together one day.'

'You're on.'

* * *

The night security men were still on duty when Sir Alexander Wheeler made his way through the office lobby. He said good morning and continued to the lift. He was a tall, elegant, distinguished looking man. His thinning hair to the front was hardly noticeable due to the efforts of a very talented barber, but he looked and felt older than his 54 years. His financial expertise was sought world-wide, and it was to the constant overseas travel that his wife Marguerite attributed his early aging. Mrs Braithwaite, of course, made his travel time as comfortable and easy as possible by never booking anything less than first class, but he never really got enough rest.

Neatly placed on his desk were his messages, as always selected in order of importance as determined by Mrs Braithwaite. He read quickly through them, and then lingered on the last one in surprise. He had not seen or heard from Nancy Harnetty for at least five years; not, in fact, since Marguerite had contacted her when they had lost one of their sons. He closed his eyes, briefly remembering how desperate he had felt. The solace she had given him at that time, to him had been priceless, so much so, in fact, that he had tried to pay her far more than her usual fee, but she had gently refused and he had asked why?

She said she needed to eat and pay the bills, but not to the extent where she became wealthy on the heartache of others. She could only do what she did because people like his son were willing to communicate because they trusted her. If she lost their trust, then she would lose the ability to receive genuine messages and help those who came to her. "People who pass over to the other side are not stupid, Sir Alexander" she'd said. "They can read and know what is truly in my heart. No. I will never be a wealthy woman, but neither will I go hungry or cold. Should my love of money overtake my vocation to help people, then I would lose my integrity. It would slowly erode and diminish, until spirits like Justin would no longer communicate with me."

He had given her his card and offered to help with any investments she might consider in the future, but she had never contacted him until now. He leaned back in his chair and sighed deeply, remembering their meeting just over five years ago and his pain and grief. His wife Marguerite had made the appointment for him and she had moved heaven and high water to make sure he kept it.

The Wheelers were a devoted couple who had three sons. Their sons had grown into fine young men who they were both proud of, but tragedy had struck when their middle son, Justin, had committed suicide at the tender age of nineteen. Justin had been diagnosed with schizophrenia barely six months before. His deterioration had been so rapid that the family were still trying to understand his behaviour and to cope with it when he had suddenly died.

The whole family had been devastated, but especially Sir Alexander; he felt he should have understood and recognised how unhappy Justin was. The more successful he had become, the less time he had been able to spend with Marguerite and the boys. He had always relied far too much on Marguerite to look after things at home. She was a good wife and mother, who rarely complained, but after Justin's death he accepted, with growing despair, that he had not given as much support as he should have. Business had taken more than its fair share of his time and he had bitterly regretted it. His unrelenting guilt had greatly affected his home life and work.

Marguerite virtually had to drag him to Barnes. He had no interest in Nancy Harnetty or others like her, but Marguerite would not be put off.

His stern face softened as he recalled all the things Nancy had told him. How he had taken Justin to school on his first day. How they used to play cricket in the garden and then watch cricket on the television with Justin on his lap. She told him of so many special occasions they had shared that were important to both of them, that he had known, without a doubt, that Justin was somehow talking to Nancy. Somehow she could see and hear him. Both he and Marguerite had just cried quietly.

But it was Justin's last message to them that had taken most of the pain away. He had made him understand that his death had absolutely nothing to do with his father or mother. Justin said he'd been blessed with parents who loved him and had always shown it, but he had become ill, not with an illness that everyone could understand as being life-threatening such as cancer, but with an illness that affected his mind, and in his case *had* become life threatening.

He said he'd been given the best treatment, which had worked so well, that he had convinced himself he was now better and did not need to take his medication any more, so he had pretended to take his tablets. The illness had returned so swiftly that he had not understood that the voice he was now hearing was not Jesus. He said Jesus kept telling him that he needed him with him, that he should be by his side. So he decided he must die; there was no other way.

Justin said he was the guilty one. He had taken his own life and was ruining and causing great pain to his father, and continuing to hurt the whole family. Justin's last words to him were etched in his heart. *"You're not to blame, Dad, so please, stop hurting yourself and me. Let me rest in peace."* He had tried to book another appointment with Nancy, but she had told him he didn't need one. Justin had said all he wanted to. Savour his memories and learn to live without him. That's exactly what he had done. His guilt had lifted and their grief had slowly lifted over the years.

Sir Alexander picked up the phone and, as he tapped in the number, wondered what was so urgent?

'Good morning, Nancy, Alexander Wheeler here, and may I say what a pleasant surprise to hear from you after all this time. I must admit I had given up ever hearing from you. Have you decided to join the ranks of investors after all, because my offer's still open?'

'Good gracious no. I think it would be too much of a temptation to call on the powers that be if I really caught the bug, if you know what I mean?'

He could sense her smile as she spoke. 'Now you've really got me wondering, so what can I do for you?'

151

Suddenly, to her surprise she, felt Angel's presence and hesitated. *'Not on the phone, Nancy. Speak to him privately. Others listen.'*

'I wondered if we might meet to discuss this matter. I wouldn't ask unless it was absolutely necessary.'

'I'm even more intrigued. Ah, let me see. Why not come to my home for dinner with Marguerite and myself, that is if you have no objection to my wife being there?'

'None at all, in fact I look forward to meeting you both again; when?'

'Is tonight too soon, about 7.30?'

'Perfect, Sir Alexander, and I can't thank you enough.'

'Oh, you'll have to drop the Sir and Lady. It's definitely verboten at home.'

He replaced the receiver and leant back in the chair. What on earth could she want? It hadn't surprised him that she wasn't seeking financial help, otherwise he would have heard from her far sooner than this, but not wanting to speak about it over the phone had. He called Marguerite to warn her they had a guest for dinner.

* * *

Nancy was decidedly nervous as she rang the front door-bell of the Wheeler's imposing residence and was surprised that Lady Wheeler answered. She had assumed it would be answered by a butler or suchlike.

Lady Wheeler was as she had remembered her but dressed much more casually. She had naturalness about her that immediately put people at their ease and a genuine smile that hardly left her gentle, beautiful face. Her soft blonde hair, streaked with grey, framed a narrow face with high cheek-bones, highlighted by two very pale blue eyes.
As Nancy followed her to the sitting-room, she reflected how stunning Lady Marguerite must have been in her heyday.

152

Alexander Wheeler greeted her warmly, offered her a drink and suggested they should eat first and talk later. 'I'm usually much more alert after I've eaten, Nancy; it's been a long day.' They were charming and interesting company, entertaining her rather than the other way round. Dining with them alone had worried her all day. She didn't classify herself as a great conversationalist, but somehow they had found common ground to discuss and after a glass of wine she was conversing with ease.

'Right, Nancy, put us both out of our curiosity and tell us all.'

'This is going to be even more difficult for me than I first thought because I had no idea your telephone would be a problem. My original intention was just to talk to you on the phone.'

'Nancy, whatever are you talking about?'

'Let her speak, Alexander, and she'll tell us.'

'Your phone's tapped, but I wasn't made aware of it until we spoke.'

His mind raced. The shares in a few companies they had decided to invest in during the last year had shot up in value with no good reason. He had suspected a leak but had found it difficult to believe. His team was the best and they had been with him for a very long time. Plus, there had been so few transactions when his instinct had been alerted, that it *could* have been natural fluctuations in the market.

'How did you know?'

She gave a sheepish smile. 'Oh, the unconventional way I'm afraid. So you'll have to get it checked to confirm it.'

'First thing tomorrow, my dear; I don't suppose you would consider an unconventional job checking these things out periodically?'

She laughed. 'No, you don't need me. Just get someone in to check every so often.' The smile left her face. 'On a more serious note, I need information regarding a person

153

who we think has business interests other than his profession, but secrecy is vital.'

'Why, Nancy, you must at least tell me why?'

'All I can say is, I have every reason to believe his outside interests are hurting a lot of people who are unable to help themselves, and I'm not alone in my thinking, but if this man or his associates have the slightest suspicion we're investigating them, people will die.'

'Good Lord, Nancy, you're serious aren't you?' exclaimed Marguerite.

'Unfortunately, yes.'

Alexander was very direct. 'Were you made aware of this man via your natural talent, Nancy, and, if so, do you usually get involved in things made known to you in this manner?' She sensed his disapproval.

'Never; this is the first time and I pray the last. I really don't think I am equipped to deal with problems like this. I've been asked by relatives and friends to help if I can.'

He studied her for a moment. 'I believe you, so I'll do what I can. I'm not in the habit of passing out sensitive information like this indiscriminately, so when you can, I want you to give me your word you'll tell me what this is all about.'

'Willingly,' she replied.

He left the table; pulled out a draw of a large cabinet and took out pen and paper. 'Right, what company am I to investigate.'

'Oh, that's just the point, I don't know, only the name of the person we suspect is involved. He's a diabetic specialist who has a clinic in Harley Street but we have reason to believe he has other interests, and if so, we'd like to know what they are.'

'Are you talking about Philip Menet?'

Nancy's eyes widened in surprise. 'You know him?'

'Not personally, no, but we're always looking for new companies to invest in that are still in the growth area. We believe that Philip Menet is the brains behind one such company for a number of reasons, but we'd be hard pressed to prove it.'

'Whatever you do, don't invest in that company.'

He smiled. 'Never fear, Nancy, I have already terminated any thoughts along those lines.'

'Why?'

'A number of reasons really. The company is far too secretive even for a research company. They are researching snake venoms, but they have never disclosed what the end result will be used for. And I get very nervous when people who we suspect are linked to a company or project, deny all knowledge of it, or even any involvement, especially when I can see no untoward reason for denying any connection. One thing I'm good at, Nancy, and that's finding out who's linked to what, even if my information is remote and cannot be accepted as proof. I didn't delve too deeply because of this but, from memory, he practises from two clinics, one in Belgium and the other in London. We don't invest in clinics so they were of no interest, but I'd stake money on it that he's the sole owner of a company in Nairobi called The African Research Group, although I'm sure he must have another affiliated company somewhere in the UK. However, I wasn't prepared to invest any more time and effort in trying to find it.'

'Why?'

'Simple. I get bad vibes about companies that go to as much trouble as this one has to hide all its connections, and it's certainly not affiliated to any established research company, because the paperwork would be impossible to hide. I know research companies are notoriously uninformative, but this was bordering on paranoia. I wasn't happy.'

Nancy looked pensive. 'I had some doubts that we were barking up the wrong tree, but the more I learn about this man, the more convinced I become.'

155

Lady Marguerite had said very little during this time but she had become more and more ill at ease. 'Whatever this is frightens you, doesn't it?'

'Terrifies me would be more accurate; terrified in case we don't succeed.'

Nancy sighed as she looked at her watch. 'I'm sorry, I feel embarrassed to say I have to leave now, especially as you have both wined and dined me so well, but in view of what I have learned this evening, I have a few things I need to attend to. Thank you for making me so welcome and especially for supplying the name of the company Menet's connected to.'

'I have to thank you, too, for confirming my instincts not to invest in that group, and making me aware of my phone problem.'

She smiled. 'Well, one good turn deserves another.'

* * *

As Nancy drove home and thought more about what she had just learned, the doubts crept back. Had they got it all wrong? She now knew Menet was indirectly connected to a research company. If that was so, their original supposition, that the case involved spare-part surgery, was looking less likely. How did snake venom research tie in with this area of medical expertise? Were they using humans to test the effects of their research for some other purpose? Whatever it was, it had to be illegal; their tight secrecy confirmed this. She sighed. It was all getting much too complicated and she had no idea how they would proceed with this new information. How could they monitor things in Nairobi, for pity's sake? And if Alexander couldn't find out the purpose of their research, how the hell could *they*? She knew it couldn't wait; she was too worried; she would have to call Alex as soon as she got home.

Nancy felt a little calmer as she closed the front door and made her way to the phone.

He answered almost immediately. 'Sorry to call you so late Alex, but I've just come from Sir Alexander Wheeler and I really need to talk to someone.'

'I gather it was a productive evening.'

'It was, but it's only made me feel even more worried than I did before. I'm really not enjoying this, Alex.'

'None of us are, Nancy. I've gained a little more insight into Menet too, so I really think it would be better to meet tomorrow and get Bill down at the same time. We'll need to discuss everything thoroughly; it's not the sort of thing we can rush okay?'

'You're right.'

'Nancy, don't fret. Three heads are better than one. I'll call you tomorrow as soon as I've confirmed a time with Bill.'

She felt better. It wasn't all on her shoulders and when the time was right, Angel would help.

***

Nancy's concerns of the previous night returned as she sat opposite Alex and Bill. As usual Alex steered the direction of the meeting. He couldn't help it; it was second nature to him.

'Right then, just to fill you in. I spoke to a colleague yesterday who confirmed not only that Menet has a clinic in Harley Street, but also in Belgium. On making a few enquiries, I discovered the other clinic is located in Ostend. Apparently his mother was English and father Belgian. He studied in both countries so he possibly has dual nationality. My source said he also did some research in Africa, but he wasn't sure in which field. My guess would be transplant research.'

'No, it isn't. Hard to believe, but it's snake venom research,' replied Nancy. 'And I don't see how snake venom research is connected to organ transplants? Alexander Wheeler says he believes he's linked in some way to The

African Research Group, but Menet won't admit to any involvement. My obvious despair, gentlemen, comes from realising we have neither the funding nor resources to track or investigate his activities on an international scale. The research company is located in Nairobi and, before you ask, I have not sensed hide nor hair of Angel. She decides when she will help.'

'Well, that just about does it then. I don't suppose you have any enlightening news, Bill?'

'Sorry, no, but, I did hear an interesting piece of gossip.'

'Well, keep it to yourself if it's the Elliman versus Menet wedding of the year saga.' Alex was annoyed and looked it.

'No, it concerns Fingers; you know: *the* Fingers.'

'Who's Fingers?' asked Nancy.

Alex looked confused as he answered. 'He's considered to be the top safe-cracker in the business, certainly in the UK, and one of the best internationally, but he's being entertained by Her Majesty's Government at the moment. This is his first time inside and he wasn't easy to catch. Real name is James Brierley.'

'He's just got out,' said Bill. 'Early release for good behaviour, but word has it he has become interested in the paranormal, big time, because most of the books he requested to read in prison in the last five years have been on this subject. Some had to be specially ordered for him, so this is not a passing interest. He was especially interested in you, Nancy. Do you know him?'

'No, but if he decided to study the subject I'm not surprised my name crossed his path.'

'Oh, but it's more than that, he has read and kept every single article ever written about you. I.......' Bill would have continued, but suddenly realised Alex had "switched off" and was staring into space. He was well aware what that meant. Nancy followed his gaze.

'I think he's working on an idea,' said Nancy hopefully to Bill. 'Shall I get some coffee?'

158

'Not a good idea, remember last time, something about creature comforts?'

She remembered; definitely not a good idea. She mouthed 'thank you.'

Bill gave her a quick wink of approval. Nancy was beginning to understand the rules, because rules there were, be they unspoken ones.

Alex suddenly addressed them. 'Let's take a quick look at the situation at the moment. Everything we have is either hearsay or circumstantial. We do, of course, have witnesses galore, but none the police would credit. In fact, Bill, I would probably lose my reputation, and you'd be asked to retire early if we tried to present what we have at the moment, but the problem is we cannot walk away from it.' He held up a hand in exasperation.

'So where do we go from here? You were dead right, Nancy, when you said we didn't have the resources to continue investigating this further, and right again in pointing out that if Sir Alexander couldn't prove Menet's involvement with this research company, or even verify what the end results will be used for, what chance do we have?'

'So you're saying we have no way of continuing,' said Bill.

'Not exactly. What I'm saying is we have no way of continuing as we would normally. Which means we have no option but to consider every other alternative, even if it doesn't sit within the boundary of the law?'

'Blimey, Alex, I'd lose my job and pension.'

'I know, so we're going to have to row you out from now on.'

Bill suddenly looked a little aggressive. 'I think that decision lies with me, Guv. It's not yours to make.'

'Don't be stupid, Bill. It's not just you who would lose out; you have a wife and son to consider.'

159

'I know, but I need to think this through.' He looked flustered as he ran his hand over the top of his receding hair, but it didn't take him long to come to a decision.

'These crimes are too evil for me just to consider my job and pension, and I wouldn't be a good copper or a decent human being if I did. Suppose it was one of ours that was suffering like these people are? I know I should give it more thought for the sake of my family, but, in the end, I know I won't be able to walk away from it.'

They said nothing because both of them understood what he was saying. Nancy looked up and heaved a sigh of relief. Angel was there.

'Tell him not to be frightened. As he willingly decided to make such a sacrifice because of the suffering of others, he will be protected. Tell him to have faith, we will not desert him, nor will his grandmother. She wants him to know she was always proud of him, but never more so than at this moment.'

'Oh thank you, Angel, thank you.'

'She's here at last,' exclaimed Alex.

'Only briefly, but not before sending you a heartening message, Bill.' She lost no time in relaying it.

Alex watched as the strain left Bill's face and a happy smile replaced it. He was finding it even harder to accept how readily Bill no longer questioned information received from a third source like this; he who had been so anti. Alex thought about what Angel had said, and was surprised he believed it too. It also made it much easier telling them about the idea that had occurred to him, an idea that never in a thousand years would he have considered a few months earlier.

'Right then, lets get back to business, and it will be a lot easier with you on board, Bill, welcome back.'

'I don't ever remember leaving.'

Alex coughed and continued. 'Unless anyone has any other ideas, as I see it, the only way forward would be to

160

gain information without the formality of a search warrant.'
He paused; there was no outburst, so he continued.

'Menet *must* hold detailed information of his clinical and business affairs either at his London clinic or the Ostend office, and my guess is London, if only because, as I understand it, he only attends the Ostend clinic one day a week. So what we need is an expert in breaking and entering, so who is better qualified than Fingers?'

Bill couldn't hold his tongue any longer. 'So we ask him to put himself at risk for another long prison stay, and for what? What financial reward will he get out of this little escapade that will make him even consider it?'

'Absolutely none; and it's imperative he doesn't even take the petty cash. Menet must never know he has ever been in, let alone out. Brierley's more than capable of that, and no-one would ever know a crime had been perpetrated. All we need is for him to photograph as many documents as he can find, which I bet will be in a safe. He wouldn't trust logging everything on a computer, just in case he was ever investigated, and I accept your argument, Bill, as to why he would even consider it? But we have to try, unless either of you has any other suggestions? He waited hopefully for a response – none came.

'We could wait and see if anything else develops, or we get some unexpected breaks; help, even, from Angel, but if we delay, how many people will he acquire, or will die during this time lapse?'

Nancy could see his reasoning and the problems. One problem stood out like a sore thumb. 'How will you persuade him to do this?'

'I can't, Nancy; the only person who can persuade him is you.'

'*Me*! You can't possibly be serious. I've told you, I don't even know the man and anyway, I have absolutely no experience of dealing with people in his profession.'

'Now, don't underestimate yourself. Look what a good job you did with Bill and me. Why, we even had Bill here prepared to put his job on the line.'

'He's right,' said Bill smiling. She found the smile irritating.

'Be real about this, Nancy. He's never going to trust a police sergeant or an ex- copper. He'd think it was a set-up and, quite honestly, if I was in his shoes I'd think the same. But the unbelievable coming from you, he *just* might.'

She sighed heavily. She was totally defeated. He was right of course. She had a very slim chance; they - none.

'I haven't got his number,' she said weakly.

'No problem. I can get it,' Bill was still smiling.

'I can't see how you can be so agreeable to this idea, Bill. I really can't.'

'Well, as Angel said, you have to have faith.'

She really wished he would stop smiling. She had never been a violent person, but at this moment she felt like smacking him in the face.

Alex was very serious as he said, 'I'm not happy about this either, Nancy; it totally goes against the grain. I've got a quick brain and have racked it for another alternative; there isn't one, but you do have a choice. You have the right to say no; Bill and I won't mention it again.'

FOURTEEN

How should she handle this? What would be the best way to approach James Brierley? The only decision she had made was not to call him by his nickname; she was uncomfortable using it and not sure it would go down well with him.
She had asked Alex and Bill for any tips or guidance, but they had both said she should follow her own instincts. The problem was, they were sadly lacking at the moment. She hadn't a thought in her head of how to convince James Brierley that it was imperative they gain access to the offices of Philip Menet.

It could all go horribly wrong. If it did, what would happen to him? The more she thought about it, the more despondent she became. Who, in his right mind, would even contemplate it, especially as there was no financial booty to soften the blow? If there was no financial benefit, why would he even consider it?

They couldn't agree to him taking a single item. That was the only way they could justify their temporary blip into crime, not only to themselves, but to others in the future, because they would be answerable eventually. They had to show that breaking the law to obtain recorded information for the benefit of those who were suffering was their only motive, and that money was never an issue.

Nancy looked at the phone but decided she wouldn't call him yet; she needed to walk, look at the trees, feed the squirrels and think.

It helped. She just needed to put one foot in front of the other, take one step at a time and not look at the whole, it was too daunting. The first step was to call him and ask if they could meet, preferably in her own home where she knew she would be more at ease. Not in a restaurant or café with others milling around. He was bound to get annoyed, be incredulous, and even raise his voice. She would handle it better on her own territory. She ambled slowly back home from the park, not wishing to bring the inevitable too soon, but, once home, got straight down to the task.

Damn, his answer machine was on. This would delay it even longer and she wanted an end to it, even the small effort of telephoning him. 'This is Nancy Harnetty speaking Mr Brierley. We've never met but I wonder.....'

The phone was hastily picked up and answered by a very cultured voice, which for a moment totally threw her. One always had preconceived ideas that villains didn't speak like that. Future experience would teach her this was a fallacy.

'Are you Nancy Harnetty, the medium?'

'Yes, I am.'

'Well, what a coincidence, I was trying to find your number to contact you.' He hesitated before he spoke again. Suspicion crept into his voice. 'Now, I know why I would want to contact you, Miss Harnetty, but I find it difficult to understand why you would contact me. My telephone number is ex-directory and very few people know it. How did you come by it?' He was no fool; he was already on his guard. The conversation was starting off on the wrong foot.

'Under the circumstances, I can understand you being wary, Mr Brierley, so I'll just be honest; it was given to me by a policeman. I need your help and...... oh, Megan would like us to meet.' She mentally said thank you to Angel.

He was silent for so long that she was about to ask if he was still there.

'When and where?'

'Could you manage some time tomorrow morning, say around 10.30?'

'What's your address?' Obviously a man of few words.

James switched the answer-phone back on. He didn't like surprises, especially ones, like Nancy Harnetty, that he could not foresee or anticipate. If the police had given her his number, then they were somehow involved in whatever she wanted. He was sure they had not known about Megan. She had died before he went into prison, but the police *might* have been aware of her and, if so, what were Harnetty's and the police's interest? His stern face softened as he thought of Megan. Megan had been as gentle as she was beautiful, but she had never had any dealings with the police, they had nothing on her. He was suspicious but intrigued. That was the only reason he had agreed to see her.

If she had not mentioned Megan he would have got rid of her quickly. But supposing she had been genuine when she mentioned Megan's name? He clenched his hands; he would know when he met her. He walked towards the kitchen; he was beginning to feel hungry. He searched the freezer for a quick meal and shoved it in the microwave. He needed to eat and to close his eyes for half an hour. He had not slept well last night.

James made his way to the long heavily-cushioned sofa and flicked through the television channels as he ate. Nancy Harnetty's call kept repeating in his mind. He switched off the TV and swung his long legs up onto the sofa, closed his eyes and almost immediately fell into a light sleep. Then, the strangest things began to happen.

* * *

James Brierley was a total surprise to Nancy as she surveyed him sitting opposite her. She'd had to raise her head when she opened the door to him. He was tall, at least 6 ft 4, broad-shouldered and narrow-hipped. Not an inch of spare fat on him. He looked and was in peak condition. He obviously hadn't neglected to exercise whilst a guest of Her Majesty. He was about 35 with handsome dark looks she suspected were a magnet to women, and immaculately dressed.

Nancy tried to make small-talk for a while, hoping Angel would make an appearance - no such luck. She was on her own; terrific.

She tried to decide the best way to approach the situation. How much she should tell him and how much she should leave out; as she looked at him, and, he her, she knew the only way was to disclose all. He was too astute. He would never be happy with part or half-truths. It was all or nothing with him. If that was the case, then he owed her too. He owed her his silence if he couldn't help them. Not for her sake, but Elsie and John's.

'I'm going to tell you everything as it happened, but first I want your word that you won't repeat anything I tell you. That's my only pre-condition. I don't expect you to believe me, or that you help me. In fact, I really can't see any reason why you would, but not a word when you leave here.'

'Understood.'

'But is it agreed?'

'You have my word.'

This was going to be much more difficult than she realised. She didn't feel threatened by him, but she found his lack of conversation very disconcerting because he conveyed nothing. She had no way of knowing how or what he was thinking, so she just told him as best she could. It took some time during which he never interrupted her once. He never questioned the unbelievable or showed any emotion or disbelief. Nothing. Nancy had never met anyone like him.

James Brierley waited for her to finish then relaxed back in the armchair, it was only then that she realised he had been sitting slightly forward.

'That was an amazing story.'

'It wasn't a story, it was the truth.'

'I know.'

Nancy couldn't hide her surprise. 'How could you know?'

'Since I spoke to you yesterday, the strangest thing happened to me.' He looked sad as he continued. 'Sometimes I forget how well Megan knew me. You see, I'm not sure whether or not I would have believed you,

166

especially as your introduction to me was via the police. We naturally don't trust each other for obvious reasons. But Megan, I trust. Now I'll tell you a little story - sorry, the truth. They say everyone dreams and I'm sure that's true. It's just that some of us don't remember them. I rarely remember mine, but yesterday it was so vivid, I can remember *every* detail.' Suddenly for the first time since he had arrived he took his eyes off her and stared out into the garden.

'I dreamt of Megan yesterday after we spoke; it was so real I could smell her perfume and almost felt as if I could touch her. She talked to me about happy times before she had died; so many lovely memories that when I woke, I still had tears in my eyes. The tears were happy tears, even though the dream became a nightmare towards the end. She said; don't be afraid my love, but I want to show you the poor souls who need your help.' He looked down at the floor and ran his hand through his dark, thick hair.

'I suddenly felt Megan move to the side of me and rest her arm on my shoulder. Then I saw this long room in low light. I was looking down the centre with beds either side and bodies on them. They had no blankets covering them, just a mass of tubes connected to each one. I knew they weren't dead, but they were not conscious either. As I looked, wondering why I was being shown this, I suddenly became afraid, even though she had warned me that it would be all right. Things began to materialise above each body. I became aware of another identical image floating above each one, held together by some sort of cord, all screaming at me to help them. They *knew* I was there and that I could see them.'

He lowered his head so that it was almost touching his chest. 'I'll never forget it as long as I live.' He raised his head and looked at her. 'Megan knew I would need a lot of convincing, but don't be offended; it's a natural trait with me. I guess she knew I had to hear it from her. That terrible sight I saw is what you've been talking about for the last half-hour, isn't it?'

'Yes, it is.' Nancy couldn't help but be amazed at the lengths to which Angel and whoever was prepared to use their power were going to. Their efforts to introduce others they knew could help and their understanding of how this could be achieved, was something she had never experienced before. James's next question totally threw her.

'Right, whose house do you want me to break into?'

'How did you know that?'

'What other reason could there be? It's my only natural talent, although I have every intention of developing others that won't conflict with the law in future. I didn't enjoy my spell in the nick. You know, Nancy, it's almost as if I have been preparing for this moment since she died. Is that possible?'

'Oh yes, I think that's why I couldn't reach Megan myself. I did try after Angel gave me her name yesterday. Verification coming from Megan, confirming what I had to tell you, was much more convincing.' Nancy sighed.

'Can I ask you about Megan? I would like to know something about her, because I couldn't have done it without her.'

His face relaxed as he returned his gaze to the garden. 'I've never been short of women, but when I met her, well, that was it. My mother always said it could happen like that, but I don't think I ever really believed her, but happen it did. I find it hard to trust others and have only ever relied on myself.' He gave a wry smile, 'it's how I evaded being convicted for so long. I always worked alone. Megan, though, I would have trusted with my life. We had four wonderful years together and one not so good; the year it took for her to die of leukaemia.'

He studied at her as he said. 'She was a bit like you, Nancy, used to sense things. Little things though, not big important things, but enough to make her totally believe in

168

the hereafter. When I'm gone, she would say, I'll let you know I'm still close to you if I can. I'd smell her perfume, sense her dancing to her favourite tunes and suddenly get a feeling of peace when I was really missing her. Somehow she came close to me when I needed it most. So you see, eventually I began to believe; too many strange things happened which I could not ignore.'

Nancy could understand that, but one thing she didn't. 'Do you mind if I ask you a very personal question, James? But tell me to mind my own business if you prefer.'

'You want to know how a man, who is obviously educated, crossed the fence to the wrong side of the law.'

She nodded. The tension between them had gone. She could ask him now; even call him by his first name, which she had, unconsciously.

'The early beginnings, I guess, began when my mother remarried after my father died. My stepfather worshiped my mother, but resented any time or love she gave to me. Not a rare scenario, I suppose; but he was clever, I grant him that. It was done in such a way that my mother didn't realise it until it was too late for me to lose the hate I had for him and the hostility I felt towards her for not realising it earlier. It certainly wasn't lack of money; he was loaded. My mother wasn't short of a bob or two either and we lived in the sort of house the up-market property magazines love to photograph.'

'I did little things to start with; got in with the wrong crowd, as they say, who taught me the basics of what I needed to know. Within a short space of time, the roles were reversed and they looked to me for guidance. But I soon realised I couldn't trust them totally with their petty bickering and jealousy. So I became my own one-man band, apart from the fences - you always need a fence. In the beginning it was to hurt others, gain some attention. Then the excitement, coupled with a very lucrative way of life for very little effort, was just too good to let go. The rest, as they say, is history. Talking about effort, Nancy, who's the unlucky recipient I will be visiting?'

'Philip Menet's London clinic. That room you saw in your dream - we must find the location. That will be the ultimate proof. We're hoping he has the information tucked away in a safe somewhere. If he has, you need to photograph everything in it, then leave everything as you found it, ignoring any money or valuables, and get out without Menet ever knowing you were there. Is that possible?'

'One thing I've learned in life, Nancy, is nothing is ever a certainty, but I don't see why not.'

'I'm really sorry to ask you to do this, James.'
He hesitated before he replied. 'I believe you.'

'Thank you. I guess the next step is to meet Alex Moorland. He's a retired Detective Chief Superintendent and Bill Palmer, a Police Sergeant at Bilston Station.'

'Moorland, I've heard of – Palmer, I look forward to meeting.' He was grinning. Nancy smiled back.

'This isn't going to be easy for you, is it?'

'Is there any way round it?'

'No.'

'Then let's do it. Only time will tell if we can trust each other.'

* * *

Alex and Bill were much more relaxed than James. Nancy supposed it was because they had been exposed to the extraordinary events far longer and accepted the unusual now as the norm. When introduced, James had almost circled them as if checking the territory for any hidden devices that might entrap him. It was like watching a panther.

He eventually sat down and addressed Alex.

'It's not exactly a pleasure to meet you, but I think it will be interesting. I remember when you were covering the Belgravia thefts and I.......'

170

Alex cut him dead. 'No reminiscences please, you might let something slip that could incriminate you and I'm still an ex-copper, so might feel obliged to pass it on.'

Alex held up his hand as James tried to interrupt him. 'I know what you're going to say. That's exactly why we're here, to discuss breaking and entering, so what's the difference? Don't let's play mind-games, you know the bloody difference. This time everyone here is trying to fight the dreadful crimes that have already been committed and I believe still are. Now if you want to know if, in the future, we will all point the finger at you and you alone, the answer is no. We all answer for this.' James had been testing him and got the right response.

Alex looked at Nancy and Bill. 'One day we're going to have to disclose how we got this information, so I want everyone here to understand. We *all* hold our hands up for this.'

'Good God, honour among thieves,' said James. Somehow his flippant remark broke the ice; they started laughing.

Bill spoke next. 'How do we get this information accepted in court, when they learn it was gained without any legal search warrant, without us all getting a record?'

'You know the answer to that one. If we are lucky enough to find what we're looking for, then we pass it onto the proper authorities who won't be able to ignore hard evidence. They'll get a search warrant and, God willing, release the abductees. Sadly, it will be too late for Elsie, but hopefully Georgie Wells will get some satisfaction, knowing he's helped end the suffering of others. But the bottom line is, James, you'll get done for burglary and we'll get charged with conspiracy to burglary.

'My hope is that the judge will treat us with leniency. After all, there shouldn't be any doubt in his mind that we didn't do it for our personal benefit or gain. In fact, he'd be a fool not to realise that we all stood to lose a lot by our

171

actions, on a personal level, especially you, James.' He looked a little uncomfortable.

'Perhaps at this stage, we should also be considering who would be the best counsel to defend you, James, but, in the end, no one can predict with any certainty how the court will decide to punish any of us.'

Nancy should have been stunned, but she wasn't. Surprisingly, she felt no panic knowing what to expect as the result of their actions. Perhaps it was because she now knew and understood what was to come. Whatever the reason, she was unusually calm.

'First things first, though. What we need to do is establish our next move and how we can accomplish it. He turned his attention to Bill. 'Any chance of borrowing that sophisticated camera again? We can't use a Box Brownie for this job.'

'I can't see any problem there, other than when he can spare it, but it should be available by the time we get this job underway.'

'Good, check on that first thing tomorrow, Bill. The next hurdle will be much more difficult. We need to get the photos developed with all speed by someone who can keep his mouth shut. I was hoping you could help with this one, James.'

He was fairly nonchalant as he answered. 'Off-hand I don't know. A good fence is more in my line, but it wouldn't take me too long to find out. But I can see problems with your line of reasoning.'

'Why?'

'Whoever develops this film is bound to read it, especially if *I* ask him. I'm known in the business, but not for this line of work. Whoever develops them will be curious, which gives us another problem. Will he make copies? Would he know someone whose speciality is blackmail, who would be more than happy to pay the right price to get his hands on this lot? More worryingly, is Luigi Spinneti's name

172

mentioned in these documents. If it is, would he run straight to him? My guess would be a definite yes. There aren't many in the business who are not aware of Spinner's existence, and to be aware of him is to fear him. I also have a certain reputation but it doesn't promote fear. I'm not known as a violent man, but Spinner, as everyone knows, is not averse to it. No, too many loopholes with this, Moorland, and I only survived as long as I did because I wasn't lumbered with a trusting nature.'

As Alex listened, he knew why Brierley commanded respect not only from the villains, but many policemen as well. 'Your right, James, and we cannot afford to take any chances. Any ideas?'

'Only one that I'm happy with. I develop them.'

'Photography a hobby of yours?' enquired Bill.

'I'd like to be able to impress you and say yes, especially at such a critical time as this, but sadly no. I do however have a friend who is a professional photographer. That's how I met Megan; she did some modelling work for him. I'll ask if I can use his dark-room to develop them myself, under his instruction of course. I'm told that with the right equipment it's not that difficult, and I'll make sure he doesn't get to see them, for his sake as well as ours.'

'I think your suggestion is excellent, James, and I'm glad you were thinking ahead.' Alex looked strained as he said. 'Its time to vote; who's in – who's out?'

One by one they raised their hand. There were no abstainers.

Nearby, an entity who did not wish to be detected was a silent witness to this gathering. Angel felt compassion for each and every one having to make such a decision.

Alex called the meeting to a halt at this point. 'I think it best we sleep on it. It's a big decision to make, so we should all give it some thought, especially you, James. You have more to lose than any of us. I would like you all to phone me tomorrow with your final answer, with no recriminations for anyone who decides to back out.

***

Surprisingly, James Brierley was the first to call to say he had not changed his mind, saying something about it being payback time for him. Nancy's and Bill's calls followed some time later

Time was all important and the next day found them seated round Nancy's kitchen table. It was decided it was better to meet there, just in case the police decided to put a spot surveillance check on Brierley. A visit to her would be far more explainable, due to his known interest while in prison. Nevertheless James had taken precautions to make sure he wasn't being followed, only because Alex and Bill were attending. He didn't want anyone putting two and two together, even though Bill and Alex would arrive much earlier and leave at least half an hour or so later.

James was sure on this occasion they had nothing to worry about.

'Okay, next on the agenda: Menet's clinic. I think this is where I hand over the meeting to you, James.'

'Well, as you all know I ......'

'Oh no, I can't,' exclaimed Nancy.

'Can't what?' Alex asked in a raised voice. 'I don't remember anyone asking you to do anything.'

'Not you - Angel. She says I have to go with James when he visits Menet's clinic, but that's the problem; it's hardly a visit, is it? Oh dear, I suppose she must have a very good reason for asking. It must be to protect him in some way and it's obviously not fair to make him take all the risks when, I suppose, I could be of some use......' Nancy rambled on as if talking out loud to herself. It was James who interrupted her.

'Hold it right there, Nancy. I work alone and always have done. If I wanted to continue with this career - which I

174

don't - I would not change that basic rule. But *if* I did decide it was necessary for someone to tag along, a rank outsider, and a female to boot, would never be my choice. So I'm sorry, no can do.'

Nancy looked agitated, 'I don't think I'm the one to convince him, Alex, you will have to because I don't think I'll do a very good job. I'd only be covering my own butt which says it doesn't want to go.'

'I said, no way.' James looked adamant.

'I don't think you could have told him about our little disagreement and subsequent episode with Spinner?' Alex asked.

'No, but you're right, it might help,' she replied grudgingly.

'No, it will not,' said James, 'and spare me any more little stories.' He was verging on rudeness now and he knew it, but he didn't want to be convinced.

'At least hear me out. What have you got to lose?'

'My sanity. If I'm swayed it will be bordering on insanity to take Nancy along on a job like this. This guy doesn't sound like a pushover and if Spinner's on his side, he would make sure all angles are covered. It will be hard enough even without her.'

Alex decided to tell him anyway, '.....so you see, if Nancy hadn't made me aware of those hidden cameras, we would have blown this case even before we really started. The whole point, James, is she can see and hear Angel; we can't, and although it's been a hard lesson for me, I've come to realise that we ignore Angel's advice at our peril. If you don't take Nancy, then, thank-you, but no thank-you, we won't need your help.'

'That's blackmail.'

'Not in my eyes. It's good sense. Think about it. If Angel is right and you need her help, it can only be for one reason; you will fail. If you fail, you will have blown our cover not only to Menet, but Spinner. In one night you will have destroyed all we have worked so hard to achieve. But it won't end there; Spinner will be looking for us. Do you have the right to expose Nancy to that unnecessary danger?'

James closed his eyes and clenched his jaw. They waited.

'All right, all right. Christ, you really know how to put the screws on.' He looked at Nancy.

'You don't move a muscle unless I tell you. You don't speak unless I tell you. In fact, you don't breath unless I tell you, otherwise it's no deal.'

Oh dear, she really *didn't* want to do this. She gulped and nodded.

FIFTEEN

Nancy jumped when she heard the doorbell, even though she had been expecting it. She checked her watch; it was 1.45am.

'Okay, let's go over this one more time,' said James. 'You stay immediately behind me and only walk where I walk once we're inside the clinic. There may be cameras which I'll have to deal with so, just to be on the safe side, keep your balaclava on. In fact, don't move a muscle unless I tell you to. Understood?'

'Understood,' she replied nervously.

'All right, let's go.' As they reached the car, James handed her what looked like a pair of surgical gloves. 'Put these on before you touch the car, it's stolen.'

'Oh dear.'

'Don't worry. I'll put it back if all goes well and they'll never know we borrowed it for a few hours.' Half-an-hour later they were parked opposite the clinic in Harley Street. James was wearing a dark track suit. He reached over onto the back seat and picked up a wide canvas belt, which had inserts that held all manner of equipment, and quickly clipped it round his waist. She noticed how he kept checking the wing mirror and windows as he worked. He pulled on a loose, casual jacket and continued to relay instructions as he reached for the door.

'Now stay here and keep your head down as much as you can. Don't draw attention to yourself.'

She nodded as she lowered herself into the seat as much as she could. Suddenly she sat up again. 'Where are you going? Why are you leaving me here?'

'I need to check things out before we go in.' His back was already disappearing into the distance.

Nancy was more than worried. She hadn't sensed Angel's presence at all this evening. Surely she wouldn't let them down tonight of all nights? Suddenly, she relaxed as she turned to look at the back seat. Not only was Angel seated there, but a beautiful blonde girl.

Nancy smiled. 'You must be Megan?'

Megan smiled back. *'Don't worry, Nancy, we have not deserted you, but I'll stay close to James for a while. I want him to feel my presence.'* With that, she was gone.

Nancy looked at Angel. 'Whatever you do, don't you leave me for a minute. Even if something goes wrong. I'll feel safer if I know you're near.'

'Not for a second. In fact, such is the power I have been given this evening, not only will you be able to sense my presence and hear my thoughts, but I will remain visible to you at all times, but Megan will leave when James returns. It's better that you work with just one communicator.'

'I can't tell you how relieved I am to hear you'll stay close.' Nancy slid slowly down in the seat as far as she could. It had been some time since James had left and she was beginning to feel nervous again. She had spotted him walking casually past the clinic a few times as if circling the block. Because she was so on edge, it seemed a very long time before the door was opened and James slid into the seat beside her.

'Now we wait ten minutes or so. They have installed a fairly good burglar alarm system, but not as good as I expected, every window and door is wired. It wasn't easy, but I've done a bypass on one of the back window circuits, and I've opened a window to see if it trips the alarm in the local station or security firm. We'll know within ten to fifteen minutes, but in the meantime we can't hang around here. We have to keep moving but stay within earshot of the clinic. We'll either see or hear a squad car racing to check the building.' James was already driving as he spoke.

'If you had tripped the alarm, we would have heard it.'

'Not necessarily. Some systems prefer not to warn the intruder. It's designed to catch them in action.' He looked briefly at her. 'I'm not sure this won't turn out to be a wild goose chase. There are much more sophisticated alarm systems on the market. His is adequate for insurance purposes but I would have thought under the circumstances, he would have invested in a better system if he really had anything to hide on the premises.'

Nancy didn't answer immediately. He was right, so she mentally asked Angel.

'Angel says the alarm system is more than adequate to keep out the normal professional, but Menet didn't expect the more sophisticated pro would be interested in trying to hit a diabetic clinic.'

'I guess that makes sense.'

'She says he expected the worst scenario would be a raid from the police, who would obviously use the front door armed with a search warrant. Remember, he also has Jean Elliman watching his back, so any police interest would not come as a total surprise.'

He looked at Nancy and smiled, and not for the first time she noticed what a good looking man he was. 'I have to give credit where credit's due. Angel's good, she's very good.'

She laughed for the first time that day. Still smiling she said. 'She also said we shouldn't count our chickens before they're hatched. I think what she means is, we're not in yet and you may find it more demanding once we are.'

'I'll bear that in mind.' He drove around for half-an-hour. Neither of them spoke. He finally parked the car, tapped her on the shoulder and indicated she should follow him. They walked to the rear of the building and surveyed the seven-foot wall and solid wooden gate. James whispered close to her ear.

'I'll put my hands together and give you a helping hand over the wall, but first put this balaclava on. I'll sort out any cameras, if I have to when we're in.'

'I'd rather use the gate,' she whispered back as she fumbled with the hood. She lifted the latch and entered the rear yard.

'How did you know it wasn't locked?'

'I didn't; Angel did.'

'I think I like working with her; stay close.'

He walked to the open, ground-floor window and gently lowered himself in. 'As each window is wired we shouldn't have to worry about infra-red circuits.'

Nancy grabbed his arm, 'That's not what Angel thinks.'

'That's bloody devious of Menet,' he joked. In an odd sort of way, they began to relax a little, almost to enjoy themselves. Almost - not quite. Nancy was beginning to understand the excitement James had previously spoken of. He searched the belt around his midriff, found the special torch he was looking for and shone it into the room. There it was, just two and a half feet from the window.

'Okay, I'll close the window; then get down on your stomach and we'll crawl under the circuit. He reached the door, opened it carefully and entered an expensively furnished waiting room. 'Now, stay where you are; don't move an inch while I try to locate Menet's office.'

'Upstairs,' whispered Nancy, 'first on the left, and we should be careful of the infra-red circuit half-way up the stairs.'

He didn't question Angel's guidance now, just acted on it. 'I'm beginning to feel claustrophobic; can I take this balaclava off?'

'You'd better ask Angel. I can't see any cameras, but I would have to check much more thoroughly to be sure.'

'Yes, it's okay. Why are we still whispering?'

'Beats me.'

'She says the only camera is in his office, but it's only switched on occasionally. It's not on now.'

James frowned. 'He obviously films certain meetings by way of some kind of insurance. Perhaps a little blackmail, just in case someone steps out of line. You're sure it's not on now?'

'Yes.' They removed their balaclavas.

They reached the bottom of the stairs and he directed the torch upwards. 'There it is; the circuit's fairly low so it will be easy to step over. 'Whatever you do don't lose your balance, hold onto the banister. I'll clear it first then shine the torch so you can clearly see it before you try.'

So far so good. They were now at the top of the stairs facing Menet's office. James opened the door and shone the torch in, 'that's a relief; no infra-red to worry about. Now all I have to do is locate the safe.' He turned to Nancy and indicated a chair. 'Sit down over there and don't move.'

'I'm happy to do that.' James moved systematically around the room checking the walls, and it didn't take him long.

'Aha.' A small glass mounted cabinet slid slowly sideways to reveal a safe. James took his belt off and started to remove various bits of equipment. 'The boy knows his business,' he said over his shoulder. 'This is one of the best safes on the market. Very expensive; too expensive by far to keep a few medical records and the petty cash in, so I would say you're right; looks like Menet's got something to hide.'

'James, stop what you're doing right now. Something's wrong.'

'Christ, not another alarm?'

'No, nothing like that; keep quiet for a minute while I concentrate on what she's saying.' She sighed. 'Oh dear, it's the wrong safe.'

Of all the things he expected, this was not it. 'I don't believe it. What idiot installs one of the best safes on the market, then doesn't use it to store incriminating evidence?'

'You're not listening, I said the *wrong* safe. Apparently, there are two in this room. You won't find what we're looking for in that one. That one is a decoy. It had to be exceptionally good so that in the rare event he was being checked out officially, no one would suspect there was another. It would also give him the added advantage of time; time to remove the real data, while everyone was concentrating on what they found in that safe. It probably contains a lot of red herrings.'

'What if I or the police had found the other one first?'

'But you didn't; the one you found is much more obvious; that's the whole point.'

'You know, Nancy, I really wasn't looking forward to this evening for a number of reasons, sorry - but you being one of them. The main one though was that I thought I would be bored out of my box, which just goes to show how wrong you can be.'

He looked around. 'I've checked all the walls. If there is another safe, Angel's right, it won't be easy to find.'

He started to examine everything again, moving his hands slowly over each picture frame or any wall-mounted structure. Angel was standing beside him although he was totally unaware of her. She looked at Nancy and shook her head, then she moved over to Menet's desk and laid her hand on it.

'James, you're looking in the wrong area. You should be checking Menet's desk.' A look of interest appeared on his face. 'He must have a button he presses which automatically reveals the safe. Nifty, but it's got to be located in the wall somewhere.' He walked around the desk, looked under it, checked all the drawers for hidden buttons, and tried pulling the legs slightly - nothing.

'Angel, I think I'm going to need a little help here. Not that I wouldn't eventually find it, but we don't have a lot of time.' Strangely enough, he was actually looking in Angel's direction as he spoke.

'She's pointing at the pen and pencil holder on top of the desk,' said Nancy. The holder was slightly larger than the average, with inlaid green and gold leather which matched the desk. He quickly walked over to it and tried to lift it. It wouldn't budge. 'That's strange; it's an integral part of the desk.'

He fiddled with it but could not get it to move or slide. He sat down in Menet's chair and studied it. His eyes narrowed then opened wider. He noticed it had a wide, raised band in the centre; it looked as if it was made in two parts. He held the top with one hand and the bottom with the other, then turned them in different directions. They heard a slight whirring noise overhead and looked up. As they did, one of the wooden panels in the ceiling moved sideways. A small lift slowly lowered a safe, supported by four thin but strong bars.

He leaned back in the chair. 'Now that's clever, Nancy; best not to underestimate this bastard.' It was strange listening to such a cultured voice speak as he did, but when you moved in his circles, some of it must rub off.

'This one's French and the other one's English. I ask myself, if you're going to install two safes, why go to the extra expense of using *two* installers, which would add to the cost of an already very expensive job? The answer's simple, of course. This way, he wouldn't intrigue the installer and start them thinking. They might even mention it to others, because they would definitely have been curious if one company installed two such high profile safes in one room. They would naturally deduce he had a lot to hide and, considering the business he was in, would wonder what? This way the British company would not be aware of the French company, and vice versa; very clever.'

Nancy brought him back with a bang. 'Can you open it?'

'I don't honestly know; I've never tried to open one of these babies. Remember, I've been out of the business for a few years, so I could be a bit rusty, but I'm up to a challenge.' He rubbed his hands together.

'Take a seat, Nancy. This will probably take a while, so no talking.'

183

As she watched, her thoughts went back to their first meeting, and marvelled at the train of events which had probably started when Megan died. A train of events that now found them calmly collaborating to break into a safe (even though they hardly knew each other), united in a common cause to gain access to the secrets of a man neither of them had ever met.

'Bingo,' he turned to face her, 'we're in.' He removed the papers from the safe, took the camera from his pocket and proceeded to photograph each one twice, as quickly as he could.

'Good thing I brought extra film. Menet has a lot to hide.'

'Why are you photographing everything twice?'

'Just in case some of them are a bit fuzzy. I'm hardly David Bailey and I don't relish the prospect of having to come back.' He faced her briefly and grinned. 'No point in pushing our luck, eh.'

At that moment, as she looked at him, she felt the affection she usually reserved for friends, and, for the first time, realised that is what they would become.

'What would we have done without you, James? You're such a professional.'

'You better believe it.'

'I do.'

'Okay, I'll just put everything back as I found it, then we'll make a quick exit.' They retraced their steps carefully and climbed out of the window through which they had entered.

'Go back to the car and wait while I reconnect the system.'

She passed quickly through the gate and made her way back to the car. They didn't speak as James drove her home. Nancy was tired, even though she had taken a nap in the afternoon. Earlier, the thought of what was to come nearly made her phone Alex to tell him she just couldn't do it. Then she remembered the courage Bill had shown in making the decision he had, and knew she couldn't let everyone down. The car came to a stop; Nancy was never more relieved to be home.

'I could murder a cup of tea. What about you?'

'Anything stronger?'

'Whisky?'

'You make your tea and I'll be back in twenty minutes. Better return the car just in case he leaves early for work.'

***

James put the three film reels down on the table and Joseph Reid looked up in surprise. 'You've been very busy, James, which surprises me; photography was never your forte. Not trying to beat me at my own game are you?'

'Trust me when I say it's not something I enjoy.'

'So, what did take your interest?'

He smiled. 'That wasn't the deal. The deal was I get to use your dark-room to develop my films, with a little guidance from you, of course, then I wine and dine you at a restaurant of your choice, which, if my memory's correct, could never be described as inexpensive. Now, I'm not bleating about the cost, so no reneging on the deal.'

Joseph laughed. 'As you're so secretive, I just wondered if we were looking at a little porno here. I wouldn't want to miss out.'

'P' lease. I thought you knew me better than that?'

'Oh I do, James, always been a boring fart where that's concerned, so let's get on shall we. The sooner we finish, the sooner we eat.' James followed him into the dark- room and Joseph started to remove some of the previously developed film, and gave James instructions which he was very careful to follow. While they were developing, Joseph suggested they have a quick glass of wine while they worked.

Joseph never mentioned Megan, although there were times when he would have liked to, but James had remained

185

sensitive about the subject. Perhaps it would have helped if he'd met someone else, but spending five years in prison had removed that opportunity. Joseph held up his empty wine glass, 'Time to refill mine while you check your dodgy films.'

James concentrated on doing just that. He could not afford to make any mistakes but was confident he could follow Joseph's instructions. They had to be legible; everything depended upon it. He took the first one down and continued to check them all very carefully. One picture was slightly out of focus, but the back-up shot was good; the rest were very good.

He heaved a sigh of relief and said, Thank you, Megan, for being with me when I needed you most.'

There it was again; her perfume, stronger than ever. He checked the films were dry, then carefully put them into the wallet folder he'd brought with him. As he left, Megan's perfume still lingered.

SIXTEEN

James opened his eyes and was immediately wide awake. It was a habit he had developed naturally over the years, initially without him even being aware of it. But as the habit became more acute, he realised it was an instinctive safety measure. Any strange noise and, no matter how tired he was, he would wake. It was a natural side- effect of working on the wrong side of the law. He would wake with a totally clear brain, be completely alert, ready to move in an instant. The problem was it was in operation all the time; it was not selective. He looked at the clock. 10 am. He hadn't got to bed until 5.30am and knew he would have slept on if something hadn't alerted his sleeping senses.

Whatever it was, it had been unnecessary this morning because, for the first time in many years, the police couldn't touch him. He had nothing to fear from them. He had paid his dues and now had a clean slate. He moaned as he pushed the duvet cover off and stood up. As he was wide-awake, best get started. He poured coffee into the percolator and switched it on, then headed for the shower. He would have to catnap this afternoon. He'd had two very late nights and this evening would be busy.

Last night's dinner with Joseph had gone on much later than they both intended. The restaurant had only been a few minutes' walk from the studio, and Joseph's home five minutes walk in the other direction. James had left his car at the rear of the photography shop and carried on to Joseph's flat for one last drink. Well, that had been the intention, but they had both ended up drinking too much wine talking well into the night.

As he poured his coffee, he realised Joseph had needed to talk much more than he did; as they conversed long into the night, he was surprised to discover Joseph had been worried about him for quite some time. He had mistaken his silence in respect of Megan as a sign that he needed help, counselling perhaps. He felt that James was damaging himself inside by rarely talking about Megan now she was gone. But that wasn't so; he hadn't locked her from his thoughts. He thought about her daily; he remembered her daily, but another bad habit he had acquired due to his lifestyle, was that he didn't bare all.

James picked up the photographs and fed them into the scanner, printed off four sets and stapled them together. He picked up one copy and drank his first cup of coffee of the day as he slowly read. There was a lot of information to sift through and four heads would definitely be better than one. It would probably be more productive to wait until he met up with Alex and Bill this evening at Nancy's flat. They knew more about the case than he did, so would make more sense out of it. He looked out of the window at the empty drive. He would have to leave early to pick up his car which he'd left at Joseph's; no point in getting done for drink-driving.

* * *

James switched on the engine of the Land Rover, and then headed in the wrong direction from where he needed to be, just in case he had a tail on him. The police had been very obliging in advising him they would keep an eye on him; they were obviously keen to get him back. He had felt obliged to advise them that he had every intention of changing his ways, basically to save them time, effort, and tax-payers' money. They, on the other hand, had been very sceptical, and although he found their attitude irritating, he could understand their logic. Evidently, they had heard it many times before. Most didn't mean it. Of course, they had no way of knowing that he had decided long ago that if he was ever to get caught again, then that would be it. He knew he would be in for a long stretch and, if there ever was a next time he would probably be old bones before he was released.

Initially, James had not been averse to the idea of them following him. The sooner they realised he was genuine about going straight, the sooner they would leave him alone to get on with his life. That was before he'd met Nancy. Now it complicated things.

It took him approximately twenty minutes to reach Kensington, where he headed for some of the little back streets. He didn't think he was being followed, but a tight, back-street diversion would confirm it. He wasn't, which helped. He was running a little late, as he'd slept longer than planned. He pointed the Land Rover in the direction of Hammersmith, en route to Barnes.

* * *

Nancy's home could never be considered large. Average-size and cosy was more accurate, but it had a calm atmosphere from which to work, the round white kitchen table being the favoured spot at this precise moment. They were all reading the copies James had given them. After a cursory look, Alex had suggested they read them and makes notes on points of interest, together with their shortened account of the operation, which would hopefully give them a clearer picture of how the donors were targeted.

Nancy had her elbows resting on the table while her hands supported her head. Bill and Alex had taken up similar positions, elbows resting on the table, each elbow clasped lightly by their hands. James's chair was pushed back. One ankle was perched on his knee with his leg draped nonchalantly sideways. From time to time, each one stopped briefly to make notes, and then continued reading. As each came across the details relating to Elsie Turnbull and John Harris, they paused and lingered. The others were names and descriptions of people they had no knowledge of, but Elsie and John were the reason they were sitting round this table; they knew something of their lives and the kind of people they were, and knew those who cared about them. It gave them a chilling feeling. Here it was in black and white, undeniable evidence which, until this moment in time, had been laughable conjecture.

At this point, Nancy picked up her coffee mug and just stared into space, gaining some comfort from the warmth to her hands. She thought about Alan and their first meeting with Georgie Wells. Her mind went into rewind as she replayed the extraordinary events that had occurred since then. Now they had confirmation of all that had happened. Her mind then switched to fast-forward as she tried to imagine what would happen in the future, because this was not the end; they still could not relax and go back to living normal lives. They were only half-way through. Alex would now have the problem of getting things moving at this point without attracting the attention of Jean Elliman.

Then what? What would happen to them? Their indictment in court, and the repercussions of what they had done to obtain the information she was now studying. Then she remembered her walk in the park before she had contacted James. Yes, it was still the best way. Take one step at a time and don't consider the whole; it was too daunting. She picked up her copy and began reading where she had left off. They read and took notes for over an hour. As they finished, one by one they left the table, either to use the bathroom or stretch their legs.

James was the last to finish, joining the others in the living-room where they had vacated their hard kitchen chairs for something a little more comfortable. As usual, Alex took charge of the meeting. 'Right, we have now confirmed that there have been far more abductions than we were aware of. Menet has been in business far longer than any of us expected; at least ten years. During that time, he sold any human body part that could be used: hearts, lungs, kidneys, eye corneas and even bones for orthopaedic use. As the body was being harvested, it was kept alive for as long as possible. They could remove eyes, leg bones or even a kidney and still wait for the right patient match to sell the heart and lungs to.' He paused and his facial muscles tightened as he continued. 'I have never in all my years on the force heard of anything so callous or inhuman.'

He paused briefly again to wipe the small beads of perspiration from his forehead with a handkerchief. No one spoke. There was nothing to say.

I'm hoping you have the list of names that Alan gave you, Nancy?'

She nodded.

'Good, I've got mine too. We'll pair off later and try to match the names on Alan's list with the names on Menet's. I did recognise some of them from memory besides Elsie and John, but we need to confirm it. Fortunately, Menet's list is very thorough and shows all their previous addresses. The biggest shock for me is how many were listed; the UK's list numbers more than three-hundred, but there are some European names and addresses which the Belgians will have to worry about.

'The next thing will be to try and establish where the donors are located. We have four addresses shown here. The London and Belgian Clinics, Nairobi, and one in Birmingham. My guess would be Birmingham, mainly because it doesn't seem to have any other function that I can see, plus it's close proximity to Birmingham Airport. They would need quick and easy access to an airport to make sure the organs were transported quickly. There's no clinic held there, but it does have rather a lot of drugs delivered, none of which seems to be Insulin, but I'm no expert and it would have to be checked out by someone who is.

'Now, we must hand over this information as soon as possible, and here we have to tread very carefully indeed; Elliman will be watching their backs.' He directed his gaze at Bill when he next spoke.

'Although it goes totally against my loyalty to the Metropolitan Police, we have no alternative but to bypass them completely in the interest of secrecy, and give this straight to the Birmingham Constabulary. There's a far higher risk of Jean Elliman getting to hear of this operation if we advise the Met. and the less people who know about this the better.'

Bill shook his head. 'Alex, whatever police force cracks this case is going to gain an awful lot of cred. We *can't* hand it over to Birmingham. We're both Metropolitan men of long-standing.'

'Have you been listening to what I've been saying Bill? This case goes beyond glory and taking chances, no matter how remote that chance may be.' He said quietly. 'We cannot afford to fail.'

Bill looked a little taken back. 'Sorry, Alex, you're right of course.'

Alex's words were not lost on them, especially James. It confirmed that Alex Moorland was a man he could trust.

'Should I try and find out who would be the best man to contact in Birmingham?'

'No, Bill, definitely not. No inside enquiries from now on, only indirect ones and I'm the best person to handle that. I still speak to the DCS in Manchester. I'll make conversational enquiries via him, on a just-interested basis on what's happening in the force. That way we have far less chance of alerting anyone.' Alex's face was in earnest as he said. 'Don't do anything, Bill unless you check with me first okay. Our cover could so easily be blown on this one.'

Bill looked slightly offended. 'I'll work this investigation as I always have in the past. You'll know what I'm doing, when I do it, and why, with nothing held back.'

'Sorry, Bill. I know you're a good officer. I guess I'm a little edgy because I won't be in charge of this operation and that's a new experience for me.'

'No sweat.' Alex rarely admitted he was wrong, especially in front of others, so Bill knew he meant it. But then he didn't make many mistakes.

'When I discover who I should liaise with in Birmingham, I'll try to get an appointment as soon as possible. Bill, let me have a couple of dates when you'll be available to accompany me. The Birmingham guy will know we mean business when he learns you're still a serving officer at Bilston. He'll know how hard it is for you to pass over this investigation. Having said that, it's still not too late for you to get out of this while you can. You have a wife and son to support and your pension's not too far down the road either. You can't ignore the fact you may well lose your job. I can't speak for Nancy and James, but I would prefer you drop out now, while you still have the chance.'

'Bill, you'd be an idiot not to. Get out now.' James meant it.

'I second that, and, to be honest, my conscience would be a lot clearer if you did,' said Nancy.

Bill didn't say anything for a while; he was obviously seriously thinking about it.
'No - no can do. I'm in and that's my last word on the matter. It's my decision and mine alone, but don't think I don't appreciate what you're all prepared to do for me. You don't come across many decent people, or friends for that matter, these days, so I can't and won't walk away.' His demeanour was suddenly sentimental.

'But it's not just that. Somehow I just know in the end it will be all right. I know my old Gran is still looking out for me and that she wouldn't have made herself known to Nancy like that if she knew me and my family would be destroyed by all this, so thank you all for your concern, but it'll be all right in the end.' He grinned. 'Anyway, Alex, you need me to add credibility to your forthcoming meeting.'

Alex smiled. 'I meant your presence would add more weight to the discussion, I didn't say I couldn't accomplish the mission without you. Anyway, if we can't persuade you to go, I'll do my best for you when the time comes.' He reverted back to business mode. 'For obvious reasons, when dealing with the DCS in Birmingham, I will not disclose our involvement, or how we obtained the information at this point, unless I have to.'

'How will you manage that?' asked Bill. 'This is dynamite; he'll want some information as to how you got it to confirm it's kosher, otherwise he'll be very apprehensive about acting on it.'

'I'll tell him it's from an inside informer whose life will be at risk if we disclose it beforehand. That's not a total lie; I can't see Spinner ignoring our existence if he learns we're on to them.'

Alex looked uncomfortable as he continued. 'Hopefully, it will give us a little extra time to tie up any loose ends before they arrest us. Whoever I hand these details over to, will know they have to act quickly; I'll give him my word that *after* the raid has taken place I will disclose how this evidence came into our possession. I don't want any of us taken into custody before they raid the Birmingham premises, and he might well feel he has no alternative if I divulge everything prior to the operation. Having said that, due to the nature of these crimes he won't hang about, so none of us have much time.'

He looked at James. 'This is going to be hard on all of us, but especially you. Better to face it now, though; I have your best interests at heart when I say that.'

'Never fear, Alex, I won't be tempted to do a runner, but thank you for the advice.'

'Okay, that's the plan of action. Did I miss anything, or has anyone got any better ideas on how we should proceed?' No one did.

'Birmingham's my first and only choice. Anyone disagree? If so, state your reason.' They were all agreed: it was Birmingham.

The more time Nancy spent in meetings such as this, the more she realised Alex Moorland had been chosen by Angel, not her. She was just the person used to introduce him to the train of events that would follow.

'Nancy, I think you're the best person to contact Georgie, Isabel and Alan. Probably better to see them all together so that they don't feel they are alone in all this. When this meeting's over, I'll advise you on the best way to handle it and how much you should disclose, which will be just enough to let them know we're making progress, but no specific details. It's also very important you impress on them how vital it is not to discuss what they're told with anyone else.' She nodded in agreement.

'Bill and I will pair up to identify as many of the missing people on Alan's list with Menet's. You two do the same.'

Later, when they had all gone home, she sat in her big, comfortable armchair and wondered if she would regret her actions in the future. Would all or some of them regret being involved when they were called to reap what they'd sown? If she was sent to prison, how would she cope with it?

She was doing it again, anticipating the outcome, which she had no way of knowing. Angel wouldn't tell her; although she had no doubt that the spirit world already knew their fate. They had promised her nothing other than to protect her, but had not specified how far that protection would go. The decision they said was hers. If she decided to continue, then she must have faith and trust them. As she stood up to clear the table of coffee mugs and wash them up, she inwardly kept repeating,

"One step at a time, don't look at the whole; it's too daunting".

SEVENTEEN

Alex asked to speak to DCS Anthony Kilbride and got the normal short form of interrogation before he was put through. 'Alex, this is an unexpected pleasure. Does this mean you'll be honouring Manchester with your presence? Rita and I will happily play "mien host".' Kilbride and Alex had always got on well together, and whenever they had been on business in their counterpart's home-town, had offered each other a bed for the night rather than stay in a hotel. It had been a system that had worked well.

'No, Tony, but when I do, you'll be the first one I call. How have you been?'

'The red tape gets longer every day, which is very irritating because there's no way round it, but I'm glad to report I remain as robust as ever. How about you?'

'I do my best to keep fit and active, mainly accomplished by three visits a week to the gym.'

'It's all right for some; I think I'll have to wait until I retire to find the time for that.' They talked comfortably for a while, something they never had a problem with, before Alex broached the reason for his call. 'Who's the DCS for Birmingham now?'

'You could have found that out just by looking in the police almanac, Alex. Why ask me?'

'Because I know you; I don't know the DCS in Birmingham and my question is important.'

Alex had caught his interest. 'Should we meet and discuss this?'

'No time, Tony, I have to move fast on this one and I need you to say nothing about what we discuss.'

'Why can't I help you with it?'

'You must know you'd have been my first choice; dealing with you would have made everything a lot easier.' He sounded tired, which wasn't lost on Kilbride. 'Secrecy is of the utmost importance.'

'What do you want to know?'

'What kind of man he is and, if I give your name as reference, that you let him know I can be trusted.'

Kilbride was silent for a while. This was an odd one; he'd known Alex for a long time and was a man he trusted implicitly, but he was no longer a serving officer. Where was this going? No laws would be broken by indulging in a little gossip, if that's all it was.

'He's an unusual man, not the kind normally chosen to be a DCS, so it came as quite a surprise when he was. He was thirty before he joined the police and was appointed a DCS within 15 years. Before that, he was a qualified plumber would you believe. His appointment was a meteoric rise by any standard. It took me twenty-five years, and he doesn't hold any major academic qualifications which might have helped. He's not a scholar, but boy, is he astute; definitely born with more than his fair share of sixth sense when it comes to dealing with crime. I like him, most people do, but somehow he's different, although I can't quite put my finger on what it is.'

He paused while he thought about it, but as he couldn't come up with any tangible reasons, continued. 'They may have taken a chance when they appointed him, but he's more than capable of doing his job, and has earned most people's respect. Anyway, if he picks up the phone to me, I'll vouch for you.'

Alex heaved a sigh of relief, he liked what he was hearing, "a man who had more than his fair share of sixth sense". It didn't mean he would readily accept what Alex needed to confide in him, but he now considered he had more than an average chance of getting him to understand the complexity of the case.

Alex smiled as he said, 'I'll need his name, Tony.'

'I was saving that little gem until last. Would you believe, John Smith?'

Alex chuckled. 'Goodness, that's a name that's been used in more than a few aliases. I'm indebted to you, Tony; we'll talk more about this when I can, okay?' He replaced the receiver and called Birmingham.

* * *

Alex and Bill stepped off the crowded London to Birmingham train and walked towards the ticket barrier. As they passed through, they walked on a few feet before stopping and looking around. 'It would help if we knew what he looked like,' said Bill.

Alex grinned. 'Not really, what is it they say about coppers? We stand out like a sore thumb. He'll find us,' and he did.

'I think you are the two gentlemen I should be meeting from London.' He was pleasant enough as he asked, 'Got any identification?'

'Always pays to be cautious,' said Bill, producing his ID card. Alex pulled out his driving licence.

'Thank you.' John Smith held out his arm in the direction of the exit. 'Shall we, gentlemen?'

'I'd like to see your I.D. too please.'

'Of course, Alex, in fact, it just confirms that like me, you're a cautious man.' He produced his badge.

'Thank you, John,' and with that, Alex was already walking in the direction of the exit.

Once outside the station they followed DCS John Smith to a very comfortable Chinese restaurant only a few minutes walk from the station. Birmingham was known for its good Chinese restaurants in and around the city. They were shown to a secluded table at the rear of the premises, which was perfect for the sensitive details they had to discuss. The only thing that worried him was it looked very expensive. Alex would have chosen a more reasonable eating place, but this was not the time to let it deter him. It was only 12

198

o'clock but as they were returning to London immediately after, they ordered as soon as they arrived.

Smith leaned back in his chair and surveyed them. Bill did likewise and estimated his height was the minimum required by the police force. He had a stocky build and fairish ginger hair, with a pale complexion to match his colouring; his amber eyes smiling, but cautious.

'I must admit to being totally intrigued as to why you have travelled here to see me, especially as anything you had to say, Alex, would have been taken very seriously in London. You may have been retired for a while now, but your reputation has stood the test of time. Kilbride did warn me to expect a call from you and he was more than complimentary about you. Even so, I preferred to make a few discreet enquiries myself, all of which were beyond reproach. Now, instead of making me feel at ease, I have to be honest made me feel uncomfortable. Could it be that you wish to discuss something that could eventually become embarrassing for the Met? And if that's the case, could it become a dilemma for whoever gets involved? Why are you here?'

'The answer to that is simple, I had absolutely no alternative, and I can't tell you how much that galls me.'

Alex's face was hard as he continued, 'So I'll speak my mind. You don't trust us. Perhaps in your position I wouldn't either, but unfortunately I had no choice but to by pass the London Met. and come directly to you. If you think that was easy, then think again. I may no longer be a serving officer but my loyalty is still with them. So if you feel uncomfortable, spare a thought for me and my partner.' Bill felt a surge of pride at being referred to as Alex's partner.

'Let's forget me, though. What about Bill here; he's *still* a serving officer in London. How do you think he will be received back at his station when his involvement becomes public knowledge?'

Alex was angry. This wasn't how he had meant to handle it, but it was too late now; there was no going back.

'Before I go any further, I don't expect you to believe what I have to say or even get involved, but if you're prepared to listen, I want your oath you will not disclose any details, and I have good reason for asking.'

Bill was now very edgy. 'Sir, you may think Alex is being a little too forthright here, but if you could bear with us, you'll understand why.'

'Don't make excuses for me, Bill; I'm more than capable of doing that myself.'

Bill nodded by way of an apology.

Detective Chief Superintendent John Smith had been watching Alex Moorland intently.

'You know, you can learn a lot by what people say and how they phrase it. You didn't ask for my "word", you asked for my "oath", which in itself is unusual. I'm not often asked, but if I am, I'm asked to give my *word*. Now the words may seem the same and in this case basically mean the same. But the word oath has very different connotations. It has spiritual and religious overtones, don't you agree?'

'I hadn't thought about it. It was spontaneous, but that's exactly how I feel about it.'

Smith held out his hand to Alex, then Bill. 'You have my oath I will not disclose any information I might receive here, without your given approval.'

The tension visibly left them. The meal arrived so they delayed their discussion at this point, they were all hungry. Smith asked if they would like any wine or beer, but Alex refused on behalf of both of them. Clear minds were needed for the next episode. Bill looked slightly miffed but held his tongue.

Alex pushed back his chair slightly and blew out his cheeks. 'Well, it will probably cost us, but that was an excellent meal.'

'This meeting's business, so it will go on my expenses, although I don't abuse the privilege. You're on a pension, Alex, and I don't suppose you have an expense tab Bill?'

'No sir.'

He looked enquiringly at Alex. 'You were very insistent that this meeting was not held at my office, or that I advise anyone who I was meeting. It almost smacked of paranoia; this better be good.'

'I wanted everything to be kept totally confidential. Had we met at your headquarters, people would have been very curious as to why you were meeting a retired DCS and a London police sergeant. Tongues start wagging and before you know it, they're all on red alert, watching, but that wasn't my main reason for insisting we meet like this, or for by passing the Met. The person behind this case has a very highly-placed police informer, who has programmed the system to alert them every time we check it for information relating to our enquiries. I can't tell you everything at this point, but I can hand over sound evidence confirming what I say.'

Smith said nothing, just listened and waited.

Alex pushed his chair further back and sighed; he didn't relish this part.

'It started with a missing person enquiry from a friend. I asked Bill to check for any developments, at which time, we became aware there was a police informer monitoring any enquiries relating to these people. The biggest surprise was who - Jean Elliman.'

Smith frowned. 'That name rings a bell.'

'It should, and you have a lot in common; she also gained promotion quickly in the force.'

'Been checking on me too, eh Moorland?'

'I needed to make sure I was speaking to the right man, otherwise I wouldn't be sitting here. She's now with the terrorist squad and currently engaged to be married to our number one suspect.' Smith whistled.

'You take it from here, Bill, as it involves you.' Bill explained how he was contacted by Jean Elliman and then tailed for a brief period. Alex continued where he left off. John Smith was used to surprises, but he was finding it hard accepting the events as they were told.

'So what you're saying is, so far you have identified three hundred missing people?'

'Yes.' Alex waited for the next question.

'Why? What's so special about these people?'

'Body parts for transplants.'

Smith flung down the serviette he had been wiping his mouth on. 'No, that's not possible; it could never happen on such a large scale without them coming to the attention of the police.'

'They did. A few of those missing were eventually reported, but because the perpetrators always cleared out their personal possessions, the police always assumed they *wanted* to disappear. The clever part was they always targeted loners who had very little or no contact with relatives or acquaintances. So no-one really pursued the investigation after the initial enquiry, because they all wrongly assumed they had left of their own free will.'

'So what made you more suspicious, Alex? What made you think differently?'

'In the beginning, I didn't, but I decided to do some old-fashioned police work on foot. Then the alarm bells began to ring. It's taken a lot of time and effort to get where we are today, so don't you screw up on this, Smith.'

Alex looked around to attract the attention of one of the waiters. 'Could I have another coffee here please; anyone else?' They declined.

'The worst part, which I still can't get my head round, is they keep these people alive, if possible, after they remove certain body parts. Take the kidneys for instance; we all have two and can operate quite easily on one, and they can still remove other non-vital parts before they get a patient match for a vital organ.'

'Christ, I'm having trouble getting my head round this; Spinetti's involved too? I'll make a few enquiries.....sorry,' he held up his hand before Alex had time to interrupt him. 'Sorry, you're right, no enquiries via the computer.'

'Dead right, you put his name into the computer or any one of the three hundred missing persons and she'll know, and I bet they have a very efficient and fast plan to close down their operation, getting rid of all the bodies or any other evidence.'

He was nervous and it showed. 'I've told you, John, total secrecy. When and if you decide to get a warrant to search his Birmingham premises, even your top men must not know where they are headed or why. The address should be given to each driver as they are ready to leave, together with details as to how to get there. We don't want anyone radioing in for last minute directions. Total secrecy. Only you, Bill, me and the judge who issues the warrant must know, otherwise you don't get the evidence and I'll deny this meeting ever happened.'

'Understood, Alex, and to put your mind at rest, we'll work together on this okay? Obviously, it will have to be unofficial.'

'Oh, I'm in all right. We've worked long and hard trying to crack this one because of the inhuman nature of the case, so I think I deserve it. I want Bill included as well, especially as he may well not have a job after this.'

'Agreed, but I think you're being a little melodramatic regarding Bill's job. The Met. boys won't like it, but they'll come to understand why.'

Of course, John Smith was not aware of the full circumstances, and Alex didn't enlighten him. Smith read through the details slowly and shuddered. He had been told what to expect, but in black and white it was much more cold and heartless. He raised his eyes. 'How did you come by this information?'

'You're going to have to trust me on this one when I say I'm not at liberty to disclose that until after the operation.'

Smith nodded; he thought he knew the answer. Someone who worked closely with Menet had passed on the copies. They would be in danger before the raid if their name became known. Whoever it was, they were probably finding it difficult to continue with what they had become party to.

'As you said, Alex, time is of the essence. When I leave here I'll contact Judge Bush; he's our best man. Won't even disclose to his wife in the morning what cufflinks he's wearing.'

They laughed. 'Sounds the ideal man to me,' said Bill.

Out of courtesy, Smith walked Alex and Bill back to the station, and then, wasting no time, continued on to the law courts. If he was quick, he might just catch Judge Bush, who he knew was in court that day. He ran up the steps of the entrance, approached the reception desk and asked to see Judge Bush. As there was no love lost between them, he requested they tell him it was very urgent; Bush wasn't averse to being unavailable when it suited him. He was renowned for being difficult, and Smith knew far more amenable judges he would rather deal with, but none with such a tight mouth.

He was in luck; "tight mouth" had condescended to see him, but not to make it easy for him.

'Make it quick, Detective Chief Superintendent.'

Not even the courtesy of using his name, of which he was well aware. Smith now regretted being as difficult as Bush in the past, but he wasn't about to crawl; it wasn't his style.

'Let's make no bones about it, Judge Bush, you and I have not always seen eye to eye in the past, but that should never get in the way of either of us doing our job to the best of our ability.'

Judge Bush had been signing papers at his desk; his head shot up angrily. 'Are you here to accuse me of that?'

'No: just the opposite. I know you'll believe me when I say, there are other judges I would have preferred to contact for a search warrant.'

He eyed him with suspicion. 'I believe you, Smith, so why eat humble pie and come to me? I can only assume I was chosen for a reason.'

Things were looking up; he'd actually addressed him by name.

You're the only judge I would trust when I say we must maintain total secrecy in dealing with this warrant. I don't think I will ever come across a more serious situation, however long I remain a serving officer.'

'I guess that's a back-handed compliment.' He sniffed, but couldn't quite hide his approval. It got better for Judge Bush.

'That I am here at all is a compliment to you.'

'Sit down then, lad, and let's get down to business. What's this all about?'

He told him as much as he knew. Fortunately, Bush had been a serving judge in London before Birmingham and knew of Alex Moorland, who he'd found to be a successful and competent officer. Like Smith, he found it hard to believe what he was hearing, until he produced the evidence Alex had left with him. He read slowly, missing nothing.

'God, there can be no doubt about it if these documents are genuine, but Moorland's no fool. True or not, we cannot afford to sit on it. When do you want to go in?'

'Smith looked at his watch; 'it's too late now to get organised for early tomorrow morning. I want my best men in place which will take a bit of arranging; the day after tomorrow would be better, sir.'

'Right, wait here Smith, I'll organise it now.'

Smith put a restraining hand on him. 'Better to leave it until the last minute, sir. We don't want tongues wagging before necessary. I believe Moorland when he says we shouldn't take any chances.'

'You're right, Smith, of course. I'll arrange it as late as possible tomorrow night and meet you outside my office to hand it to you personally. Does that meet with your approval?'

'It does, Judge Bush, thank you.' Smith looked worried. 'You know if these people are there, it's going to be a massive exercise getting them into hospitals. We have no idea how many we'll find, and for obvious reasons I can't organise bed space in advance. As I understand it, these people will all be in a comatose state. It's going to be a massive exercise, and I need to know in advance the right medical specialists to contact as soon as this operation is under way; have them standing by, so to speak.'

Judge Bush looked at him with sympathy. 'I don't envy you, John, and I'll do everything I can to help you. I hope you'll spare the time to keep me informed.'

'We'll shake on that sir.' Smith noticed he'd been elevated to first name terms now, which surprised him in some ways, and not others. This was the sort of case that overrode any former differences, if in the end you never lost sight of the true purpose of the job you were being paid to do. They needed to work together very closely on this one; Smith never had any doubts about Judge Bush's sense of fair play, only his interpretation on some occasions.

It was nearing six before he walked back into his headquarters. He approached the front desk. 'Where's Bryant?'

'He's off duty sir.'

'I don't care what he's doing at this moment. Get him in now!'

'What if he's out sir?'

'I don't care if he's on Mars; get him in!'

The duty desk sergeant was already rummaging in the personnel telephone book as he replied, 'Right sir.' The duty sergeant felt a twinge of excitement. Something was up, something big. The DCS spoke with quiet authority as always, but his facial expression and manner were different. His face was set in a hard line as he gave his direct order, but his eyes looked as though he was elsewhere, as if he was thinking of more than half a dozen things at once. The DCS himself was organising a sting; he'd bet money on it.

'Hello, Bryant, its Cobb speaking. The DCS said for you to get down here right away.'

'Now, hang on a minute, I've just finished a ten day stint without a day off and I'm in the middle of turning my jungle back into a garden. Put me through to him.'

'If you'll take my advice, Bryant, drop everything you're doing, ignore the formality of showering and get your arse down here now.'

There was a short silence, 'I'm on my way. Are you sure about the shower?'

'Positive.' The phone was slammed down.

Thirty minutes later, not actually holding a trowel in his hand, but looking like it, Bryant knocked on Detective Chief Superintendent John Smith's office and entered. If he noticed Bryant's state of dress, he never acknowledged it. He didn't waste any time either.

'Sit down, Bryant; we've got a lot to get through.' He shoved a list at him and Bryant studied the names of twenty men. 'I want all those men ready for an operation by 4am the morning after tomorrow.'

Bryant looked surprised. 'This is very short notice sir. I'll have to check if their all available. One or two of them are already working high profile cases, but I'll do my best.'

'This is not an invitation to attend if they can spare the time Bryant, it's a fucking no excuses order. I need twenty of our best, and they're it, so I don't care if Buckingham Palace has invited them to tea and they've waited all year for the privilege. Get them to cancel.' He hadn't meant to, but his voice had gained an octave or two.

'Yes, sir, I'll get right on to it. Can you fill me in on what's happening?'

'I'm sorry, Bryant, no, not until just before we leave the station which will be about 5.30am the day after tomorrow: Thursday. Oh, and I want at least two officers to be armed. I don't really anticipate any problems of that kind, but I can't take any chances. Listen very closely to my next instructions, because they're very important. No details are to be entered on the computer, and I'll have any man or woman's job if they do. This is to be a word of mouth job only, via the personnel concerned.' Bryant was visibly frowning now.

'One thing I will share with you, Bryant, so you understand how easily it could jeopardise our operation. Even without the address, *any* big sting operation in this area could well alert a highly placed police informer if there was even a whisper.'

'Christ.'

Smith smiled for the first time. 'No, it's not him, but they still carry a lot of respect in the force, so we have to tread very carefully on this one.'

Bryant returned his attention to the list. 'One name I'm not happy about, sir, is Reynolds. His wife has just gone into hospital to have their first child. He won't be happy under the circumstances.'

'Understood, but let *him* make the decision. I think he will regret that he missed out on this exercise if he was never given the chance.'

'This case is that big, sir?'

'I doubt whether either of us will ever work on anything as big again.'

Cobb was right. Getting his arse down here was all-important, and his attire and lack of a shower wasn't. 'I'll give him the chance, sir.'

'Right, most of the organising we'll do together from my office. Start by getting the officers' home numbers on the list I've just given you; they won't all be on duty, and then we'll both start calling. I want them all assembled here by nine this evening. I'll leave Reynolds's call to you. He won't feel so intimidated or obliged coming from you rather than me. Any questions you think I can answer?'

'No, sir, that area seems to be very limited. I'll just phone home and let them know I will be late, then I'll check who's on duty from this list and make sure they stay on for tonight's meeting, after which I'll be back with the phone numbers.' He nodded, turned and left.

Bryant was the right man to be his second-in-command. It also made sense to phone home, something which had totally slipped his mind. He buzzed the desk. 'Get my wife on the phone, please.'

EIGHTEEN

Nancy stood on tiptoe to raise her head above the crowded platform at Euston station, and waved. Bill saw her and waved back. She was apprehensive as she hugged them, but hoped it wasn't obvious.

'I was very lucky: I found a parking space only a few minutes' walk from the station.' They made their way to the car, then Nancy headed in the direction of Alex's home which was the nearest.

'Thanks for meeting us. It's been a long day, but we could have got a cab you know.'

'I know, but I knew I'd be on tenterhooks all day wondering how you got on. This way, you can put me out of my misery and tell me all while I drive.'

Bill couldn't wait to relay what had given him the most grief. 'There was a moment when I thought Alex had blown it. He actually got angry and took Smith down a peg or two before we'd even got started.' Alex frowned briefly at Bill, but not enough to make him regret his outburst.

Nancy glanced quickly at Alex seated beside her, then silently mouthed the words "Oh no" as her eyes returned to the road.

Alex was on the defensive. 'I find this case very emotive and he irritated me. It was almost as if he was pontificating; he actually said he felt uncomfortable that we had approached him. Can you believe that' How did he think we felt?' He huffed slightly to emphasise his annoyance. 'Fortunately, I seemed to find the right words after our little disagreement, so the good news is, Menet's Birmingham premises will be raided in the early hours the day after tomorrow.'

Nancy felt her arms go weak; after all this time something positive was actually being done. 'You did well, guys, really well, I'm proud of you both.'

'Let's not count our chickens before they're hatched, I don't know what we'll do if they don't find anything,' said Alex.

'They're there, I just know they are,' replied Nancy more calmly than she felt.

'Did you manage to see Georgie Wells & co yet?'

'Yes I did. They were so keen to hear of any new developments, that they all made sure they could make it.'

'How did they take it?'

'Georgie and Isabel were very emotional. Alan said he had been very worried about it, but now hoped he would sleep better. They were all just relieved we were making some headway, and I was very careful as to what I told them,' she looked sideways, 'as per your instructions Alex.'

'Good, we'll make a good copper of you yet.'

'Thank you, but no thank you.' They laughed.

***

John Smith surveyed the men seated before him. They were two short but Reynolds wasn't one of them. 'This case will probably be the biggest case any of us will ever work on, so I will personally hound out of the force anyone who does not obey my direct order when I say you will not discuss any detail with anyone who is not sitting in this room. That is not a threat, it's a pledge. Is that understood?'

To a man they agreed.

Unbeknown to them, they had a visitor. Angel moved silently behind them and closed her eyes as she tried to project her thoughts to them.

'All right, I will go over as much as I can tell you at this point, such as the time of the raid, the equipment we will carry, the radio silence I expect and the timing required to guarantee this operation runs smoothly. Hardy and Rogers

211

will carry firearms. I want to make sure you're prepared as much as possible for the operation, without knowing exactly what it is. Any questions?'

'Could we at least know what kind of crime is involved without giving any details?' asked Hardy.

'No. Had I been able to, I would have, so the next silly sod that asks will be shown the door.'

The tension in the room had been slowly mounting, but an air of excitement too. None of them wanted "out the door", so they all made a mental decision to listen and say now't.

'Right, gentlemen, Bryant will take you through some of the details, and then I'll explain what we do and how we do it.' The meeting took no longer than an hour and as the team filed out, they had already come to the conclusion they knew what they were dealing with.

Hardy and Rogers followed each other out to the parking lot. 'It's got to be a drugs bust,' said Rogers.

'Can't be anything else,' Hardy replied.

'Then why is Smith so touchy about it? Surely some of the guys who cover narcotics must have some idea who we are dealing with? Normally we'd be told if it's a drugs bust, if not exactly where.'

'It has got to be a new lead the narcotics team are not aware of, which somehow came Smith's way. What I'm not sure of is why he withheld it from them. All I can think of is there's a leak somewhere, and if that's the case, we'd better keep our mouths shut.'

The invisible image of Angel smiled. She had accomplished her mission. They had come to the wrong conclusion, but nevertheless a conclusion which would stop the men involved continuing to seek answers by covert questions, and inadvertently spreading the word.

***

Although it was 4am in the morning, everyone looked and was totally alert. Hardy nudged Rogers and pointed in Alex

Moorland's direction. 'I'm sure I know that guy, he's with the London Metropolitan. What's he doing here?'

'Could be where the lead for this exercise came from. Who's the other guy with him?'

'Him, I don't know, but he's probably from London too.'

Detective Chief Superintendent John Smith stood facing them with Bryant alongside him. 'I'll go over the details one more time, but before I do, I'll introduce you to two gentlemen who will accompany us on this operation. This is Alex Moorland, who is a retired DCS from the London Metropolitan, and Sergeant Bill Palmer, who is a serving officer at Bilston Station in London. We don't have enough time to dally over introductions, so let's finalise the operational details, not only for your benefit, but to introduce Alex and Bill to our plans.'

Out of the side of his mouth Hardy asked, 'What the hell is a retired officer doing here?'

By way of response, Rogers shrugged. Others were also asking the same question and Smith raised his hand to stem the murmur, raising his voice as he did so.

'You'll all know soon enough why Moorland and Palmer have graced us with their presence, so unless anyone has any objections I want to get on with the business in hand,' Smith's mouth was clenched in a hard line. No one raised a hand. 'Right, back to business.....'

At 5am precisely, they were all loaded into vans and ready to move. Bryant moved from van to van giving last minute orders, especially about maintaining radio silence, and then they moved out. They drove at a steady pace towards the outskirts of Birmingham in the general direction of the airport, no sirens blaring, just twenty officers from Birmingham, one from London and Alex Moorland.

Of course, it had been impossible to stop them speculating on what kind of raid this was, and, to a man, they had all decided it was drugs, but they had not mouthed one word to anyone who had not been chosen for the exercise. There had been a great deal of speculation via those not privy to the operation. People were aware meetings had been held at the highest level with DCS Smith, so it was inevitable some of them were approached and discreetly asked what was going on, but none let slip even the remotest detail. John Smith's unveiled threat probably had a lot to do with that: they all knew him to be a man of his word.

They drew up outside the long two storey building and quietly alighted from the vans. Smith and Bryant were already silently directing the officers chosen to surround the building, covering every aspect. Six moved round to cover the only known rear exit, and eight moved to cover the front door, others were dispersed to cover others areas, including the windows. The building was quickly and quietly surrounded. Bryant had been assigned to the rear as the senior officer, to cover any attempted escape or assault.

Smith rang the front door bell and was surprised to find it was opened within a few minutes; he hadn't expected it to be so easy. He would learn at a later date that they sometimes received deliveries late at night from Nigeria, and that one was overdue by two days. The night security guard who answered was astonished as uniformed policemen pushed past him, but regained his wits quickly. He tried to duck round them to reach the front foyer desk, but Alex and Bill had anticipated this move. Alex.had already sprinted round the desk and Bill had grabbed him from behind and then grappled him to the ground.

'John, take him into custody, he's trying to warn others by pressing an emergency button behind the desk,' warned Alex.

Smith didn't need telling a second time. He was already instructing two of his officers to handcuff him, then, with the security guard still struggling, they dragged him outside to one of the vans. Smith looked at Alex enquiringly.

'Sorry, I was warned it could happen, but wasn't sure.'

'Right, Rogers, up front, but move with extreme caution.'

'Will do, sir.' They moved slowly from room to room, not knowing what to expect. Each room was hardly furnished, the odd desk here and there, sometimes supporting a computer, otherwise empty. It was almost as though the building was not in use at all; empty boxes were strewn in the halls or rooms, but other than that - nothing. Alex and Bill began to feel a knot tighten within their stomachs; they had almost covered the ground and first floor of the building, so far without success. In the end, their worst fears were upon them. The building was virtually empty.

John Smith turned round to confront them, 'Well, unless the security guy is an escaped prisoner, we have zilch.'

Alex held up his hand. 'I need to make a phone call; just one.'

Smith nodded. He couldn't see the point of refusing; they were already doomed. Alex switched on his mobile and rang Nancy, who had been waiting for his call.

'I know: you can't find them.'

'You got that right.'

She sensed his anxiety. 'They are there, Alex, and I know how hard it is for you working like this, so just take a deep breath and I'll get Angel to guide you.' There was a short silence. 'You're on the wrong floor. Go down to the ground floor and keep the phone to your ear.'

Relief written all over his face, Alex spoke as he moved in the direction of the stairs.

'We're on the wrong floor; we need to go downstairs.'

Rogers had lost all confidence in Alex and he didn't try to hide it. Smith, on the other hand, followed with regained interest.

'As you get to the bottom of the stairs, turn left,' said Nancy. 'Go to the room at the far end and then inspect the central heating pipe-work. There should be a basement off there which houses the boiler.'

'Of course, the boiler,' repeated Alex excitedly.

'Are you going to share your instructions with us, Alex, or must we remain totally in the dark, because, under the circumstances, I find it unacceptable.'

'Sorry, John, I've been with this case so long, I sometimes forget I'm not in charge anymore. Hopefully, we'll get instructions which will lead us to what we're looking for. The central heating is on in here, and although we've searched every room, we haven't seen a boiler. Evidently, there's a basement housing the boiler with access to another part of the building. We've already covered the whole of this building, so if there is a basement, it must be hidden, and if so, why?'

'You're bloody right sir,' said Rogers, his confidence in Moorland returning. At the bottom of the stairs Alex turned left and continued with renewed vigour to the last room, with the others hot on his tail.

'I'm being told we should concentrate on where the pipework leads. That should point us in the right direction.'

'Makes sense,' said Smith. They followed the line of the pipes which disappeared into the ground. They crouched around the floor area studying it then, noticed a fairly large section where there were gaps between the large dark-coloured ceramic tiles.

'This looks as of it could be some kind of entry point.' Bill was pointing to and outlining the area that had caught his eye. They started to check if any were loose and would lift up, then the skirting boards for any parts that moved or held hidden devices.

They all heard Nancy yell at one and the same time. 'Pick up the damn phone, Alex.' Alex had placed the mobile on the floor while he helped them search.

'It's a woman,' said Smith in surprise.

'What is it, Nancy?'

'What's the point of calling me to help if you're not going to accept it?'

'Okay, how do we get in?'

216

'There's one too many pipes, check the cold ones.'
He checked the pipes. 'You're right; it looks like we have one too many cold feeds into the basement.'

Rogers leaned over and studied the pipes. He didn't know who Moorland was talking to, but he was glad she was on their side.

'Half-way down between the wall and one of the cold pipes, you will find a small lever, pull it down, but tell the others to stand clear.'

Knowing where to look was a bonus. They moved back. Alex pulled the lever and the whole section swung noiselessly down. When it was in place, they heard a slight whirring noise from below as steps glided into position under the opening.

'The missing people must be down there, Alex. I can't see any other reason for this elaborate and, I would estimate, costly conversion,' said Smith.

Rogers had been squatting in front of the entrance with his gun arm extended, but stood up and confronted Alex. 'People, what missing people, I thought this was a drugs bust?'

Smith answered his question. 'Nothing could be further from the truth, Rogers, but we don't have time for explanations, so let's get this over with because I'm really not looking forward to it.'

Alex briefly placed his hand on his forehead and rubbed it. Bill stepped forward and laid his hand on his shoulder. 'Not long now, Guv.'

'No, not long now.'

Smith moved to descend the stairs. He felt a restraining hand from Rogers. 'Excuse me, sir, but I think I should go first. I'm armed and we don't know what we will encounter.'

Smith stepped back and Rogers moved slowly down the stairs, his gun held straight ahead supported by both hands. Rogers' mind raced as he edged forward. He now vividly recalled Smith saying this was probably the most important case any of them would ever cover, and they had all imagined a big drugs bust. Every part of his being now knew it was much bigger than that, much more important. He now understood it involved some kind of humanitarian rescue, which was so serious that the three people who knew what to expect were deeply affected by it. His arms became stronger and straighter, his mind more focused and he lost all fear. He had no idea what to expect, only that when this was all over his actions would never be called into question. They never were. Only Rogers would question and regret his actions.

They entered a long corridor which was scrupulously clean from floor to wall, which resembled a hospital hall (except for the padded walls) only much cleaner. The padded walls showed not the slightest trace of any dirt or stains. Everything was pristine. There was only one door situated at the end of the hall. Rogers walked quickly down to the end and positioned himself to one side for cover.

Alex held back and raised the mobile to his ear and whispered 'Nancy, are you still there?'

'Yes.'

'I think we've found the room we're looking for, but we haven't entered yet. It's probably locked anyway.'

'Hold on a minute, Alex; Angel is trying to tell me something.'

'Nancy, tell them not to try and force their way in. Tell Alex the door will open without force if they will allow me five minutes. The woman inside is in a highly emotional state, so it is better I reason with her from within.'

'You can do that? Can she see you?'

'Do you doubt me Nancy?'

'I'm still learning.' Nancy hesitated. 'I'll tell Alex, but I want you to know my heart is with you.'

'My place now, is with the souls that suffer.' Angel faded slowly before her eyes as Nancy blew her a kiss.

'Alex, there's a woman inside who, according to Angel, is in a very emotional state. She wants you to make your presence known, but not to try and enter for at least five minutes, then Angel say's she'll open the door without you having to force it.'

'Thanks, Nancy, but don't hang up okay?' It was a silly thing to ask as she had no intention of doing so. Alex relayed Nancy's instructions to Smith, who decided enough was enough.

Smith's jaw-line hardened. 'We're the acting police officers here. Has this woman any experience in matters like this?'

'Not one iota, but if we hadn't listened to her earlier, we would all have been out the door now with egg on our face. I'm told you've got a gut instinct when dealing with criminals, but Menet's not your average villain, so shouldn't be treated as such.' Alex raised his voice as much as he dare at this point. 'But if you now ignore what I consider to be very good advice, then on your head be it.'

'She hasn't let us down so far, sir,' said Rogers. Smith's eyes narrowed while he thought. 'You're right of course, Rogers.' They all heaved a sigh of relief.

Smith addressed Alex with a slightly cynical air. 'I suppose it's acceptable if I negotiate with this woman?'

Alex held up his hands and stepped back. 'It's your show John and nobody could handle it better.' None of them knew at this point how true his words would prove to be.

John nodded. 'I've only been on this case a couple of days, and already it's getting to me.'

He stopped whispering at this point and hammered on the door. 'Madam, we know you're in there. We have no wish to harm you, and it would be better for us all if you opened the door, preferably now, but I am prepared to give you five minutes or so to think about it. Have you heard and understood what I am saying?'

Delores Heeja ran to the door and pressed a speak button. 'Who are you?' Her English was spoken with a strong African accent.

'I am Detective Chief Superintendent Smith and I have a warrant to search these premises. I want you to open this door, but I warn you, Madam, I'll wait no longer than five minutes, after which I'll have no alternative but to break it down.'

Delores cringed behind the padded door with her back to the wall. She slid slowly down to the floor and almost started to hyperventilate. She was terrified, and not only by the police presence outside the door.

She slowly raised her eyes; not wanting to, but almost as if she were compelled to. *They were all watching her.* They never ceased to watch her. Sometimes, she felt she could have coped with their watching her every move, but it was their *wailing* that had escalated her inability to think clearly. They'd held no fear for her in the beginning; after all, she was the daughter of a witch doctor. She had been used to seeing many strange things from childhood, and she didn't frighten easily. In the beginning, Delores could neither see nor hear them, but as the years wore on, she had become aware of them in short, sharp bursts. Quick images that momentarily intruded on her vision, which escalated until she eventually became aware of their souls floating like tied tormented puppets above their bodies. Her eyes gave her no rest from the sights that now affronted her daily.

Then a year ago she began to *hear* them and her life had become intolerable; the wailing, the crying, the screeching, and with the hearing, came the awareness of their true torment. It had taken ten long years for her mind, body and soul to deteriorate to the almost out-of-control being that now cringed and snivelled like an animal behind the door. Those who watched her knew others were near who held their salvation and their lament increased. Delores' hands flew to her ears, trying, but not succeeding, to block the almost deafening noise that now assaulted her.

There was only one other being Delores feared more. What would he do to her if she opened the door to them; how would he punish her? It would be terrible, she knew that. Perhaps he would even make her into one of the living dead before her, because that's how she now perceived them. She screamed and then began to wail in time with them as she rocked backwards and forwards, still with her hands pressed tightly to her ears, so tightly that they now marked her face.

She must warn him, she must. But first she must calm herself. He must not know how weak she had become over the last few years, otherwise he would replace her. It wasn't that he would replace her which made every waking day and night terrify her, because it was her daily dream to leave the place that had become a living nightmare, no, it was that she knew he would never let her leave alive. She knew too much and he was a vengeful man; her passing would not be easy. Had he known how unstable she had become, she would have already been removed. But she had been careful, taking heavy sleeping draughts before he visited, knowing that the short respite from the continuing sights and sounds would make it possible for her to appear normal and in charge for the half hour or so when he was in attendance. Had it been hours, she knew her strength would have failed her.

She opened her eyes and looked at the desk. She must warn him. All she had to do was pick up the phone and press number one in the memory and his emergency number would dial. Wherever he was, he would answer. Yes, it would please him if she warned him. She turned her body around so that she was on all fours. She felt weak; she needed the support of the door handle to help her stand. She pulled herself up and turned to walk in the direction of the desk – then stopped dead.

A woman faced her, barring her way to the phone and her deliverance from the wrath of Menet. How did she get in; who was she? Then something else assailed her senses. What was it? Then she knew – *the silence.*

Delores surveyed the woman in amazement. It was her; she had silenced them, but how? Delores studied her more closely. Of course, she was like them, but not in torment. They felt at peace with her, but why? Delores suddenly became aware of a slight glow surrounding her, and then she knew. The woman had been sent to help end the suffering of those she had held captive all these years. This was a good and powerful soul sent from God to right the wrongs she had helped others perpetrate.

'I cannot allow you to warn him, Delores. This evil must, and will end now.'

Delores nodded and started to cry. It was all over and she knew it. She spoke to Angel with reverence, as if she was in the presence of a godly spirit.

'I am truly sorry for what I have done, I don't know whether you can believe that, and I know I must pay for my sins, but will you at least grant me a little peace?'

'Your sins have been great, but you have already suffered as much as those you see before you. Never forget, Delores, God welcomes all those who truly repent, but your conscience will create your own hell. The love from above is all-forgiving, but you will have to forgive yourself and only time will help you do that, but I can promise you peace from the souls who have plagued your every waking hour. Now stand clear from the door, Delores.'

Delores turned in surprise and watched as the security code was miraculously punched into the side panel by an unseen hand. The door slowly swung open and she faced those without. Her head turned back in Angel's direction. She was gone.

Smith and Rogers were first in; Alex and Bill followed. Each one stood as if mesmerised by the sight that met them.

It was a long room that ran the length of the building; movable trolleys were sporadically placed to include as many bodies as possible. On each trolley men and women of different ages lay as if in a coma, each one connected to tubes which fed what looked like drugs or liquid feed into them, and tubes which seemed to drain off any unwanted excess. This sight was horrific enough, but it was the all pervading feeling of evil that seemed to permeate even the fabric of the room that made them stop and hesitate to enter any further. It was as though they had walked through an invisible barrier, that, once entered, entwined each and every one of them, making them lose the courage to go any further.

Rogers was the first to snap. He rushed outside and braced himself up against the wall for support, as if it offered some hiding place from the evil that was entrenched within. It was so strong, he knew he had no protection from it. He had to leave the room before it contaminated him.

He shouted. 'Sorry, sir, I can't go back in there,' His voice shaky and uneven.

Smith forced himself to regain some kind of composure. 'Stay where you are, Rogers, it's all right. Then, hands visibly shaking, he called Bryant on his mobile and gave him instructions as to where to find them and said. 'There's a woman down here I want taken into custody right now.'

'On my way, sir,' Bryant was a little alarmed by the sound of Smiths voice. 'Are you all right sir?'

Smith didn't answer, just switched off the connection. No, he was not all right. What he had just experienced was an abomination. It took all his self-control to use the mobile again and call the detective he had left on standby duty at the station. 'Open that sealed envelope I left you, and start phoning all the people on the list, and I don't care what they have planned, tell them it's an emergency and to get down to this address as quickly as possible.'

'Yes, sir.'

Anger mounted in Smith as he faced Delores Heeja. 'How could you be party to something as unholy as this? What kind of human being are you?'

'A human being that will fear her death for the rest of her life: knowing, if there is such a thing as hell, it's where I'm bound.'

As Smith looked at her, there was no compassion in his heart to help ease her pain. He could offer no solace. Her eyes were dead.

By the time Bryant arrived downstairs, they had removed Delores from the room and pulled the door shut, to hide the horrific view of all the inert bodies. Bryant handcuffed Delores Heeja and read her her rights. Suddenly he noticed Rogers pressed into the corner. 'Are you all right Rogers?'

'I'll take care of him,' said Smith kindly.

Alex and Bill were now leaning against the wall opposite Rogers. It wasn't just the sight that met them; that had traumatised all who entered the room. It was something else; something they sensed but could not see. Something that made the hair stand up on the backs of their necks and touched their psyche like nothing else ever would. Yet, even more horrific, was the realisation that this sensing of evil would not ease or fade with time.

No one knew how, but in spite of the horrific *circumstances* Smith was doing exactly what he should be doing.

Only Smith knew. There was no-one else. Otherwise he would have positioned himself up against the wall with the rest of his fellow men and joined them in shock. Later, others would ask why it had affected them so much. They would answer with the truth as they saw it. So many years of evil had been committed in that room, that it was impossible for any who entered not to be aware of it, or touched by it. But Smith had the greater burden to bear. He had *seen*.

NINETEEN

Someone was pounding on the door. Alex lifted bleary eyes to his watch and noted it was 2pm. He bellowed to whoever it was to come in before the door left its hinges. Mrs Horton wandered in and apologised as she place a large steaming mug of tea beside the bedside table. 'Hope I didn't give you a fright, Mr Moorland, banging on the door like that, but you were in such a deep sleep I couldn't get an answer to my knock,' she smiled. 'You won't be able to complain you didn't sleep well in our beds; lummy, it was like waking the dead.'

He thanked her and she withdrew. His head hit the pillow again; he could have slept well on into the evening. It wasn't that he was exceptionally tired; he'd done longer stints than last night and this morning. It was the heavy load that had been lifted off his shoulders; they had found them. It wouldn't be easy or plain sailing from now on, but, as far as he was concerned, the part that had worried him the most was the finding. James Brierley was now his major concern. None of them had long to wait now before they were all charged, but James would fare the worst. His admiration for him increased with each passing day. It took a special man to do what he had done.

He wearily swung his legs out of bed. Bill and he were due for another meeting with Smith at 3.30; just enough time to have a quick shower and something to eat. Smith had chosen a pub that let rooms within spitting distance from the station. He walked to the bathroom and, for the first time, noticed the bath had no shower attachment. Damn. Twenty minutes later he met Bill in the hall downstairs.

'Not much on the menu, Guv, so I ordered their standard cooked breakfast, which they were none too happy to supply

225

at this time of day; you know, the usual objection, breakfast ends at 10am etc.'

Alex nodded and followed him into a small dining-room. As they seated themselves at a small but bright table by the window, Alex caught Bill's gaze.

'What's on your mind, Bill?'

'Well, the worst is over, but I guess today is D Day. How will we handle it?'

'I've been thinking about that. I'm not sure whether we should reveal everything to Smith now, or invite him to London and explain it to him and the DCS at Bilston at the same time. If we decide on that, then I think Nancy and James should be present. They should be party to what we have to say and it will give them a chance to speak for themselves. Also, it won't be easy to explain how this case evolved, so, all round it's probably best we're all available for questioning, rather than in dribs and drabs. My money's on London; what about you?'

'Ditto.' They finished their breakfast in silence, paid the bill, picked up their overnight bags, and then made their way to the police station.

As they pushed through the double doors, a couple of uniformed officers who were just leaving the building, stepped back to let them pass. What happened next took them both totally by surprise as one of them spoke.

'Sir, you both did a really good job.' He held out his hand and shook hands with them. Others followed suit.

Cobb was on the front desk. 'The DCS is waiting for you, sir. Would you like to come through? I'd just like to add my congratulations to you both: it couldn't have been easy.' He directed his last remark to Bill Palmer. Cobb was a serving officer of the same rank; he knew what Palmer was in for. As they walked through the corridor to Smith's office, men and women patted them on the back and shouted their support. Neither of them had ever been received like this before, and, in a slight daze, they entered Smith's office and were immediately joined by Bryant.

'You look tired,' said Smith, 'but I'm not too sympathetic; some of us haven't been to bed yet.'

Alex smiled. We would have helped unofficially if it had been possible, but you know Bill has no jurisdiction here, and certainly not me. We couldn't risk some smart-arsed lawyer stating that as normal procedure wasn't followed, they had some kind of let-out.'

'Too true, Alex.' Smith also looked tired, but happy.

'What about Menet and the rest? Please don't tell me any of the bastards got away.'

'No, I had a long conversation with the guy who took over from you at Bilston, name of Draycott. He moved pretty quickly. I told him about Spinner's little camera operation so they were prepared for his back exit manoeuvre. Jean Elliman was the one he had most trouble with; pulled more rank and threats than the prime minister. I even had a very nasty phone call from her boss, and after listening to him rant for a few minutes, told him to do his worst, but that I wanted it in writing so that he could be called to answer for his intervention at a later date.'

'What did he say to that?' asked Alex.

'He went dead quiet; said he would check with Elliman before he pursued it. I told him to be very careful, because if he secured her release on bail, which I think was the main reason for his call, she would do a runner. In fact, I'm sure that all she wanted was for him was to buy her a few hours. She knew she was dead in the water, and that what we had on her was so horrendous, she would become as notorious as Myra Hindley and never ever get the chance of parole. I'll lay odds we won't get anything in writing, or hear from him again.'

'Menet?'

'Ah, now he was weird. Draycott personally got him out of bed early this morning; said he came down the stairs as

227

cool as a cucumber and never lost his poise for a second, even though he must have had some idea why the police were there. He showed no emotion; he didn't panic; no denial, just a slight smile which I'm told never left his face. Draycott said he found his demeanour very odd indeed. The arrests were timed simultaneously just in case one of them was fortunate enough to escape, and warn the others. All in all, a very fruitful night, for which I'm indebted to you both.'

'Lost your concern about this case being embarrassing, then?' Alex couldn't help himself.

'I'll regret that assumption till the day I die, Alex, but if I had to start from the beginning, I would probably make the same mistake.'

Alex nodded. It was an apology of sorts, and in the presence of Bryant which couldn't have been easy. Anyway, he deserved a pat on the back after last night, not recriminations.

'I couldn't have handled it better myself, John, and I don't hand out compliments willy-nilly.' He looked at Bryant. 'You and your men did a good job, as good as the Met any day.'

Bryant beamed. 'Thank you, sir.'

Smith leaned forward with his arms on the desk and looked expectantly at them. 'Right, gentlemen. I've been patient and kept my side of the bargain; now it's your turn to keep yours. How did you acquire this evidence?'

Alex leaned back in his chair and although he wasn't aware of it, his mode slipped into stubborn.

'I'll keep my side of the bargain, but I will only discuss that information in London with those present who are also involved. They have a right to hear everything we discuss and, out of courtesy to them, I would ask you to bear with me and set up a meeting in London.'

Smith's natural habit of narrowing his eyes when thinking was something Alex now recognised, so he waited. If he wanted to fight him on this - so be it. Then much to his surprise, Smith smiled.

'Is there no end to your sense of honour and fair play, because I hope not, Alex. It may be irritating on occasions but I'll always know where I am with you.' He picked up the phone. 'Cobb, get the DCS at Bilston station on the line for me.' As he replaced the receiver he said, 'Let's see how quickly he can fit us in shall we?'

'Let me have a word with Draycott after you, John, if you don't mind?'

'Not at all, Alex, as long as I'm party to your conversation,' he added as an afterthought.

Alex nodded by way of agreement with a slight wry smile on his face. Smith wasn't sure why the Met had to be present when he disclosed his informant, but he didn't want any last minute surprises. The Birmingham arrest and discovery of the missing people was his bag, and he wasn't about to hand it over to anyone else or let them share the glory.

'Draycott would like us to be there at ten tomorrow; okay with you?' Smith passed the phone to Alex as he agreed. There was no special bond between Bernard Draycott and Alex Moorland. When Alex had retired, the men had been slow to pass their loyalty to Draycott, but this quite often happened when a team had grown to respect their chief. Unwisely, Draycott had taken it personally, and in so doing, it had taken him far longer to get his team to work closely with him. Moorland had been a hard act to follow and he had resented it. Bill was in for a hard time. Draycott would interpret his actions with Moorland as a continuation of that loyalty.

'Hi, Bernard, I'm happy to attend the meeting tomorrow, but you'll need to interview two other people who are involved, so I'll have to check with them first, but I will get back to you quickly on that.'

'Okay, Alex, I've no problem with that, what intrigues me is the reason for this meeting, Smith's not totally sure either. I'd like some idea as to why the Met are suddenly to be included in information first-hand, which previously was being handed down via Birmingham? '

Alex decided to ignore the sarcasm. It wasn't unexpected and he knew there was much more to come. But he would deal with it when the time was right. Now was not that time.

'A crime was committed in London, which the police and the victim are not yet aware of and which directly ties in with the Birmingham arrests. You, of course, will want to arrest the main participants in the crime. I, on the other hand, will do my best to protect them.'

Smith and Bryant exchanged worried looks.

'Christ, you really know how to land them don't you, Alex?'

'Can't disagree with you on that one, but if it's any consolation, its goanna hurt me more than you.'

Bernard Draycott smiled as he replaced the receiver. It was.

Smith addressed them both. 'Seeing as I also have to travel to London tomorrow, why don't you both travel back with me and get yourselves some well earned rest now?'

'Actually, that suits me if Bill agrees?'

'Good idea,' replied Bill.

As they stood up to leave, Smith said, 'If you need any help, Alex, I'm your man.'

'Thank you, John. Bill and I will need all the help we can get, but reserve that offer until after tomorrow's meeting; you might want to change your mind.'

'Don't need to. The offer's up and running as of now. What little I know of you, whatever you did would have been for an honourable reason. Bryant and I will pick you up at about 7.30 tomorrow morning.'

'We'll be ready.'

Checking back into the pub down the road was no problem, but Alex took the most expensive room they had, for one reason: it was the only one with a telephone, with the added bonus of a shower. He didn't relish standing in the hall using the public pay phone to call James and Nancy. His mobile had a habit of cutting out on extended calls; he made a mental note to change it as soon as he could. Then it struck him that mobile phones were not allowed in prison, so it was pointless. Prison; until now he hadn't really wanted to address the problems that would cause him. There were plenty of inmates who would love to get their hands on him. No doubt about it, he would get a rough ride.

His only consolation was that James wouldn't have to cope with that kind of aggression as he would be considered one of them. He was also the kind of criminal they respected; one with brains.

Alex flung his bag in the corner, sat on the bed and picked up the phone. As usual, James' answer phone was on. 'James, if you're there, pick up the phone; it's Alex.' He did.

'Tell me anything, Alex, except you didn't find what we all hoped for.'

'Thanks to you and Nancy, a medical team is at this moment organising the evacuation of all the people found in a hidden unit located in the basement.'

'How many people did you find?'

'Forty-one, but three of them were dead.'

He sighed. 'How on earth could people do this, Alex, and can they help the survivors?'

'I guess it's too early to say. They have samples of the drugs used to keep them all in a state of limbo, but they will have to do tests to see how they can reverse the effects. Menet is being interviewed to see if he will help, but at the moment he's not being very co-operative.' Alex filled James in on all the details as far as he knew, but at the back of his mind was the knowledge he would have to discuss the interview.

'A meeting has been arranged for 10am tomorrow and I would like you and Nancy to be there. I don't want to discuss our involvement in how we illegally gained access to this information without you and Nancy being present. You both have a right to be there and hear what's discussed. It's not going to be easy for any of us, but it will be worse for you, James, because you're the one with a record, but I stand by what I said. We all answer for this; you're not on your own. I don't have much clout now because I'm retired from the force, but I want you to know I'll do everything in my power to help you.'

'I know that. I didn't at first, but I do now. I'm just relieved it wasn't all for nothing; that you got the evil bastards. I couldn't sit back and do nothing, knowing what was happening, so sleep easy, Alex, I have no regrets.'

'You're a good man, James.'

James laughed. 'I never thought I'd hear a copper say that to me.' Alex saw the funny side too and chuckled. His mood became so much lighter now he had spoken to James.

'Have you spoken to Nancy yet?'

'No, she's next on my list. So I'll see you at Bilston Police Station tomorrow at 10am?'

'That you will, and a very interesting meeting it will be too; wouldn't miss it for the world.'

Alex revised his opinion of Brierley. Not only was he a decent man, he was brave too.

* * *

Nancy replaced the receiver after speaking to Alex. She was relieved; it was the waiting and not knowing she found the hardest. She had known they would find the missing people, but that was all. Like James, she wanted to know the outcome: had Menet, Elliman and Spinetti been apprehended? How many had they found? Did the poor people they find have so many organs removed from their bodies that they would never be able to lead normal lives again? Would they be able to survive at all without the aid of artificial machines, continually pumping life back into them? Could they bring them out of the coma-like state Elsie Turnbull had been subjected to? So many questions; so many disturbing questions, that she was unable to concentrate on anything else.

Alex had been gentle, kind and considerate when reliving his experience, but she knew it had affected him badly, especially when confronted with so many bodies lying on beds. He said he could feel the evil, almost smell it; so much so, that he could not stay in the room. She sent up a mental prayer to Angel to give them some healing. Doctors and medication would help, but they also needed the power of healing, a loving, caring, spiritual healing drawn from a godly power. Nancy sighed. She wasn't looking forward to the meeting tomorrow, but glad the waiting was over. She needed to know her fate and that of others she cared about.

She headed in the direction of the kitchen. What she needed was a strong cup of tea. She sat at the kitchen table and thought about Elsie and John. Their abduction had been successful because they were loners, preferring their own company. That was the key to Menet's success, and because their sudden disappearances were carefully orchestrated and planned. That's what had made it all possible.

It was wrong, totally wrong. People had a right to lead their own lives as they saw fit, so long as they were not harming others. Elsie and John certainly were not, and she suspected neither were the other poor souls who had been abducted.

Her mind wandered on this aspect and she remembered a friend talking about Tibet. Tibet was virtually a closed country to the world. They were a peaceful and contented people, with strong religious beliefs. The few who had visited the country, said it was like stepping back in time at least a hundred years. No real roads, only tracks to follow which made it very difficult to get from one village to the next, let alone cross the country. The Chinese had decided they needed more land to accommodate their growing millions, so they had just walked in and taken Tibet, transferring thousands of Chinese to populate the country, and they were still there to this day.

No country had made determined efforts to help them. No one really *knew* them. They had not sought or cultivated friends outside their country. They had no enemies (or so they thought) but they had no friends either; no powerful countries to speak up on their behalf, which China was well aware of. Tibet could be taken without any outside interference, and crushing the peace-loving nation within was easy.

As she cupped her tea in her hands and her mind continued to wander, she decided it was important to have a few friends who looked out for you.

TWENTY

'So all this started with a fucking psychic, meditating in a dark room with a crystal ball?' This was better than anything Draycott could have wished for; he was really enjoying this.

Nancy couldn't help herself. Try as she might, she was unable to control the tears welling up in her eyes. She couldn't take this; it wasn't fair after all she had had to cope with over the last few months. Why was he being so aggressive? Did it really matter how it all started? At the end of the day, the only thing to bear in mind was the result; surely he could see that, even if he didn't approve of her, many suffering people would now be helped. What was she supposed to do; lie about how and when it had happened?

Alex had expected some opposition from Draycott. He knew he and Bill were in for a hard time; Alex had known Draycott would not miss any opportunity to make things as difficult for them as possible, but he had gone too far. In his effort to humiliate them, he had overstepped the boundaries of fair play and had used anyone or anything to achieve his goal. He had taken every opportunity to interrupt and ridicule, and now was being downright offensive.

Alex did not take his eyes off Draycott for a minute as he moved in Nancy's direction. He placed his hands on her shoulders and gently pulled her up. He checked his watch, it was 11.03. He'd had enough of this crap. At this point, they had not disclosed their criminal involvement, only that a crime had been committed, so Draycott would be hard-pressed to retain them against their will. Brierley and Palmer were already on their feet, as they waited for Alex to take control of the situation.

His hard eyes met Draycott's. 'I find your treatment of Nancy Harnetty both unprofessional and intimidating, so I am terminating this meeting now. I will, of course, make sure statements are drawn up in the presence of a solicitor and get copies to both you and DCS Smith as soon as possible. '

Too late, Draycott realised his mistake. Even Smith was looking at him with contempt. He turned to his second-in-command, Detective Hardcastle, for support. There was none.

'You can't close this meeting, Moorland; you don't have the authority. I'll tell you and everyone else here when this meeting is finished.' Draycott's voice no longer carried the confidence he had felt at the start of the meeting. *He* was in charge. It was going to be *his* day to get one over on Moorland, but it was all going belly up.

Smith stood and Bryant followed his example. 'I want it on record that I totally support Alex Moorland's decision to suspend the meeting at this point, for reasons already given, and I expect a copy of this recording to be sent to me within the next few days. Now, if you will excuse me, DCS Draycott, I have other business to attend to.' John Smith no longer addressed him as Bernard, and any future contact would be out of necessity, not choice. He did not suffer fools gladly.

Smith caught up with Alex and the rest in the police courtyard. 'I would still like to know unofficially, Alex, how all this happened; I think you at least owe me that?'

'That I do, John.' He turned to face Nancy. 'I'm sorry you had to endure all that nonsense, but he will regret it. Because it all started with you, Nancy, it was logical that you gave your version first. Are you all right?'

'I've been better.'

'I know how you feel, and it's not over yet, so we're just going to have to be strong for each other. I'm as surprised as you are at how Draycott handled that meeting. I knew he'd make the most of it, but only as far as Bill and I were concerned. You have to believe me when I say that if I'd had any inkling of how unprofessional he was going to be with you, I wouldn't have given him the courtesy of arranging this unofficial get-together.'

'I know that, Alex, and I regret reacting as I did. I don't know what I was expecting, but it wasn't that. It's been so frightening for me these last few months.'

'Do you feel up to us continuing this meeting with John and Bryant? I wouldn't ask this normally, but they went out on a limb for us, and they've come a long way.'

'I would appreciate it, Nancy, if you would, and I would like to set your mind at rest when I say that I found Draycott's behaviour totally out of order.'

'I just want to go home, so if you're happy to talk there, I will.' She needed to be on safe territory and have something to eat to steady her nerves. She hadn't managed a bite this morning.

Smith and Bryant followed Alex's car with Nancy, Bill and James. They had all met at her flat earlier because they needed each other's support and parking one car would be easier. Alex still felt the need to give a friendly warning to both Smith and Bryant.

'This is going to be far more difficult for us than you, gentlemen. You will hear things you'll find hard to get your head round, as it was for us. But it all happened just as we will tell it, so I would ask you to refrain from any comments or questions till later.'

Smith answered for them both. 'Agreed.'

So they told them. The Birmingham episode had been sensational. The events leading up to it: even more so.

***

The timing of today's meeting had worked well; due to Delores Heeja's evident fatigue and depression, the doctor had advised them to allow her a few hours' rest.

As Smith now looked into the dead eyes of Delores seated opposite him in the interview room, he waited as Bryant

237

went through the motion of switching on the recording machine and stating the necessary dialogue before the official start of the interview.

Delores Heeja was not tall; just over five feet, with a wide, muscular body. As he studied her, Smith decided she was of mixed parentage; her colour was light for a Nigerian. As she spoke he noticed her full, perfectly-shaped mouth and imagined her eyes would be beautiful, had they conveyed any expression; something they seemed incapable of. She answered each question by rote, without any inflection or feeling, and her command of English was excellent, which surprised him. Had Delores Heeja walked a different path in the last ten years, Smith knew she would have been considered a beautiful woman. Pain, worry, stress, hate and a permanent state of fear, had very nearly eroded all signs of her former looks. Try as he might, he still felt no compassion for her. Only someone with a cold heart would agree to the inhuman duties her position had required.

'When did you first meet Menet?'

'Twelve years ago when he came to Nigeria to work for a company that was researching snake venom.'

'What particular area of research?'

'He was involved in the usual areas of interest for venoms; snake venom antidotes and for use in heart drugs. But Menet has a brilliant mind, so it wasn't long before he wanted to research other areas of possible use, but the research company were not happy with his ideas, so they blocked every new area of research he suggested.'

'Why?'

'They considered them to be bordering on the unethical.'

'So he couldn't continue.'

'Oh, it didn't stop Menet. It just made things a little more difficult; he was used to getting his own way. He talked about his mother a lot and I would say she was the only one he ever truly loved, which I would say was mutual. She gave him everything he ever asked for and, on the rare occasion she refused him, he manipulated her by asking for help with something else, which usually paid for his original request.'

'If Menet was refused the facilities for new areas of research, how was he able to continue?'

'He worked during the day for the company, and as many hours as he could at night on his own project, when the laboratory was closed.'

'How was that possible? Surely any premises that held highly poisonous substances would have strict security.'

'He became very friendly with Adoke, a highly-qualified and respected technician who held a set of keys to the restricted research area. Menet arranged to get another set cut.'

'Did he work alone at night?'

'No, Adoke worked with him as often as he could.' Delores' eyes had been firmly locked on the table until now but she raised them to Smith as she said, 'Something he came to regret. Eventually, Menet needed a human guinea pig and decided, willing or not, it would be Adoke; he became as the living dead you saw yesterday.'

'What did Menet do?'

'For the first time, he was afraid. He didn't know then how to reverse the effects, yet couldn't ask for medical assistance to care for Adoke while he tried to reverse the coma. So he killed him; then continued his experiments until he had perfected the end result.'

'Which was?'

'You already know the answer to that.'

Smith raised his eyes in surprise. 'Was this already planned before he went to Nigeria?'

'I can't be sure he had definite plans - no, but as I said, he is a brilliant man, so I would not be surprised.'

'Why did he decide to take this very dangerous path? After all, he could have used his talents in so many other fields?'

'Money; being a brilliant research scientist will never make you rich. He came to realise that very quickly.' She smirked. 'Mummy was very generous, but her wealth would not last a lifetime, not the way he intended to live.'

'Delores, I can't believe that Menet had any premeditated thoughts of producing this serum when he arrived in Nigeria, so I can only assume, at this stage, it wasn't his initial intention?'

The merest smile touched her mouth, but not her eyes. 'Then you presume wrong. He had a fascination for snakes and their venom from the very beginning; that was the only reason he came to Nairobi. Of course, he couldn't know, or guarantee in advance where his experiments would lead him, but from the moment he discovered the drug, he immediately recognised its potential and planned his next few years very carefully.'

'How?'

He chose an area of medicine that would not be too demanding and would allow him time for his real venture and interests. That's why both his clinics were private. He then went to India where he perfected the art of removing organs for transplant: after all, he could hardly employ other surgeons to work for him and keep their mouths shut.'

Bryant wiped the slight perspiration from his forehead.

'How did you get involved with Menet?'

'I was a staff nurse at the local hospital, so we met occasionally when Menet lectured on antidotes for snake venoms.' She raised her head slightly as she said, 'I'm the granddaughter of a witch doctor who is feared by many where I come from.' She sneered slightly, as she continued, 'Of course it would never do for a senior staff nurse to practice the art of black magic, either outside the hospital, or within it. I was guilty on both counts, and somehow Menet found out. He threatened to expose me unless I worked for him.'

She raised her eyes briefly. 'To me, this was no threat at all; my grandfather could have dealt with him quite easily, but I liked the idea of working in England. Like Adoke, it was a decision I came to regret.'

Delores Heeja's head slumped. She'd had enough. Smith remembered the doctors' warning, and terminated the interview. Delores had given them more than enough for today. It had also been a long day for Smith and Bryant.

* * *

Nancy rested her head in her hands and wondered how she would cope. If today's meeting was an example of what she and the others could expect in the future, they were in for a hard time. She was weary of it all. She would never regret being part of the fight to stop Menet, but she still had little faith in her own resilience to cope with the kind of aftermath it would inevitably create.

'Where are you Angel? I need your support and comfort now; so *where* are you? I *told* you I was the wrong person to cope with all this; you should have chosen someone much stronger....' She was shouting so loud she had not realised the phone was ringing.

Her voice was still raised as she said, 'Hello.'

'You sound distraught, Nancy, its Alexander Wheeler here.'

'I'm sorry, I didn't mean to sound so abrupt, but I have rather a lot on my plate at the moment. How are you?'

'I'm very well, Nancy, but I'm phoning to see how you are. The television and newspapers were full of the people who were found in Birmingham yesterday and to be quite frank, it didn't need a brain surgeon to put two and two together to realise why you wanted information on Menet. But that's not why I'm calling. You need help and you sound very distressed, so, with your approval, I want to come and see you.'

'When?'

'No time like the present. I could be with you in less than an hour.'

Angel's gentle voice whispered in her ear, *'I had not forgotten you Nancy, neither has Justin, Alexander Wheeler will help ease the months ahead.'*

'Do you still have my address?'

'You bet, and depending on the traffic I'll be there within an hour.' Alexander looked concerned as he picked up his keys and walked through to the next office. 'Cancel anything else I have for today, Mrs Braithwaite.'

She looked up in surprise and as their eyes met, knew it was unwise to enquire as to why.

He arrived at Nancy's home within forty minutes. She was waiting for him and opened the door as he approached. She looked smaller than he remembered, and vulnerable. The change in her was quite dramatic. When he had last seen her, she had appeared unsure, but determined. Today she looked as if the guts had been knocked out of her.

'Would you like a drink?'

'No, I would like us to sit down and just have a quiet chat.'

She told him everything as calmly as she could and he was visibly shocked. As she relayed the events he felt every emotion: sorrow, compassion, rage and revenge. To be of any use, he knew he had to control the last two.

'Right, the first thing you need is the best lawyer we can get, and I know just the man.'

'Is he really the best?'

'They don't come any better than Reece Cohen.'

'My goodness, even I've heard of him. What makes you think he will take the case?'

'Because I will ask him as a special favour, but, in all honesty, I think he would want to represent you whether I ask him or not, because this is such an emotive case. Not only will the UK be watching developments with great interest, but the world, so it won't do his career any harm either. Not that it needs any help.'

'Could he represent all of us and how expensive is he?'

'No, you will all need separate counsel and you needn't worry about costs; I will sort out the financial side.'

She hesitated. 'Alexander, I know you won't like what I have to say, but it's the only way I can accept your help.'

'Right, what's worrying you, Nancy?'

'I'm not the one who needs the best counsel. Good counsel yes, but the best - no. The best lawyer should represent James Brierley. He's the only one of us who has a criminal record, and the sad thing is, he really had decided to go straight. Can you imagine how much he gave up to help all those poor souls that Menet had trapped in that den of evil?'

He stroked his chin and sighed. 'Oh Christ, Nancy, you're right.' He stood up, walked to the window and stood staring out, then squared his shoulders as he made a decision.

'Right, Cohen's for Brierley and I'm off to see him right away. I'll also ask who he would recommend not only for you, but Moorland and Palmer.' He hesitated. 'I'm not happy to leave you like this, you need a little TLC. Why don't I pick you up later tonight and you stay with Marguerite and I for a while?'

'Before you arrived, Alexander, I really couldn't see the wood for the trees, but now, with such good friends, how can I fail. You've made me strong again.'

He bent and kissed her gently on the forehead. 'You may want to take up my offer in the near future, Nancy. Once the press become aware of your involvement, they won't give you a minute's peace. Trust me; you'll need a bolt hole. My home is far more difficult to penetrate than yours.'

'I hadn't thought about that. Can I take a rain check?'

He smiled and nodded as he left. She closed the door with a frown on her face.

Oh dear, the press!

James Brierley parked his 4x4 in the car park of the prestigious offices of Cohen Goldsmith & Rayburn and wondered at his good fortune. Nancy certainly had the right contacts. Cohen would never have considered representing him in a million years had he tried to contact him direct. He was also very expensive. Could he afford him or would the state grant him legal aid? Oh well, he would find out soon enough.

He entered the large, elegant glass doors of the building and approached the very pretty and immaculate receptionist. She raised large intelligent eyes to him and asked who he was there to see.

'Ah yes, Mr Brierley, please take a seat and I'll let him know you are here.'

The large intelligent eyes followed his progress across the marble floor to the waiting area with admiration and interest. James tall frame ambled over to the large sofas and he picked up one of the many magazines on display. He expected to have to wait, but he was proved wrong.

'Mr. Brierley?'

'Yes.'

A smiling middle aged, but equally immaculately dressed woman held out her hand to him and introduced herself simply as Maggie, P.A. to Reece Cohen. She chatted amiably as she escorted him to the lift and then to Reece Cohen's office, which was located on the top floor with spectacular views over London.

Reece Cohen held out his hand to him and asked him to make himself comfortable, which he did. Cohen was a very direct man. Time was money and he had none to waste.

'Did you really decide to go straight? No lies please. What you say in here is privileged information, and I'm not about to repeat anything that could be detrimental to my client, but I will not tolerate fabrication of any kind. I want that understood from the outset.'

'No fabrication, Mr Cohen. I knew from the outset that if I agreed to break into the offices of Philip Menet, I would have to admit all, and in answer to your question - yes. I had always told myself that if I was ever caught, that would be it, because if I went down again they would probably throw away the key. So to continue would not have been a smart move.' He smiled, leaned back and sighed. 'This little episode really came at the wrong time for me, wouldn't you say?'

'Then why do it? You had far more to lose than any of the others.'

The lazy smile left his face. 'Because, being made aware of the inhuman things that were being done to innocent people, I knew I couldn't walk away from it and live with myself afterwards. I just couldn't. Now, it did cross my mind that perhaps I could bypass the responsibility, and recommend someone else for the job, but, to be honest and not arrogant, I'm the best there is. I knew that whoever did the job should be the one with the least chance of failure: they couldn't *afford* to fail. Too many people were suffering. Is that honest enough for you Mr Cohen?'

He answered by way of a statement. 'As we're going to be working together pretty closely, James, call me Reece. I consider it a privilege to act as your counsel, which, take my word for it, I have rarely said before.' He rubbed his hands together. 'This is also going to be a very rewarding and interesting case and I will move heaven and earth to stop you going back to prison.'

'Is that possible?' James's mouth was slightly agape with surprise.

'I will not consider anything less, but nothing is guaranteed, James.'

'Good Lord, that's the last thing I expected. How much is this going to cost me and if I can't fund it all, will the state help?'

'Oh, as I said, I consider representing you a privilege, so I'll work for nothing. Of course, there are always some expenses. Sir Alexander Wheeler has graciously decided to pick up that tab, so from now on, James, don't worry about a thing and leave everything to me.' He winked. 'As you said, dear boy, you're the best. But then, so am I.'

James couldn't hide his surprise. 'But I don't *know* Sir Alexander Wheeler; there must be some mistake.'

'No, no mistake. You don't know Alexander, but Nancy does. Alexander contacted Nancy as soon as he heard of her plight. He wanted me to represent her, but she wouldn't hear of it. She said you were the one who needed the best counsel and I have to agree with her. So sit yourself down and let's get on with it.'

'No, this isn't right. You must help Nancy. She could never cope with prison but I on the other hand, can.'

'As far as Nancy is concerned, it is highly unlikely that would happen. Not so with you, dear boy. But I don't want you worrying about Nancy; I have been very busy on her behalf and retained a very good barrister who's nearly as good as me.' Modesty was not one of Reece Cohen's virtues.

James stared at this very confident man and really took his measure for the first time. He was a large man, as tall as James, somewhere in his late fifties. His face was slightly ruddy, but not from drink, almost like a seafaring complexion. A strong face and body, but carrying far more weight than James. He was about to protest when he suddenly felt Megan's presence and smelt her perfume. It would be all right. Nancy and he would be looked after. But no prison sentence for him? Reece Cohen was being very naïve and overly confident.

Reece Cohen suddenly raised his head and sniffed. 'What's that lovely smell? Can you smell it?'

'I can,'

'Well let's get on, boy. We have a lot to get through and we need to get your statement to the police as soon as possible. As we speak, Nancy is doing the same. Alex Moorland and Bill Palmer, as it turns out, did not require my help in retaining counsel; a Detective Chief Superintendent Smith helped them there, and I must say I approve of his choice. It would appear people are queuing up to help you all.'

He suddenly grinned wickedly. 'Just one other point which may be of interest. I had two messages when I got back to the office last night, one to call Wheeler, the other to call Philip Menet. Wheeler and I go back many years, so I rang him first.'

'And Menet?'

'Oh, that was obvious. He was looking for the best counsel to represent him, but he will find it very difficult. The four best legal brains in Britain have been retained by your lot; offered me a disgusting amount of money to change my mind.'

'Now it's my turn to ask you, why?'

'I have been blessed with an excellent legal brain which has earned me more than I can ever spend. It's no longer my god. Now, it's the case that interests me and the ethics of the crime, and I didn't like Menet's ethics. Even if Alexander Wheeler had not asked me, James, I would have chosen to represent you. Only a man with a very good heart would have taken the path you did.' He rubbed his hands together, 'Anyway, boy, we have a real fight on our hands and there's nothing I enjoy more!'

Detective Chief Superintendent Bernard Draycott was a very unhappy man. All day he had been present as each statement had been given on behalf of those he considered to be the infamous four. The problem was his views were not shared by all those present. They were being regarded as some kind of martyrs, because of the actions they claimed they had been were forced to take. What made it worse, to a man and woman, Bilston's serving officers supported not only Moorland, but Palmer too of all people. How could that be? He had personally betrayed every serving officer at Bilston.

It had been three years since Moorland had retired, and yet Draycott knew he was still the one they looked up to. It was as though his three years as their DCS had never been. He raged inside with a hate he found hard to control, yet control it he must.

The infamous four's respective counsel, in word, were superb. He remembered with distaste the arrogance of the 'great' Reece Cohen. His total control over the meeting *he* should have been directing. Yet, try as he may, Cohen took it totally out of his hands with an ease one had to see and hear to believe. He virtually opened the meeting; he administered the direction it would take; he terminated the session when he saw fit. Collecting up his papers and briefcase and heading for the door in one fell swoop, ushering James Brierley out the room as he did so, having argued successfully for police bail.

Bilston Police Station had never had such senior council grace their humble doors before, and probably never would again. He had even managed the impossible as far as Draycott was concerned. Brierley was out on bail for a ridiculously small retainer, stating that his client never had any financial purpose in breaking and entering. His only motive was to help those long-suffering souls whose bodies were being raped daily of their god-given organs, and in doing so, he had put his own freedom at dire risk purely for the benefit of others. Had he wanted to evade the arm of the law he could have done so, therefore bail was the only decent and humane option in respect of his client.

Draycott cringed at the memory of his oratory which seemed to mesmerise all those present except him. Even Brierley had the good grace to show his amazement. It was almost as though he were speaking to a live jury and pleading his case. Christ, he'll be asking to make him a fucking saint next.

A thought suddenly occurred to Draycott. His facial colour until now had been a slight shade of red matching the inner rage he felt. Now he began to pale. Surely Cohen didn't think he could get Brierley off without a prison term? Draycott strode purposefully down the corridor in the direction of his office. Sergeant Bill Palmer was waiting there as directed. In fact, Draycott had taken great pleasure in making him wait all day before deigning to see him, and had forbidden any officer to speak or communicate with him in any way, other than the general courtesy of offering tea or coffee. He didn't want Palmer to feel relaxed at all. Draycott's intention was to make him sweat.

'Right, Palmer, what have you got to say for yourself and your total lack of loyalty to me and your fellow officers?'

He was not expecting Palmer to handle the situation well; he had a lot to lose. Draycott held the aces in his hand and intended to use them all. He would give Palmer a hard time; he had the power to do that.

'I have nothing to add to my statement, in which I have already given my reason for withholding last minute information due to security problems. Prior to that, not only Bilston, but every other police station would have found it impossible to act on the information we were given, due to

249

the nature of it and the source.' His face was calm, as he said, ' I have no intention of regurgitating my actions over and over again, sir, so may I respectfully ask you to advise me of any decision you have come to regarding myself, or continue this discussion when you have.'

As Bill's inner strength grew, the rage within Draycott escalated to the point of eruption. How dare he. He was doing a Reece Cohen, stating *his* terms, with the condition that he contacted him when he had decided his punishment and future. No, that was not how it was to be played. He was to grovel and feel fear in the face of the control Draycott believed he had over his life at this given time.

'Fucking suspension is my immediate decision, Palmer, with a dishonourable discharge pending, which, as you are already aware, means no fucking pension.'

Palmer sighed. 'I would not have expected any less from you, sir, and you have not disappointed me. Now, if you will excuse me, I think it's time I went home.'

Bill turned and walked quietly out of the door, followed by a barrage of abuse and threats which was not lost on any of the officers nearby. They patted him on the back as he left, by way of showing their support and in contempt of Draycott's earlier orders.

Bill felt strange. He should have been worried. His career was in tatters; his pension was gone and he had to tell his family, although it would be no great surprise to them. He had warned them. But he had held on to a faint glimmer of hope which he guessed was part of human nature. Palmer had reasoned that, bastard or not, Draycott was nevertheless still a human being. He had hoped Draycott's compassion for those held in Birmingham would override the knowledge that Palmer had not confided in him and that it had not been Bill's decision to make. It was circumstance that had decided the outcome.

Now he knew. Draycott would not waste any time or energy showing any compassion for him. So be it. So why didn't he feel the panic and apprehension he thought he would, now all hope had gone?

He left the building and was confronted by a sea of press and was surprised there were so many TV companies from overseas. He had known they were there earlier; his great surprise was they were still there waiting for him.

Bernard Draycott sank wearily into his office chair and reached down and unlocked the bottom left side drawer in his desk. His hand caught hold of the virtually full whisky bottle and placed it on the table. He looked at it for a minute or two before he filled the waiting glass on the desk. He took two large gulps to settle his agitated body; it helped. It helped a lot.

He leaned forward placing one elbow on the desk as he ran his hand through the back of his hair. How had it all gone so wrong? He had planned it meticulously. Palmer in first for interview; then make him sweat all day waiting to be called in to hear his fate.

Next was Brierley's interview, which he had every intention of enjoying. After all, he was a convicted criminal, and only six months out of prison. Hells bells; what a fiasco that turned out to be.

Then there was the woman, Nancy Harnetty. He had not intended to give her a hard time, mainly because he was no fool. He'd come to realise she was some kind of celebrity and well-respected in her field. She had also been the main whistle blower on all this, which had gained her a lot of support. He had no intention of making the same mistake twice.

It had been part of his strategy to interview Moorland last. He had wanted him in and out as soon as possible, anticipating the retained respect and loyalty the officers still held for him. He had not got that one wrong.

He reached for the bottle again....... and again. It wasn't the first time he had resorted to this kind of comfort when under stress, even though he knew it was a dangerous weakness for someone in his position, and he had curbed the habit. It was now exceptionally rare for him to lapse into a few whiskies while on duty. He waited until he was in the sanctuary of his own home if he felt the need.

Today had been intolerable; he had felt one of those rare rages surge through him, which he had never been able to control in the past, but it was imperative he either keep it at bay, or hidden. That was easier said than done and he had never managed to control one as strong as this before. His survival instinct had kicked in; too many influential witnesses. He had taken temporary breaks on different pretexts while Brierley's and Moorland's statements were being recorded, and disappeared into his office for five minutes' solace while he fought with his devils. He knew medication would have helped him at such times, but not his medical record, or his job. Now that arrogant pleb, Palmer, had bounced out of his office, and the full force of his rage was beginning to return. He needed another drink. Just one!

Rob Atkins, the Senior Detective on duty that night looked at Draycott's closed office door and wondered why the hell he didn't do them all a favour and go home. His inability to handle the proceedings professionally today had embarrassed them all, and he had been in since 7am: thirteen hours were enough for anyone. Atkins, like most officers at Bilston, did not like Draycott. He classified him as a first-class idiot. How he had ever succeeded Moorland, no one had ever been privy to. His dislike for him, bordering on hate, had developed over the last few years as he watched him use his power in such a way that the morale of the station was now at an all-time low. So much so, that many good officers were now looking for transfers.

Atkins looked up as Draycott's door opened and his eyes narrowed. Draycott left his office with what would have seemed to a layman, a straight walk. Atkins noticed the merest tremor.

Draycott called to say he was off home and that he would be in the office early next morning, without meeting anyone's eye.

Atkins waited for the command that never came. He'd been on the juice, but had not requested a squad car to take him home. Why? Then it hit him. Draycott didn't want anyone to know how much today had affected him. His pride would not let him.

Rob Atkins tried to contain his anger. Everyone knew he drank when under abnormal pressure, but it was rare. To his knowledge it had only happened three times since he had taken over at Bilston, but he had never been stupid enough not to request a squad car to take him home on some pretext or other. Rob Atkins didn't hold with drink driving. His best friend's little girl had been killed by a drunk driver. Atkins remembered little Maisie with sorrow. Her death had devastated his friend; she was their only child. He had been Maisie's godfather. He swore as he walked towards his office....... then stopped.

Abraham Betts and he had been best mates since junior school. One of those rare friendships they both knew would last a lifetime. They trusted each other implicitly. Atkins eyes were still narrowed, but now with determination as he picked up the phone. Afterwards, he always wondered where he got the balls to do what he had.

* * *

Abraham Betts sat in the police car in a slightly obscured lay-by just off the A3 with the engine and lights off. His partner, Patrick Murphy, was enquiring in a jovial way why Abraham had parked where he had with no lights on.

'Come on Abby, come clean. Why this hidey-hole at this time of night? Don't tell me one of your black dudes has taken you into their confidence about a drugs bust tonight?'

Abraham was black, very black, but he never took offence at this sort of banter. He knew when the comments were racist and when they weren't. Anyway, Abraham dished out more than his fair share of "paddy" jokes. Patrick was pulling his leg as usual, but he couldn't tell him why they were parked where they were, not ever. Rob Atkins had contacted him while he was on a break. It would be both their necks if anyone ever had any inkling what they were up to. It wasn't easy to go after a Detective Chief Superintendent and get away with it. It would have to appear sheer chance. Rob and he would never rat on each other and they both had strong reasons for this spontaneous stake-out, but it would be best for Patrick if he had no idea what Abby was really up to.

'You know me, Patrick; sometimes I need to meditate and mull over our next dynamic move.'

Patrick roared with laughter.

'Besides, I'm a little tired tonight, so a quiet half hour in a lay-by won't hurt either of us.'

'Now you're talking, Abby. Little Natalie had us up half the night. She was a right little...... sorry Abby, I wasn't thinking, really.' Abraham's little girl had been killed less than a year earlier.

Abby nodded. 'I know, Patrick, but it only makes it worse if you keep pussy-footing around me. Wrapping me in cotton wool won't help. My mother says only time will heal, okay? So quit apologising every time you mention Natalie. She's part of your life and it's only natural she'll come into our conversation from time to time.'

Abby suddenly switched on the engine and lights and moved out slowly as he positively identified Draycott's car, allowing it a little distance so as not to arouse his suspicion.

Patrick Murphy interpreted Abraham's decision to drive at that precise moment, as his way of changing the area of conversation they had inadvertently slipped into. He would never learn the true reason. What happened next went beyond Rob Atkin's and Abraham Bett's wildest expectations. Detective Chief Superintendent Bernard

Draycott fell asleep at the wheel and virtually demolished the side of a Silver Shadow Rolls Royce, which was not merely bad luck. After all, he lived in Esher which as most people know, is stockbroker belt. Rolls are more prevalent in this area than Minis.

* * *

Draycott had the book thrown at him, and six months later was still on suspension while they tried to decide what best to do with him.

The elation Bilston Police Station experienced was instantaneous and virtually all came to the conclusion that providence had stepped in to lighten their load.

No one ever guessed the real reason Officers Betts and Murphy had been in the right place at the right time, and Abraham Betts and Rob Atkins never felt the need to enlighten anyone.

Later, much later, when all the facts of the case had been well discussed and reported, Abby and Rob quietly wondered if Angel had anything to do with the outcome?

As they would discuss and think about Angel a lot, she picked up their thoughts as to her involvement. She smiled, and would have told them if she could that this was not the case, but not everyone is clairvoyant, certainly not Abby or Rob. No, she had not and would not have intervened in DCS Bernard Draycott's case. He had engineered his inevitable fall from grace all by himself.

Bernard Draycott was one of those rare people who were very good at interviews. He said and did the right things at the right time, which gave an undeserved impression to interviewers of what he was capable.

The truth was he had other rare talents which had helped instil their faith in him. He had a true genius for watching and spying on others. In this area, his talent was boundless. Acquiring information and ideas in such a way that no-one had ever really been able to point an informed finger at him.

He had been promoted, albeit more slowly than if he'd been blessed with natural talent, because it took time to gain access to, and implement other people's ideas, especially as he had missed some good ones along the way. Nevertheless, he had eventually arrived, but to a position which necessitated true leadership and talent. It didn't require a MENSA member to confirm that he found it difficult to maintain the perceived image and expectations his superiors had of him. He now had his own office, and was therefore segregated from others, which didn't allow him as many opportunities to survive on the backs of others.

Of course, following Moorland had not helped. He had been and was a true leader. Instinctive, perceptive, clever, he had the ability to promote loyalty and ambition in his serving officers. Draycott had not understood this, or had chosen not to. He chose instead to ignore his own imperfections and lack of ability and look for someone or something to blame. Moorland was his obvious choice. The only surprise was that Draycott had lasted so long, but then Moorland had left a good team behind him.

It had only been a matter of time before Draycott fell. Every day his inefficiency was witnessed and discussed by all.

When Rob Atkins and Abraham Betts next met and pondered their good fortune in legally and rightfully bringing about Bernard Draycott's downfall, they discussed the possibility that perhaps they had received a little paranormal help from Angel, but it was not so. Her only intervention had been to help the tormented souls trapped in a void.

TWENTY TWO

The press are either the bane of governments, companies or people, or their saviour. In this case, they could only be regarded as saviours, not only in this country, but the world. The world had been gripped by the story. Newspaper circulations had increased as people's interest in the case gained momentum. They could not get enough of it, so every newspaper, magazine and journal had obliged.
The media loved the case. It had everything as far as they were concerned.

The victims - subjected to vile actions.
The unusual - Nancy.
The good coppers – Moorland and Palmer.
The highly placed bent copper – Elliman.
The villain with a heart – Brierley.
The evil but clever villain - Spinetti.
The closet villain - Menet.

Each and every one of them had received offers to tell their exclusive story when the case was concluded. They had declined, but the suggestion had stayed with one of them: James Brierley.

During the six long years he had spent in jail, he'd had plenty of time to mull over ideas as to how he could earn his living when he was finally released. Two had remained for a couple of reasons. One, he felt he could be successful at them, and two, they might well compliment each other. One was to market himself and offer consultancy services as a security expert and the other was writing. When his consultancy expertise was not in great demand, he could write and vice versa. One problem he had already foreseen with the security consultancy was his criminal record. People might not be happy showing him round their homes or business premises, just in case he ever decided to use his new found status to occasionally relapse into his previous field of expertise. Now the gods had smiled on him. Due to the nature of the case and his decision to act as he had, no one he'd met so far doubted his integrity, or that his intention to go straight was genuine. Now, they were being asked by the media to give their accounts, and getting paid very handsomely for it.

He didn't want to interfere with any of the others recouping some profit from their personal experiences, but he had asked if anyone had any objection to him writing a book from start to finish. He had been humbled by their response.

'I can't answer for anyone else,' said Alex, 'but as far as I'm concerned, you have my total support. It would make me feel better if I knew you'd gained something out of this. God knows, we asked enough of you, and you had more to lose than any of us.'

Nancy stood up and came over to him. 'Give me a hug.' He had obliged. 'This is so right for you, James, and no-one could tell it better.'

'You've got my vote too, boy,' smiled Bill. 'I don't think I will need the money. Alex and I have got plans of our own, which could be very lucrative.'

James had left on cloud nine. He remembered his mother's words spoken in anger many years earlier, when he was being particularly difficult. 'You only get out of life what you put into it, James.' He regretted waiting so long to test her theory.

He thought of Megan and sent up a mental thank you to her. He knew she was doing all she could to help him. He wondered if getting caught and serving a prison sentence had been engineered by Angel and Co. or was it his natural time to pay his dues – he suspected the latter, and his sudden interest in life after death and his eventual awareness of people like Nancy Harnetty, was due to Megan's untimely death. Nevertheless, he would have bet money that, there had been some manipulation by Angel in bringing them all together.

But they had not been abandoned; help seemed to pour in from all quarters, most of it unexpected. He pondered the opportunities that now presented themselves, but James Brierley was no fool. Opportunities or not, he was the one who had to make them happen.

Tomorrow was the first day of the trial and, not for the first time, he began to speculate on how long his prison sentence would be. There it was again, her perfume.

* * *

Bill came down the stairs carrying the empty mug of tea his wife had woken him with earlier. He hadn't slept well last night and was dreading the trial. Yet all his being wanted it over and done with. It was the not knowing that kept his mind awake and alert. Still, not long now. Tomorrow they would stand side by side in the dock, and because they had all pleaded guilty, they would not have to wait too long to hear their fate. It would not be one of those trials that dragged on and on.

He sighed. He didn't know why he was feeling so nervous. James was the one he should be thinking about - and he was. It was because he had never stood the other side of the dock before, that was the reason he was so impatient for the trial to arrive. Many of his worries had been satisfactorily settled since Draycott had been suspended; others had decided his fate with much more compassion. He was fined six weeks pay, and one month's suspension, which meant he would not lose his pension.

He had wanted desperately to return to work. He felt the longer he was away, the harder it would be to resume his old standing with his work colleagues; that the time lapse would somehow put a barrier between them which would prove difficult to lift. He eventually came to realise his thinking was way off-course, that, in fact, he needed time to look at

259

his life and contemplate his future, and to realise Bill Palmer was no longer the man he had been.

In the last few months too much water had passed under his bridge for him to be totally content and satisfied with the job he had done quite happily for nearly twenty- five years. He thought about the long discussions he'd had with Alex, and the eventual decision they had made. They would start a Detective Agency. Bill had initially assumed Alex was offering him a job. His true intention had surprised and filled his heart with pride.

'If we ever get the chance to start this business, Bill, it will be equal partners or nothing.' He'd grinned then, 'Though I might insist my name goes first. You know, like Moorland & Palmer.'

'Suits me, Alex,' he had replied, and it did. He had opted for early retirement and although he would not receive a full pension, it wasn't far off it. He walked into the kitchen and sat down at the table.

His wife glanced sympathetically at him. 'I'll get you another cuppa love and your breakfast won't be long.'

'His son Leslie passed the newspaper over to him. 'Here, Dad, you have a read.'

'No, son, you finish reading; I've got all day.'

'I'll be leaving for work in a minute, so you grab it before Mum does.' Leslie winked at his mother.
Bill patted his arm as his wife Gina poured him another mug of tea.

'I'm not going to fight you for it, love,' said Gina. 'I'll look at it when you've finished with it. Anyway, you must be tired. You didn't sleep well again last night, so after breakfast you put your feet up in the sitting room and rest. You've got a lot on your plate at the moment, so I don't want you worrying and getting too tired, all right love.'

Gina Palmer's face was full of concern as she busied herself. Her generously sized body was pushed into a pink track suit and her thick, voluptuous, naturally curly hair, had been left to its own devices as usual, but her slightly wild mane more than complimented her attractive middle-aged face. She transferred the eggs and bacon from the frying pan to a plate and set it down in front of him.

'Looks good, Gina.'

'Mother always said, the way to a man's heart is through his stomach.'

Leslie placed his hand on Bill's shoulder. 'I'm off, Dad, but get some rest like Mum said, okay?'

Bill nodded. Since the case, the attention they had all received had been difficult for them to handle. They were ordinary people who, because of circumstances, had been propelled into a barrage of publicity which they were not equipped to handle. Bill's counsel had advised him and his family to say nothing, which suited them.

Leslie had found it very hard to cope with. He had now stopped answering the "supposed" well-meaning questions from friends and work colleagues, after he realised they were being printed in the next day's national newspapers.

Gina had experienced similar problems with neighbours. She went out as little as possible now and had all their food delivered. The whole family wanted it all to be over and for their lives to return to some normality, but they had not spoken one word of anger, or blamed Bill in any way. They had just tried to show their support by trying to make his life at home as easy as they could.

Bill smiled inside. Normally, Leslie would not have relinquished the morning paper without him directing a few stern words in his direction.

Bill pushed a half-finished plate away from him, picked up his tea and paper, and made his way to the sitting room. Gina was right; he might as well take it easy while he could. Tomorrow he would have to fight his way through the crowds and spend an unknown amount of time in court.

Half an hour later, Gina left the washing-up and went to collect Bill's mug. He was dozing with the television on.

She quietly picked up his mug and crept out, turning the TV off as she left.

* * *

The doorbell rang; Alex turned the radio off and went to answer it. He knew who it was before he opened the door; she'd been like a mother hen checking on him every day, either telephoning him or calling round.

'Hello, Leila,'

'Hello, Dad; thought you might like some fresh croissants for breakfast,' she bustled past him.

He didn't, but thanked her anyway. It was strange, but he had come to realise her efforts to comfort and help him were as much for her benefit as his. She was worried for him. Alex knew this, but did not understand the whole.

Leila needed to be near him. She was afraid of losing him if they sent him to prison; afraid that she would not be able to get in her car and drive the short distance to see him. It made her realise how much she relied on him, knowing he was always there for her if she needed to talk. Most of all, she was afraid for him. He had been very successful in sending law-breakers to prison; many would welcome the opportunity to meet him again on their terms.

She feared for his safety and she was beginning to miss her mother again with the strong ache she had felt when she had died. The ache that had dulled over the years until it had virtually disappeared: was now reborn. Or perhaps the ache she now felt for her father had joined forces with the remembered pain for her mother. Whatever the reason, she was unhappy, and had a constant tightness in her chest.

He kissed her lightly on the top of her head. 'Got time to join me, love?'

'I thought you'd never ask.' She smiled. 'Shall we put them in the oven for a few minutes?'

'Why not.' He filled up the kettle and threw the switch.

262

Leila quickly placed the croissants onto a baking tray and shoved it in the oven. 'Are you worried about tomorrow, Dad, or just glad it's here?'

'Both. I want to get it over with. Did you know DCS Smith and Draycott's temporary replacement have written to the magistrate handling the case on our behalf?'

'No, how does that help Dad?'

'Depends on the magistrate, of course, but it could help quite a lot. They have said that without our involvement this case might never have come to light, and that our help in securing a conviction had been immeasurable. He's not obliged to take it into consideration, but it certainly won't hurt us.'

'Oh, Dad, that really is decent of them.'

'Yes it is, and I never cease to be surprised at the support I've been shown.' He smiled. 'I think I can hear the croissants knocking on the oven door. You let them out and I'll make the coffee; is that fair?'

He had always been able to make her smile. She walked over and hugged him. 'That's fair.'

The phone rang and he walked to the next room to answer it. 'It's John Smith, Alex, how are you?'

'Let's just say, I'm glad the waiting is nearly over.'

'I don't doubt that. Anything I can do?'

'You already have. I just heard you wrote to the magistrate on our behalf.'

'It's the least I could do, and I meant it when I said we might never have secured a conviction without your help. I also know the magistrate is under a lot of pressure from the press and public. They're all on your side but it doesn't guarantee anything, Alex. I have to be honest and say he might decide to make an example of someone.'

'You're not telling me anything I don't already know, John, but I'm still grateful for the support you've given me. I just wish there was some way I could return the favour.'

It was a few seconds before he answered. 'Actually, there is. I wasn't going to mention it yet, so it's strange you should say that now.'

'What can I do?' Alex was sincere.

'Oh, it's not what you can do, rather that I would like your honest opinion on a matter. It is highly confidential by the way.'

'Shoot.'

'I had a phone call last week and a short unofficial meeting with the powers that be. Apparently, they have come to realise they have a very disgruntled and unhappy station at Bilston, which has made them think long and hard about who will replace Draycott. Believe it or not, they have asked me. I said no, I wasn't interested. They, on the other hand, insisted I think about it. What I want to know is, if I decide to accept, would I have your support?'

'I couldn't think of anyone more suited to bring Bilston up to scratch again, and they deserve a decent DCS. It's a good team; they just need a man who knows what he's doing, but you shouldn't have asked me, John.'

'Why?'

'Because: I'll be bloody annoyed if you don't accept.'

John laughed. 'I have to be honest, I'm still not sure, but I'm having my arm twisted at the moment.'

'Oh, who by?'

'The wife, would you believe. She's a Londoner and born not far from Bilston. She has strong family ties there.'

'Dad, the croissants are not happy,' yelled Leila.

'That's my daughter calling, John, I have to go now. All I can say is you get my vote, but the decision will have to be yours.' Alex thought for a moment. 'I'm not really sure why you needed my advice on this one?'

'I wasn't sure if you regretted leaving the force and had a desire to return. I didn't want to step on your toes, especially as I'm not unhappy at Birmingham.'

'No, rest easy, none at all.'

Sir Alexander Wheeler and Lady Marguerite sat in their large, beautiful conservatory before dinner, overlooking a garden clothed in vibrant summer colours and pondered while they waited for Nancy. Nancy had not coped well with the incessant phone calls from reporters, the continual barrage of questions, and the cameras permanently posted outside her small flat. She had eventually been forced to accept Alexander's offer and temporarily move in with them. Alexander picked up his whisky and recalled their first meeting. He had been surprised not only with her natural gift, but also her outright refusal to take extra payment, or his offer of free stock market guidance. It wasn't often one met a truly honest person. He was glad he had thought to offer Nancy a safe haven for a while. He wasn't usually so helpful; not because he didn't want to be, but because he just didn't think. It was a natural consequence of being so busy. He had mentioned this to Nancy one day. She'd been distracted at the time, but had suddenly looked up.

'Oh, I'm sorry, I thought you'd realised. It wasn't your idea, it was Justin's. He must have felt so strongly about it that you picked up his thoughts.' She had gone back to being distracted, leaving him to wonder about what she had just said.

'How's she been today,' he asked Marguerite.

'Not good. She has hardly eaten all day, which hasn't helped, and has just stayed, in her room. I have tried to coax her down, but in the end decided I wasn't helping. I think she really needed to be alone. I made sure I didn't go out, just in case she wanted to talk.'

'I think you did the right thing.'

'Mind you, I did insist she came down for dinner with us this evening. She will need something inside her with the start of the trial tomorrow.' Marguerite sighed. 'The biggest problem she's had to come to terms with, as far as I can see, is that she can't understand why she had to be the one to start this whole terrible business. She seems to think someone with more experience should have been chosen; like mediums specialising in helping police, who then go on to write books about it.'

Alexander took a sip of his whisky. 'None of them have perfected their gift as well as she has. She has the ability to pick things up with total clarity. There's no straining or fumbling to interpret, or get it right. She just can, and does. There could be no allowance for fumbling in this case. Think about it, what would have happened if she had not been able to see and hear clearly when she and James were looking for vital evidence at Menet's clinic?'

'Yes, I see; I hadn't thought about it in that sense. Things could have been disastrous on many occasions. Why can she not see that?'

'If I was in her position, I would probably think as she does. It must have been very frightening to have these horrors unfold before you, knowing that one wrong move could jeopardise everything. Remember, they all took most of their direction from Nancy. It must have been a terrible responsibility, one that anyone with any sense would want to off-load, especially if you had never had to deal with anything like this before, so I can understand her reasoning that psychics who work with police should have been the natural choice.'

'Yes, but as you said, *none* of them had such a developed gift as Nancy.' Marguerite frowned and looked at her husband. 'That's why you're so good at what you do, Alexander; it's your ability to think things through.'

He smiled. 'Well if you mean I look at stocks and shares and try my utmost to anticipate and analyse where they will be next year, yes dear. But it's a little more complicated than that.'

Nancy entered smiling, looking tired and thinner. 'I thought it was a golden rule you never discussed business at home.'

'Quite right, Nancy, lets hear no more of stock and shares. Sit yourself down and drink that sherry that has been waiting far too long for you.'
She picked up the glass and gazed out onto the lovely garden. Gardens had a very therapeutic effect on her. She put her glass down and looked from one to the other.

'I haven't been the easiest house guest, I know that, but you will never have a more grateful one. I just want you to know that, whatever happens tomorrow, I will never forget your kindness to me during what has been the worst period of my life.'

'Sometimes, Nancy,' said Alexander quietly, 'we are given the chance to help those who have helped us during a period we also consider to be very painful. So let's not mention it again.'

The tears were never very far away. 'No, we won't.'

'Right, let's eat. I have lovely champagne waiting on ice as a surprise for you both.'
Marguerite was already walking in the direction of the dining room.

'Well, what are we waiting for? After you, Nancy,' said Alexander.

* * *

Virginia Draycott opened the door of her husband's study as quietly as she could. When they had married some twenty years ago, Virginia had had a slight stutter, evident only on very stressful and rare occasions. Today, it was very pronounced.
Her stutter had grown over the years, as had her husband's intolerance of it.

'Beeer-nard, your din-eeeers getting cold.' She closed the door just in time to miss the flying object.

Christ. How on earth had he ever been so stupid as to marry her? He picked up his drink. He wasn't drunk, not yet. He had to finish this letter to his superiors. He smiled and took another drink. Superiors! That was a laugh. He was far more capable than....

He lost himself again in a melee of self pity. It was one of the things he did best.

Eventually Virginia crossed his mind again and his original question, to which he already knew the answer. He had married Virginia Rowan (one of *the* Rowans) because her family was not without a bob or two and knew the right kind of people. It had helped for a while, but they had soon seen through him, though not before they had helped him up a ladder or two. As they no longer saw fit to continue their support, he no longer saw fit to treat Virginia with the respect they thought she deserved. In many ways it was a relief. Initially he had been fond of her, but had never loved her.

He studied the rim of his glass as his mind reviewed the wrongs he had been subjected to over the years. He had desperately wanted a son. He smashed the glass down on the large and immaculate Edwardian desk as he remembered. The bitch wasn't even capable of that. She had miscarried their one and only child, and never conceived again. The Rowan's had put the blame squarely on his shoulders for both misfortunes, using the doctor's terminology of a "stress related miscarriage". How did they think up this fucking crap?

With her family's removal of support, he no longer saw the necessity of giving the impression he still had any feelings for her. It had become tiring anyway, and he had done all right with help from others as time passed, many of them unaware of it. He took another drink. Maybe now was not the time to finish the letter of disapproval for his outrageous suspension. Perhaps it would be better phrased after the infamous four had appeared in court. He longed for

268

that day. It was the only thing that had kept him going. He now no longer cared if the woman and Brierley were let off lightly. It was Moorland and Palmer he prayed nightly would go down.

He refilled his glass and decided it didn't need the water he usually added. Half an hour later, stretched out in his leather chair, he was unable to hear Virginia Draycott struggling with her suitcase down the stairs, or the sound of the engine as her car sped away.

TWENTY THREE

Nancy awoke feeling slightly groggy but rested. Lady Marguerite's doctor had prescribed something to help her sleep and thankfully it had worked. She rolled from her side onto her back and stretched, raising her arms above her and sighed.

It was the second Monday in August and they were all due to appear in court for the start of their trial. As they had all pleaded guilty to the charges, it overruled the necessity for separate trials, but they would still be represented by their own counsel. She was glad they would be tried together; it gave her an inner strength, knowing they would be near, and she needed to know how they would fare as and when it happened. Waiting each day and having to imagine the fate of the three men she had come to regard as close friends, would have been much harder and taken more of a toll on her; Nancy worried incessantly about them. She was the reason they were in the position they were – she had instigated their plight. Her apprehension increased as she thought about James. Wearily she raised herself from the bed just as there was a slight knock at the door.

'Come in, Rose.'

Rose was a motherly looking woman in her early fifties. She set the tray down with a sympathetic smile. 'Shall I pour your tea?'

'No thanks, Rose, I can manage.'

Rose placed the tray on the small table overlooking the garden where Nancy now sat. Then, without warning, Rose suddenly bent and hugged her. 'I have been praying for you, Nancy, and I know I'm not the only one.' Nancy nodded as she took her hand and squeezed it.

She needed time to sit quietly for a while, before she made her way downstairs. Lady Marguerite was waiting for her in the breakfast room and although Nancy had no appetite, she had insisted she try to eat something before they left for the Magistrates' Court and would not take no for an answer. Marguerite was very proficient at not taking no for an answer; gentle but firm. Alexander and Marguerite had been a tower of strength for her in the last few weeks and she had not wanted to burden them further, especially with the hassle of her court appearance.

'Of course I shall come with you, Nancy, you cannot possibly go alone. It will be a madhouse out there and you will need at least one friend beside you for support.'

She was right, of course, and Nancy was grateful.

* * *

The Magistrates' Court was twenty minutes late in starting. Not hundreds, but thousands had crammed into every square foot surrounding the building and they had to send for extra police to help the defendants gain access to the court. There had been a near riot as the public fought to get a seat in the public gallery. Some had been physically removed from the building after they had tried to push their way through when told it was full.

Eventually, chaos was replaced by control, and Nancy Harnetty, Alex Moorland, William Palmer and James Brierley were led into the dock by the Court Usher.

The Stipendiary Magistrate looked at them with interest as one by one they filed into the court-room. His gaze wondered to the public gallery; they were transfixed.

This was a most unusual case, the likes of which he never thought he would ever be asked to preside over. Anyone connected with the case, directly or indirectly, would gain fame or infamy in some way or other whether they desired it or not. He himself was known and respected by those in his profession. Now, he was virtually a household name and he guessed (rightly) would always be referred to as *the* Magistrate who presided over the case of those before him.

There had even been a number of newspaper articles about him, reporting even the most insignificant details of his life just to fill space, which was ridiculous. He was now recognised in the street and had been approached to sit on news panels in the future, to give expert legal advice as and when required, which to be honest, he found very embarrassing. There were far more competent lawyers available, who had the added charisma required for the cameras. The Crown Prosecution Solicitor stood and addressed the court.

'Your Worship, it is alleged that on the….'

Nancy listened, as in a dream, as the date, time and place of the Menet burglary charges were outlined, detailing each offence they were accused of. Nancy Harnetty and James Brierley were accused of Burglary; Alex Moorland and William Palmer of Conspiracy to Burglary. 'How do you plead: guilty, or not guilty?'

One by one they pleaded guilty.

As the events had started with Nancy, her barrister Edmund Drummond was the first to speak. 'Your Worship, although my client admits to the charges brought against her, the mitigating circumstance as to why she committed this offence is staggering.' There was a mumble of "here, here", and "quite right" from the public gallery.

'When someone commits burglary, the purpose is for financial gain or for their own personal benefit in some way. I would respectfully remind Your Worship that in this case nothing of value was taken and that this was never Miss Harnetty's intention. She did not even remove the evidence she sought, only to photograph it. Now, we must ask ourselves, if personal gain was not her intention, then what was? The only conclusion and true answer to that, Your Worship, was to help others who were suffering such heinous indignities, that not only the United Kingdom, but indeed the world is horrified. Having established the motive for her crime, what had Nancy Harnetty to gain personally by her actions, which she had already decided she would not seek to conceal? The answer to that is nothing, other than a criminal record and the possibility of imprisonment. In fact, there could be no personal gain, only personal repercussions. I therefore ask Your Worship not only for leniency, but to show great mercy when sentencing.'

'She ought to be given a bloody medal, not standing in that bloody dock,' Georgie Wells shouted somewhere from the back of the court.

'Let her out, you bugger,' shouted someone from the public gallery. The uproar started.

The magistrate banged his gavel several times before order was restored.

'I am aware how painful this must be for you, Mr Wells, and you deserve and have my genuine sympathy for your loss, but I will have you removed from court if I hear any more outbursts from you. It serves only to delay this case and prolongs the discomfort of the defendants. Do you understand?'

Georgie Wells nodded. He didn't trust himself to answer. He did not agree, but had no choice in the matter.

The Magistrate nodded for Nancy's counsel to continue.

'I am sure you have read all the evidence presented prior to this case, Your Worship, so my client and I will await judgement.'

Reece Cohen QC was next to plead on behalf of James Brierley and he milked it for all it was worth. There was barely a dry eye in the public gallery, when half an hour later the Magistrate decided, enough was enough.

'I am now fully conversant with your client's dilemma and reasons Mr Cohen, which have been presented very professionally, so if you see fit to close.'

Cohen did, he didn't get where he was by being a fool. He could have cut the time in less than half, but that might not have been long enough to get the gallery and press totally on his side. He smiled graciously at the magistrate and sat down. He'd achieved what he wanted.

At this point, the Magistrate decided to call a lunch break. An hour and a half later they all resumed their seats. Alex Moorland and William Palmer's solicitors duly addressed His Worship, but the real hard work had already been done for them. No magistrate could be unaware of the sacrifice each and every one of them had made. No-one in their right mind could arrive at any other conclusion, but it was a hard case, unprecedented in his and most of his legal colleagues' experience. Nevertheless, each one had committed a crime.

'I will adjourn this court for today and will pass sentence tomorrow morning at 10am. This court is now closed.'

There was an air of disapproval from the gallery. They were not sure they would be able to get back in tomorrow.

***

Next morning, the Magistrate had indeed made his decision; not one the defendants were happy with.

'Due to the unusual nature and circumstances, I have decided to pass this case over to the Crown Court for sentencing.' He faced the defendants in the dock. 'You will all be advised at a later date when you will be required to attend Crown Court.

Reece Cohen nudged Edmund Drummond. 'Told you so, old boy; you lost the bet, so you can pay for my lunch today. I told you he wouldn't risk sentencing. It's such an emotive case, too much hangs on it. One really unpopular or unwise sentence could stay and haunt him (if you'll excuse the pun). No, better to play safe and pass it on.'

Drummond smiled good humouredly, 'I always cough up, Reece. Who do you think will now get the honour of sentencing?'

'Ah, now that's what worries me. Only one judge is afraid of no-one and nothing; Judge Appleton.'

'Christ.'

'Exactly, never know which way he will swing.'

The defendants left the court at staggered times, allowing their counsel to make a short announcement on their behalf. Then the media circus fight and the struggle through the well-meaning crowd all over again.

They would have liked to meet up after their court appearance for a quiet dinner, but as that was not possible, spoke to each other on the phone instead.

'Why didn't he make a decision, Alex; he had all the facts? We denied nothing. Why pass it onto the Crown Court?' Nancy asked.

'Oh, that's simple; he's a magistrate and not a judge. Normally, a case like this would go before a judge, but as we all took the unusual step of pleading guilty, they had no alternative but to hear it in a magistrate's court. Now, although it's an open and shut case, technically it would be very difficult for any magistrate to pass sentence because it's a very emotional case; the sort that could cause a sentencing magistrate a lot of unwelcome repercussions in his career, if he is deemed to have made mistakes when doing so. So although we are not happy to go through this again, I can see where he's coming from.'

'Oh dear, I see. I didn't realise how difficult this would be for him, and I don't want anyone else who doesn't deserve it to suffer because of what has happened.'

'Edmund Drummond should have explained this to you.'

'He put a lot of his cases on the back burner when he agreed to represent me, so he's well behind with his work, and, to be honest, I didn't think to ask him at the time. He said he'd call me later tonight, so I guess he will go over everything then. He had to make time to represent me which I appreciate. He's had to work a whole lot harder by fitting me in, but I know he's doing the best job possible.'

'You're right Nancy. I guess I'm still a little edgy.'

'I know; we all are.'

'You're still staying with the Wheelers?'

'Yes, Marguerite wouldn't hear of me going home. Said I'd be besieged, and she's right. I'm so grateful to them.'

'Yes, you're in the best place and they're good people.'

* * *

Exactly thirty-two days later, they stood shoulder to shoulder in the dock of the Crown Court and faced Judge Appleton for sentencing. Reece Cohen eyed him with suspicion. Judge Appleton was a tiny man, with an enormous reputation for ruthlessly administering justice without fear of repercussion. Cohen was sure he must be propped up on cushions the other side of the bench from which he presided, and his wig looked far too large. He had a narrow nose positioned below two piercing eyes that at this precise moment looked very stern indeed. Not for the first time he raised the gavel, then brought it to bear on the desk with a crashing blow. 'I will not ask again; I will have silence in this court before I pass sentence.'

Nancy had braced herself for this moment; she was ready. Why wouldn't they all stop murmuring and let the judge get on with it? She looked briefly at Alex; he winked by way of encouragement; then clasped her hand.

All eyes were now on Judge Appleton as they came to order. Georgie Wells and Isabel Jennings were present, anxiously waiting, as were the rest.

'James Brierley and Nancy Harnetty, you are charged with Burglary. Alex Moorland and William Palmer, Conspiracy to Burglary to which you have all pleaded guilty. However, it is clear from the testimonies given that you were not actively seeking personal reward, and indeed, each made a considerable sacrifice by his action, which in my opinion, could only be described as bordering on insanity.' There was a murmur of voices as he picked up his gavel and banged the desk.

'If you do not keep silent, I will clear this court.' Judge Appleton waited for the murmuring to cease.

'I can only attribute the lack of self-preservation to one reason; your compassion for your fellow man, which these days, is indeed rare. The only logical assumption for this indiscretion is that it was committed purely on humanitarian grounds. It would therefore be unjust to punish you further. In the light of this and the extreme extenuating circumstances, it is therefore my decision that you all receive an absolute discharge. This court is now closed.' The uproar was deafening as Judge Appleton stood to leave the court.

Cohen regarded Drummond. 'You see what I mean about Appleton; afraid of no-one and nothing. That he would let the other defendants off lightly, I can understand, but only *he* would dare let my client off without even a smacked wrist. There will be those who will attempt to besmirch his reputation through Brierley, but if you'll excuse my French, Drummond, he won't give a shit.' He smiled as an after-thought occurred. 'Mind you, Brierley did have brilliant representation.'

Drummond laughed. 'Now you owe me a lunch; obviously I had more faith in your oratory power than you did.'

'I'm more than happy to concede to you on this one.'

Outside the court the press and public had a field day. The general public cheered and even threw flowers.

The trials of the accused duly followed. Philip Menet, Luigi Spinetti and Delores Heeja all received life sentences with no chance of parole. Jean Elliman, a life sentence.

TWENTY FOUR

Nancy's eyes lingered on the phone as she replaced it. Many calls these days were offers to appear in theatres or TV shows or to give lectures. Some had even suggested she name her own price.

It was tempting, very tempting. But deep down she knew it was the tragedy of the tormented souls and the infamy of Menet that drew their interest. They had read all about it anyway, so what more did they want? In her heart she knew it was wrong to cash in and make money out of their suffering. No, she would continue with John Dale who had organized her American and Canadian tour, with the understanding that she would not discuss the case. Hopefully, this would attract the same kind of people as before. Those who had a genuine interest in her knowledge of medium development and meditation; she had no desire to become a side-show.

Her mind wandered to James. It was different writing a book. They would read the facts sympathetically written by someone who cared, and he genuinely needed another source of income. She did not. It was more honest, as far as she was concerned, that someone closely connected to the events, with a true understanding of the dilemma they had all experienced, should put pen to paper; she could manage well enough without the extra revenue. A large house required a large and permanent income, and she had everything she needed or wanted in her one bed-flat.

She turned to walk away just as it rang again. She would ignore it; she'd had enough for one day. Suddenly, she stopped. She had to answer it; she had the same feeling as when Goergie Wells rang, almost a compulsion to pick it up.

'Hello.'

Nancy, how are you? It's Edmund Drummond here.'

'I'm doing very nicely thank you, Edmund. What about you?'

'Well, busier than ever which is a bonus really, because it means I am in the enviable position of being able to choose the more interesting cases. The money's a great comfort too.' She laughed.

'I had a strange phone call today. I'm at a stage in my life when I think that nothing can surprise me anymore, but I have to tell you I couldn't have been more wrong.'

'What's the matter, can I help?'

'It's not a matter of helping me, Nancy, it concerns you.'

Suddenly, she felt cold. 'Oh.'

Philip Menet's counsel rang me, but at least he had the grace to be embarrassed by his request.'

'Go on.'

'Evidently, Philip Menet has requested you visit him in prison.'

'What! Why on earth would he want to see me?'

'He said he would not discuss that with anyone other than you. His counsel did quiz him for quite some time on the matter and explained to him that you would want some explanation as to the purpose of this visit, but he refused to say. The only response he could get out of him was that was it was a matter which concerned only the two of you.'

'That is totally unfair. I can't see any reason why he and I would want to meet, not under any circumstances. I don't even think I could be in the same room with him.   I have not forgotten the pain of Elsie Turnbull, nor will I.'

'He won't budge, Nancy, so you'll have to make up your own mind on this one. For what it's worth, I wouldn't go; he's one sick bastard. I know this has been a shock for you, so take your time and think about it. Let me know your decision when you're ready. There's no rush; he's not going anywhere.'

'I will, Edmund, thank you.'

Nancy had been on her way to do a little weeding and tidying up in the garden. It was the end of March and, although chilly, the sun had pushed through, making everything look and feel different. She sat down in her favourite armchair and looked out at the comforting evergreens which had bravely survived even the iciest frost nature had slung at them this winter.

What could he want? She couldn't possibly go. He would remind her all over again of the continuing pain she had felt during that evil time. She sighed. Of course, that was it. Edmund was right; he was mentally ill. He had to be to do what he did. This was some kind of sick game he now wanted to play. Oh dear, she wanted an end to him; she needed time to heal inside. She would phone Edmund tomorrow and tell him there was no way she could see him.

She walked towards the bedroom. She would need a thick sweater if she was to tackle the garden. As she entered the room, she stopped. Nancy had not seen her for a very long time, but there she was again, calmly looking out of her bedroom window. Angel turned with a sad smile. It was then it hit her.

'I can't do it, Angel, I just cannot do it.'

Angel turned and faced the window again.

'You have a pretty garden, even at this time of year. They say someone who creates a garden, creates happiness.' Angel faced her as she said. *'He is not happy, Nancy. It was not my intention he should suffer; that is a very earthly trait. When we pass over; we try to aspire to better things.'* She sighed. *'He asks it every day, but he does not have your gift; so he will never know the answer he seeks until he leaves his earthly life. But what he seeks, he has the right to know. This is the one and only time I will ask this of you, and I will respect your decision whatever it is.'*

Nancy couldn't understand Angel's request. 'As far as I'm concerned, he gave up all his rights when he played devil with other people's bodies. Why? Why does he have the right to know?'

'*To give him the chance to repent; he has no remorse or sorrow in his heart for what he has done. He refuses to accept or understand the enormity of his actions, but the answer he seeks will in some way make him acknowledge there is a fine line in life, which if we cross, we do so at our peril; that there is a force greater than us. His earthly being does not realise that it is his own soul that makes him ask this question; that inner voice that will always try to guide us on the right path, no matter how hard or difficult that path might be.*'

'This isn't fair, Angel; I am not the only medium on this planet. Why can't you find someone else to help him?'

'*I will not trust another as I do you. I did not choose you Nancy, but those who did chose well.*'

She'd heard those words before. 'I can't promise anything, Angel, I really can't. I don't know whether I can handle this, but I will seriously think about it, okay?'

She smiled gently at her. '*Take care, Nancy.*'

Nancy did what she always did when she had a problem. She got in her car and drove to Wimbledon Common and went for a long walk. She had a great love of Wimbledon Common; it never ceased to bring back fond memories of the many Sunday afternoon picnics she and her friends had enjoyed there as children. Armed with an abundance of jam and paste sandwiches, and her old mongrel Sally, they would catch the bus the short distance to the common, climb trees and generally run free all afternoon. She was never sure who enjoyed it most, them or Sally. Sometimes they would take empty jam jars and catch tadpoles from the nearest pond. It wasn't until a few years ago when she bought a book about the common, that she discovered how blessed she had been to have such a haven so close to home. The common was over 1000 acres in size, had sixteen miles of horse rides, an 18-hole golf course, playing fields and ten ponds. Here, there was more than enough space to be alone with her thoughts.

The sun had now disappeared, but the day was still bright. A wind now blew so she had wrapped herself up well. It was difficult to think if you felt cold. She looked up into the branches of the trees and noticed how the wind fought to remove the last of the brown leaves that had resolutely refused to fall.

She guessed she had walked for at least half an hour before her mind became more peaceful. It was silly letting it unsettle her as much as it had. She had free choice whether she went or not, with no recriminations from Angel. She was looking at this problem from the wrong angle. If it was her choice, why was she so worried?

It was because her imagination had worked overtime as to the power he would exert over her in a confined space. She had only seen him once in court, yet she had been aware of the strength of his aura. The dark side within him was magnetic, almost as if it could taint those who came too close to him. Then there was the remembered pain of Elsie and John and all the other poor souls.

That was it! She feared him. That was the true reason she did not want to meet him.

Nancy was not happy with this analysis, for she knew it was a weakness that should be mastered. But if one feared, how could one overcome it? The answer was easy, of course; they usually are if you are prepared to really look at a situation from every angle. She must face her fear; that was the only way to overcome it. Easier said than done; she would gain no strength visiting a counsellor or psychiatrist to prepare her for such a meeting. How could she overcome her fear in such close proximity? She knew the energy from his aura would affect her, and if that was the case, they would not be meeting on equal terms, which was imperative.

Nancy looked up and realised she was just about to pass the Windmill Café. A coffee and a bun would help. Even though the temperature had dropped, she decided to sit outside. She preferred to be alone with her thoughts and most of the customers had opted to sit inside. Only the man at the far table, feeding his dog half his rock cake, sat outside. Nancy sipped her coffee as her thoughts returned to Menet.

The problem was, she was afraid of him which was not a good thing, not only for now, but for any other situations which might arise in the future. So far, she had only dealt with everyday people who had never been a threat mentally or physically. She had been blessed with meeting people who had just needed comfort from a short reunion with someone they loved. Most of these encounters had been a gentle experience, which had brought out the best in those who came to see her. There had been a few difficulties, but that was life; it was never intended to be all roses. But she had never met someone who actually generated a malevolent presence such as he did. Most people would not be aware of it; those who did would feel uneasy about him without realising why.

Delores Heeja was the exception; she had no illusions about Menet. Delores was one of those with an inborn knowing, who mistakenly thought that because of her insight and knowledge of voodoo, she would be able to protect herself; Delores would never make a more destructive mistake. Greed had impaired her instinct. The longer her contact with him and her participation in his inhuman actions, the greater was the decline in her ability to keep her mind and body strong. Menet on the other hand, although he had not truly understood the reason, had grown stronger.

She knew the power of good was as strong as evil, but only when met with equal strength. Was she as strong as him? No. Then how could she meet him on equal terms?

Then she knew. She would gain strength, as he had, from others. But whereas he had drawn from that which was bad, she would draw from that which was good.

She sipped her coffee and sighed with relief. All one had to do was ask the right questions and eventually they would be answered. One had to search from within. She needed Angel. Her thought was enough to summon her.

'You knew this, Angel, didn't you? Why didn't you just explain it all to me?' Nancy was facing out onto the common as she spoke quietly. She didn't want any near onlookers to think she was talking to herself. She faced only a few distant walkers.

'Yes, but sometimes we have to answer our own questions to truly believe them.'

'I want you to stay close to me. I'll need your strength when I meet him.'

'As close as when you faced Elsie's torment. But you are as strong as he is, Nancy, you are just not aware of it because you have never had to draw on this inner strength until now.'

Nancy turned to face the one no-one else but she could see, and she no longer cared if anyone thought she was muttering to herself.

'I know you would never lie to me, Angel, but if I have it, I can't feel it, so I want you to promise you'll stay close and not leave me.'

'You have my promise. Now go home, you're getting cold.'

* * *

Alex had insisted on accompanying her to Wandsworth Prison and she hadn't argued; she was only too happy to draw on his support. He wouldn't be allowed to sit in on the meeting with Menet, but having him drive her there and back, plus the comfort of knowing an old friend was close at hand, made here feel somewhat stronger in coping with a meeting she dreaded.

As they approached the prison, the architecture surprised her, it looked almost medieval. The high wooden gates were surrounded by a large ornate stone arch, built into a very high wall. It was built in 1851 and just by looking at it one could almost feel its history. It was strange; she lived only a few miles from Wandworth Prison but had never seen the building before. She had only vaguely been aware it was there.

Alex parked the car and turned to face her. 'Remember, you don't have to do this, so if you get any abuse, you leave immediately.'

'I know, but I don't think that's his intention, otherwise Angel would not have asked me to come.'

He nodded in agreement. She was right, of course. He had only met Angel briefly, but he knew she would not subject Nancy to such treatment. They were a few minutes early and it was almost as though the prison officer was waiting expectantly the other side of the door. Alex could never remember such a quick response to ringing the bell at any prison. The prison officer acknowledged Moorland with respect, and then he turned his attention to Nancy.

'May I see your VO please, Miss Harnetty?'

Her brow creased.

'He wants to see the paperwork, your Visiting Order,' said Alex.

'Oh yes, sorry.' She felt in her pocket and passed it to him.

They were ushered in. 'Could I ask you to empty your handbag onto the counter please?'

She emptied her bag out and waited as he searched the contents. Nancy noticed a Labrador dog which stood nearby, watching her. Its nose seemed to be twitching slightly and she realised it was sniffing for drugs. It remained standing which confirmed she carried no illegal substances.

The officer then handed her a key and requested she lock her handbag in the locker provided. Having done this, she pocketed the key and followed the officer into an empty waiting room.

'I thought there would be other visitors.'

'Evidently your meeting is outside normal visiting hours. I won't be able to come any further, Nancy, but I'll be waiting for you here when you return, okay?'

She nodded and smiled. She did not want to show how apprehensive and nervous she felt. She looked around the clean but basic room and tried not to let her imagination run riot. Even if she had not known he was near, she would have sensed his presence as she did now, which surprised her. She had not been aware this could happen and she didn't like it. Where in Heavens name was....

'I am here, Nancy, never fear.'

At times like this, Nancy communicated with Angel telepathically. *'His presence is so strong; I was unprepared for this. How will I manage if I can feel his aura from here?'*

'By drawing on that inner strength that resides within. You have an abundance of this power and protection, but I will stay close.'

She sighed and resigned herself, realising she would only find this inner strength (if indeed she possessed it) when it was tested; when they were face to face. She wasn't sure how long it was before another officer came to escort her to the visiting block; she would only remember how she started when he called her name.

'Miss Harnetty, if you would like to follow me please?' She must have been miles away; she hadn't heard him come in. Alex was already standing.

'Oh yes, I'm ready. I'll see you soon, Alex.'

'I'll be waiting, and remember, don't let the bastard give you any stick.'

She nodded and followed the officer who was already halfway out of the door. She had an eerie feeling as she followed and fell into step beside him. She noted the other officers were watching her with undisguised interest, and realised they were as nonplussed as she as to why Philip Menet had requested this visit. Menet was their most notorious resident, so anything out of the norm which might give them a greater insight into this man, was of interest. She didn't know it, but those officers eligible to be party to this meeting had vied for the privilege. She could feel the intense interest as their eyes followed her. If she met their eyes, they looked away. It did not help, only serving to increase her unease, burdened as she was with the knowledge she must find the strength to match Menet's own.

She walked into a sanitised and impersonal room which was brightly lit. He was standing with his back to her, facing the wall on the other side of the long narrow table that separated them, his hands casually lodged in his pockets. He had obviously heard her enter, but did not acknowledge it. She knew instinctively this was to let her know he was in charge, almost as though she had been summoned to the headmaster's office. He was stamping his authority from the outset.

An unexpected and forceful anger rose within her. 'Have the grace and good manners to acknowledge me, or I will leave now. I have no time for your mind games.'

There were two officers in the room. One stood on Menet's side of the table, one on her side. Officer Swanton was nearest Menet, Officer Benson, Nancy. Their eyes met and the merest smile passed between them. She was not afraid of him. Neither were Swanton or Benson; they had been hand picked to deal with him. But they were slightly intimidated by him. It had been a slow process of intimidation, not by threats, but something more worrying than threats: something intangible they could not honestly define. There was something almost unholy about the man; that was the only way they could describe it. It had been taken on board by the Governor and he had decided no officer would do more than three months duty with Menet.

He would keep changing the officers to allow them an interim period before they resumed their spell of duty with Menet.

Menet turned his head slowly to look at Nancy over his shoulder and smiled. He was pleasantly surprised. Just because one had the ability to communicate with the dead, didn't mean one was also possessed of the power of reasoning and logic. He was bored silly with the tiny minds that now surrounded him daily. She would be a worthy adversary.

'You are quite right, Nancy; where are my manners?' He turned and held out his hand indicating the chair. 'Please be seated.' He sat at the seat opposite and appraised her, taking in every detail. He was well aware that this intimate scrutiny unnerved people.

'I didn't come here to discuss what face cream I use, so let's get on with it.'

He laughed long and hard. Swanton and Benson could not hide their surprise. He had not laughed once since he had been committed to Wandsworth. Humour was hardly his bag.

Still smiling he said. 'So we meet at last, Nancy.'

'Not of my choosing. What do you want?'

God he was enjoying this, and it was so unexpected. He feigned sadness. 'Are you not even going to ask me how I am, Nancy? Don't you want to know how all this has affected me?'

'I know how you feel.' Interest kindled within him. First she had made him laugh; now she had surprised him.

'How could you possibly know how I feel? I don't even share my feelings with these morons.'

'I was told. But how you feel is not why I am here. I'm told you have a question that I can help answer. What that question is, I have no idea, so I can't guarantee this meeting won't be a total waste of time for both of us.'

Would she never cease to surprise him? 'How could you know this?'

'I have someone who helps me who I call Angel – she told me, and, so far, she has never been wrong. But if she is, then say so, I don't want to waste any more of my time?'

Nancy knew he had not missed the inference that wasting time did not include his time. She wanted this meeting over and done with. He on the other hand wanted to milk it for as long as he could. She had to start to push him. She suddenly realised with a jolt that she had lost her fear of him from the moment she had seen his stance. He wanted answers, but only via manipulative means; where was the pleasure in just asking?

Anger had replaced fear. She still saw his menacing aura, but it had not and could not touch her now. As the energy from his aura was propelled in her direction, it just bounced back to its natural source: Menet. From the moment this happened, it had been her, not him who was the strongest. She was the one in charge of the events now being acted out.

He lost none of his confidence as he asked. 'Who is this lady?'

'I don't know; as I said, I call her Angel.'

'Ah; now this angel, she intrigues me; I must admit my knowledge in these matters is sadly lacking. I was unaware people like you called upon angels to help you.'

'She's not an angel as we know it; it's just a name I gave her.'

'Just a name you gave her; interesting.' He stood up, walked a few steps and faced the wall again, his hands back in his pockets. Now, it didn't matter, it had no effect on her. Posturing stances and manipulative moves just delayed the outcome, but would not affect it.

Swanton and Benson were enthralled, hanging on every word. They wouldn't have missed this for the world, although they'd been offered a lot to feign sickness.

'I would like to know how she became involved in all this.'

James Brierley's book will be out in print soon. I suggest you read it. Why am I here, Menet?'

His back rose slightly as he tilted his head back and sighed heavily with affection. 'Oh come now, Nancy, after all that has happened between us, I think we know each other well enough for you to call me Philip? At least let us be civilised with each other.'

Swanton and Benson were staggered. Praise indeed from him who was barely civil to anyone.

Suddenly, she felt very sorry for him, and for no logical reason she could explain. 'I'll give you a few more minutes... Philip, but if you don't get to the point, I will leave and never return.'

His shoulders hunched a little. 'You know the more we talk, Nancy, the more you interest me.' He pointed sideways briefly. 'Take Swanton and Benson for instance. They don't like me for obvious reasons, but it goes deeper than that. I make them very uneasy, which believe it or not, is in their favour. They are uneasy with me, but they are not *afraid* of me; there's a significant difference.'

Benson's eyes quickly locked onto Swanson's; he knew, but how did he know? Both he and Swanson had used all their training techniques to conceal this fact.

'Most people that I have contact with over any length of time, eventually come to fear me. Sometimes it's an advantage, other times not. Take Spinetti for instance; I had to work very hard as time progressed to keep him working for me. I needed him you see; he was the best in his line of work. His eventual growing fear of me was very irritating. I continually had to boost his confidence when in my presence.' He smiled slightly to himself. 'But not you Nancy, you have no fear of me and I suspect even with time, never would, and I find myself wondering why? Not that I

290

don't appreciate it, only God knows how I have craved to meet someone like you.'

He swung his shoulders round briefly and mockingly saluted her. 'I now accept you as a worthy opponent, which indirectly gives me solace. I would have drawn no comfort if my downfall had been at the hand of some unintelligent Joe Bloggs stumbling inadvertently onto my operation. No - better to go down with a worthy opponent.'

'Why am I here Philip?'

'Who is Angel?'

'I don't know.'

He turned and faced her in anger and disbelief.

She remained calm. 'You can be as disbelieving as you like but I'm telling the truth.'

She couldn't hide the surprise in her voice as she said. 'Ah, at long last I know the reason I am here, but this of all things is not what I expected.' She was firm as she said, 'Sit down, Philip.'

He walked slowly back to his seat. There was no defeat in his manner, but his attitude had changed. They were equals and he knew it. The arrogance had gone and was replaced with a respect he had shown only to one other. The slightest perspiration appeared on his forehead as he clasped his hands together and sat down.

'I did ask Angel that very question a long time ago, but she said that who she was wasn't important, but I'll tell you what I know of her if you think it will help?'

He nodded.

'When I first met her I was in Toronto taking a meditation class when she suddenly appeared at the back of the room. I told her I wasn't there to give messages and I was sorry if she wanted me to relay one to someone there. That's when I got a surprise. She said she didn't know anyone there, and the only reason she had come was to observe me. I will always remember what she said when I asked her why?'

Nancy looked at no-one as she remembered that brief encounter. 'She said that we would be together in times that were to come, and that it was her responsibility to protect me.'

The perspiration had increased on his forehead. 'Do you know what she looked like?'

Nancy felt a cold chill run down her spine. Suddenly Angel was very close.

'Answer him, Nancy.'

Nancy didn't want to, but for the first time ever, felt pressure from Angel to do so.

'I er, would say she was in her sixties when she passed over. She was tall with a very slim frame. Her face wasn't exactly beautiful but it was a very elegant and interesting face. She had long, thick hair with a lot of grey in it, tied back in quite a sophisticated chignon......'

She couldn't continue. The effect on him was dramatic. All his arrogance and confidence seemed to slip quietly away as she heard his tortured voice exclaim what she already knew.

'MOTHER!'